A Night for Jack-o-lanterns and Scarecrows

A Collection of Halloween Tales

A Night for Jack-o-lanterns and Scarecrows

A Night for Jack-o-Lanterns and Scarecrows
A Collection of Halloween Tales

L.J. Stephens

ISBN 9781076015242

A Night for Jack-o-lanterns and Scarecrows

L.J. Stephens

To Antoine, as promised and the first of many ...

"OH, HALLOWEEN! THAT SOUNDS FUN!"

I'm first to admit I was raised rather unconventionally. We were more of the "stay-cation" family, primary because we couldn't afford lavish summer trips like the ones my classmates bragged about when another school year started. In replacement of traveling or traditional holiday festivities, my household adapted Halloween as the most fun time of the year—it was cheaper than Christmas. However, in the 80s and 90s, growing up in a family that preferred Halloween over a vacation was seen bizarre by most.

Recently, it seems Halloween has evolved from an ominous holiday to an accepted lifestyle. Many communities have adopted it as an interconnected moment for all to prepare for the end-of-year celebrations rather than some special day for those who consider themselves "different than most."

I've written in journals volumes of perspective entries of such societal evolutions with eccentric phobias since my coming-of-age years. Expressing these thoughts on paper really assisted with the internal queries to where the self-therapeutic habit became something more goal-oriented: wanting to write a book.

At first, I struggled like any novice writer: not sure how to actually write like an author; had so many rough—and I do mean *rough*—drafts that seemed to just take up space on my hard drive; never finishing anything I'd started. When many colleagues and instructors suggested that I start simple and write about what I knew, I could only think of two personally strong topics: Halloween and what scares me. When I shared this, many amusingly responded with, "Oh, Halloween! That sounds fun."

I'm a sucker for supernatural stories, I'm still a huge fan Alvin Schwartz and R.L. Stine. Cannot forget Stephen King and Dan Simmons, too. So, of course, there will be such tales as "Let Her Sleep," "Household Silence," and "Pumpkin Spice Tea" in this collection.

However, what really frightens me are reading stories that could actually happen to someone. Gillian Flynn and Paula Hawkins influenced me to create some of the more realistic stories. When I wrote "Cue Ball," I had unpleasant flashbacks of similar moments that influenced the story, wondering what would've happened to me if I had made the other choice. The images from "Girls' Night In" had me double checking my locked doors and invoked some genuine nightmares during its process, due to my scelerophoia. "The Retractor" hits too close to home on many levels—fear of heights and engaging with others. Personal events even inspired some of the more devilishly blended stories, like "Legend of the Dancing Cowboy" and "The Lucky Soul."

When I began to share my writings, people were entertained and wanted to know where to get more. I told them I was compiling a collection called *A Night for Jack-o-Lanterns and Scarecrows*. I got praised for the project, but many commented on the lengthy title. I simply responded with, "Jack-o-lanterns and scarecrows are my thing." In lieu of this fact, I made sure I somehow referenced a jack-o-lantern and a scarecrow in each story in honor of what I love the most about Halloween.

I know this collection isn't going to be for everyone. And I'm sure even those who are reading it now aren't going to appreciate every story (and that's fine!—Pease give a genuine review). Nevertheless, this book has been one of my three lifetime achievements. It has felt like a partner along a epoch journey. I wanted to share my therapeutic process for the sake of helping someone, either personally or emotionally or just needing a good moment of escape. Regardless, thank you for your support, and I hope you enjoy these tales as much as I enjoyed writing them.

– Lindsey "L.J." Stephens, Jr. January 2019

CONTENTS

A Night for Jack-o-lanterns and Scarecrows

THE LEGEND OF THE
DANCING COWBOY

1.

"You know Cowboy Bill comes alive at night."

Finn's piercing words from behind startle Mike, Anthony and me that we nearly rock off the sidewalk edge. We were too honed into looking up Macon Street to had heard his big feet crunching on the fallen decay leaves.

"Yes, Finn." I sigh, to cover for being startled. "We've heard the ghost stories at school, too."

"But he really does move." Finn's tone is more so sardonic than convincing. "Late last Halloween, like, past one, I came home—"

"Breaking Mom and Dad's curfew once again, I see," I taunt.

"—and saw Cowboy Bill totally dancing at the end of the street," Finn continues, ignoring my jab. "He'd crossed the highway from Old Man Larry's junkyard and right at the stop sign at the end of Macon Street. I swear, it felt like that thing was calling to me. Wanting me to join him."

Finn's tone turned grave enough that the three of us stare down the street again.

The animatronic figure continues its stiff, repetitive movement. One hand rests on a hip while the other holds a flickering lasso Old Man Larry contorted from Christmas lights.

"That's not true," I say, in an attempt to disrupt the awkwardness. I turn toward Mike and Anthony. "I'm sure Old Man Larry just forgot to turn off Cowboy Bill that night."

Why am I even entertaining Finn's nonsense?

"Old Man Larry never forgets to turn off Cowboy Bill," Finn says, arrogantly.

"Yeah, Jonas," Mike chimes. "Dad told me one night that Old Man Larry is stingy with how he uses his electricity for the shop. I really doubt he'd forgot to cut off Cowboy Bill."

The trivial information from Mike's mouth never ceases to amaze me. And it's odd that his father would even share other people's personal business like that from his job—isn't that illegal, or something? Mike's family's weird.

Mike adds, "Well, except during trick-or-treating on Halloween nights, of course."

Mike seeks any reason to shift our conversations into Halloween. It's like he's obsessed with the day. And don't get me wrong; it's a cool holiday and all, but we're in eight grade now. Mike just needs to mellow out that kids stuff.

"Finn's always saying stupid stuff like that to try to scare me," I say. "Be thankful you're an only child, Mike."

Finn laughs too loud. "So, *that's* why Mikey's such a troll?"

Anthony huffs. "What's your damage, Finn? We've been hearing this cowboy-robot-comes-to-life mess since first grade, man. Go somewhere with that noise."

I agree. "Nobody—other than dumb little kids—has actually said they've seen that thing ever step from The U-Lasso-U-Pull's front."

"Not true," Finn says, sounding offended. "Rebecca Little—"

Anthony exhales smoothly through his teeth. "She's so fine!"

"—told us at lunch a few weeks ago," Finn continues, "that she and her parents were coming home from that new Italian restaurant in downtown Mayville when she caught Cowboy Bill totally watching them as they passed Old Man Larry's junkyard."

"Duh!—That's what it does, Finn," I retort. "The thing's an animatronic. They're programed to move, loser."

Finn shakes his head in a way that seems he's about to throw one of his fits. "She said the head did a complete three-sixty—"

"I think you mean one-eighty," Anthony corrects. "I don't think Cowboy Bill is capable of turning its head like the girl in that Exorcist movie."

"Old Man Larry could've updated the animatronic to pull in more business," Mike interjects with a random and bizarre theory.

Finn disregards their comments, like a brat not winning an argument. "And Cowboy Bill watched them go all the way down the highway. She said it kept staring at her with those big, black eyes peering beneath the hat brim."

"And so many from school has shared *so* many stories about them spotting Cowboy Bill stepping off his perch every Halloween night, Jonas," Mike pointlessly refers back to the rumors. "So, maybe Finn did see it happen last year. May it did watch Rebecca Little's family driving down the highway."

I want to tell Mike to chill with his wild, random rambles—and to stop backing up my jerk of a brother—but this statement gives me pause. I leer back up Macon Street in silence. The junkyard's robotic lawn ornament remains in its spot, repeatedly shifting from left to right. I'm too far, but I still hear in my head the rusted creaking with each rigid motion.

Finn chuckles over my shoulder: "Yeah, I've heard Cowboy Bill stalks trick-or-treaters who stay out too late. He mesmerizes them with his gyrating for them to dance with him. The lamer their costumes are, the more Cowboy Bill wants them to stand with him before Old Man Larry's place ... forever. And only the true weirdos fall for Cowboy

Bill's Jedi mind tricks … so watch your back tomorrow night with these two losers, Mikey."

"Hey!" Mike shouts, sounding wounded.

I turn and lightly, yet firmly, shove Finn. "Back off, freak."

Finn snickers. "Oh, I'm the freak? I overheard you butt-heads out here, yapping about how tomorrow's your official last year for trick-or-treating. But trust me, you three will still be the biggest dorks at Mayville Middle School, whether you go trick-or-treating or not."

We about face, start cussing out my older brother, but Finn just laughs as he walks toward the house.

2.

We stand at the edge of the front yard and watch Cowboy Bill flashing across the highway for a few moments longer until the familiar green Dodge pickup exits the junkyard gates. The truck stops, and Old Man Larry eases from the driver's side. He limps to Cowboy Bill and leans on the animatronic's left side while reaching behind it. A few seconds later the bulbs from the robot flicker off. The automaton slows to a stop with Cowboy Bill slumping forward.

The old man struggles back into his truck, officially ending another work day. We watch the truck turn onto the highway while listening to the radio on Anthony's boom box, the DJ reflecting on the Mets winning the World Series and the recent death of the entertainer, Joan Dornacker.

"Let's go scope it out," Mike says after Old Man Larry's no longer in sight. "We should go down there right now."

Right on cue, the radio starts blaring Ringo Starr's 'The No No Song' while Anthony and I both stare at Mike like he just grew another head—I'm shaking mine, and Anthony is, too.

"Guys, the three of us have been talking about doing this every Halloween since the second grade," Mike rebuts.

He's correct. It started with us obsessing over the scary tales of Cowboy Bill's annual resurrections, and we used to dare each other to go up there alone during late summer nights. By fifth grade, we stopped daring each other and started developing scenarios to debunk the myth. Now that we are in the eighth grade at Mayville Middle, the energy we used to spend on the town's ghost story has shifted toward more constructive extracurricular activities.

This past summer, the coaches at Mayville Middle recruited Anthony to play safety for the football team. Some of the star high school varsity-team players helped the coaches with summer training, which meant Anthony's older brother dogging him, since he's the main defensive guard for Mayville High's Bulldogs—one of South Carolina's top fifteen high school football teams. Anthony's scrawny body has started toning up from the grueling drills, and other athletes at our school are now calling him "The Machine."

I was nominated to be a band aid for the high school marching band, which meant summer band camp. We were on the high school's football field, charting and constantly practicing for the season's halftime shows, under the blistering sun. By late July, I was getting compliments on my massive weight loss.

Mike spent his summer at some theatre camp in the North Carolina mountains. Anthony and I didn't hear much from him—neither of us had much time on our hands anyway. When he returned, Mike had adopted a rather eccentric style: overgrown bangs, gothic outfits, and eyeliner. He seems more articulate now—and flamboyant.

When the Trio comes together for our last year in middle school, we could barely recognize one another.

We try to ignore the talk in the school halls, but both the students and even the teachers are saying it: The Mayville Trio is growing apart. We deny it, sharing we walk to school together. However, we don't leave together like in the past school years.

Football season intensifies with autumn approaching. Anthony and I practice four days a week in preparation for the weekly games. Meanwhile, Mike's wrapped up in Mayville's drama club. They've been rehearsing in the high school's auditorium for the fall semester's play, The Crucible.

So distracted, we didn't even hold our annual brain-storming session to debunk the Legend of Cowboy Bill this year until the actual week of Halloween. Even then, the discussions have been short … and usually provoked my Mike.

"This has to be the year," Mike continues. "It has all built up to this moment."

"You're sounding like a fool, man." Anthony says in a low, firm voice. "A plum, dumb fool."

Mike gets defensive. "Why's that, Anthony? Are you scared, Mr. Football Star?"

"You're damn right!" Anthony's arms stiffen, and he tilts his head toward Mike. "Scared of my parents. They'd whoop my ass if they caught me sneaking out the house late. They might even take me off the football team. I hear them riding Donte just for coming home fifteen minutes late."

Mike's hands fly into the air. "Anthony, we were just talking about doing this yesterday afternoon, walking home."

"*You* were, Mike," Anthony responds. "You were talking about it. You're always talking about Cowboy Bill."

"*We all* have always talked about visiting Cowboy Bill at nightfall since that Halloween," says Mike, referencing the Halloween night when we were in the fourth grade.

"Yeah," Anthony says, clearly annoyed. "The night only you saw … whatever it was you said you saw."

"Jonas said he saw it that night, too," Mike snaps. "Didn't you, Jonas?"

They both turn to me, but I keep my focus down the road.

Cowboy Bill has been wearing the same weathered leather vest and oversized, brimmed hat for as long as I can remember. The red in Cowboy Bill's plaid shirt has faded over the years. Finn always jokes that the robot's matted mustache underneath his pointy metallic nose is fur from the stray dogs Old Man Larry has caught roaming his junkyard.

Anthony returns to his bickering with Mike. "That was also before you got your glasses, Mike. And since the glasses, I haven't heard any other stupid sightings."

"You're just scared, Anthony," Mike repeats, more weak this time.

Anthony sucks on his teeth. "I ain't scared of a hunk of old metal."

Mike's voice takes a terse tone. "This was an oath we made. And the three of us have always stayed true to our words, regardless. Isn't that right, Jonas?"

I remain stoic, and they return to fussing with one another. Their bickering fades from my hearing as we stroll closer to the junkyard and Cowboy Bill comes into focus. I don't recall actually walking toward the thing, but feel like I'm being drawn to the animatronic. The fabric and accessories on Cowboy Bill seem more glossy in the sunset's rays. Maybe it's because I'm not blinking, but the robot appears to tremor upright. The vibration intensifies and it's now blurry. I can hear the metal rattling. Then it ceases without any warning, erect. And Cowboy Bill's head turns— he's looking right at me!

I squint for a better look, resist blinking. My vision becomes watery, tears sting my eyes, and I wipe the back of my wrist across my brow. I glace back at the robot.

Cowboy Bill bends toward the ground, and his features are again vague from the distance.

We still stand where we were just fussing with Finn. The three of us had never moved from the front of my house. We never walked toward the highway and Cowboy Bill.

"Let's walk down there tomorrow night," I suggest.

The two stop bickering and stare at me. They look stunned. I'm a bit thrown myself, not really sure I even said that until I meet their eyes to confirm the words actually came from my mouth rather than remained in my mind.

"Mike has a point," I continue. "We've always talked about it. And we've always done what the Mayville Trio has always agreed to do: we've explored the banks along the train tracks, snuck into that abandoned house in the woods behind the park, and hung on the school roof those summer nights back before our seventh grade year. This mission is minor compared to those, so we can't leave it undone."

Anthony lets out a hiss. "Don't you have a game tomorrow night, Jonas?"

"It's an away game tomorrow night. Band aids don't go to away games."

"I'm in, Jonas," Mike says. "We will become legends in the school halls."

Anthony laughs, and inspires me to do the same. "I don't know about all that, Mike."

"Think about it," Mike exclaims with jazz hands. "If we do this and share our story, not only would we be the ones from Mayville Middle who confronted Cowboy Bill, but everyone would stop hounding us about splitting up."

"We go way back," Anthony says. "We've been hanging out since kindergarten … and we all live on the same street, bro. We'll always be friends."

I want to believe it, but deep down, as we look at each other, we know this moment signifies the beginning of the end. I mean, sure we'll stay in touch—like Anthony says, we live on the same street. But it won't be the same by the time we enter high school. Being brave enough to stand down Cowboy Bill in the dark would bond us forever.

"I think we need to do this tomorrow night," I say. "This oath needs to be fulfilled."

The silence that follows confirms the decision for the Mayville Trio.

3.

My eyes open and the VCR clock reads 12:02 a.m., October 31—I thought I heard giggling. I close my eyes and try to drift back to sleep, but snickering interrupts it. I squint at the ceiling to adjust to the darkness when a commotion alarms me enough for my eyes to spring wide open. I prop myself in bed to flip on my nightstand lamp. I nearly knock my lamp onto the floor when I reach for it when the snickering shriek into laughter.

Is this a nightmare? No. This has to be a prank from Finn, not letting go of this afternoon.

I let my suspicious curiosity assist and learn the laughter is coming from outside my window. I'm anxious about getting out of bed but the laughter is getting louder and more sinister. The curiosity gets the best of me. I tip toe to my window and peek through the blinds.

It's Mike, standing in the middle of the road, staring down Macon Street and wildly laughing. He's wearing only tighty-whiteys and a tee shirt. His long hair is standing up and disheveled. He isn't wearing his glasses.

I rap my knuckles on the window to get his attention, but Mike remains in a trance of laughter. I snatch my bathrobe from my desk chair, hustle to the front door and step onto the porch, bundling up to shield against the cold. A weak glow flickers from the eyes and mouth of the jack-o-lantern on the steps.

A second after I blow out the candle, Mike's laughter reaches a crackling howl. His roaring echoes in the otherwise silent October night. I scan the neighborhood, perplexed as to why no one else has come outside to investigate this unsettling disturbance.

I call to Mike in a stern voice, with the hope that someone would hear me. Mike keeps his focus down the street.

I'm contemplating getting my Dad—or even Finn—when Mike begins these herky-jerky gestures with his arms and legs. I'm dumbfounded, staring at Mike. He's always been odd, but I've never seen anything like this. I hear the wheezing beneath his giggling, as if his running out of air in his lungs.

I step off the porch. "Mike, where's your inhaler, man?" I try to control my tone, but the cold—mixed with my fear—hinders my vocal cords. "You need to get inside."

He keeps laughing while gazing down the street.

I approach Mike but look down the street, in the direction he's staring at. "Your asthma, dude … You need to chill with that breakdancing—"

A tall, dark figure with limber limbs and convulsing near the stop sign at the intersection of Macon Street and the highway caught my attention. It dances under the streetlight but promptly slides into the shadows, as if it knew I'd spotted it.

Seconds later, while I'm still processing it all, I realize it is boogeying down Macon Street.

I grab Mike—his skin's frosty to the touch. I tug on my buddy and beg him to snap out of it. At the same time, I can't take my eyes off the dancing silhouette.

It glides along the pavement with impressive moves. I swallow hard before taking a deep breath that burns my esophagus, and force myself to break the gaze.

"Mike, man, we really need to get in—"

I hold the icy breath in my throat when Mike and I lock eyes. His pupils are bloodshot, his grin wide, and his stained teeth are chattering in his clenched jaws. Mike's laugh is muffled and tears are frozen on his puffy, red cheeks. Snot is running down his double chin. And he keeps dancing.

I look back down the street. The figure has picked up the pace; and he's close enough for me to decipher the familiar metal face and ragged clothing.

I remove my robe to bundle Mike and maneuver to his other side. Adrenaline floods my blood stream, and allows me to power Mike's stubby body up my driveway, despite his gyrating.

Mike stops straining his eyes after I nudge him onto the stoop with my knees. By the time I get him into the house, his lips are relaxed, but his teeth are still chattering.

I can't resist turning around one last time before entering the house. I need a better look at it. The silhouette ducks beneath the shadowy trees at the edge of my neighbor's yard, but the brim hat in the moonlight gives it away. I slam the front door, void of any thought from what I had realized just followed us up Macon Street.

• • •

Mike firmly holds the steaming mug of hot cocoa with both hands.

I sit across from him at the kitchen table and take my first sip when I hear my father's footsteps stumbling down the hallway.

After we—well, mostly *I*—answered Dad's questions, Mom comes in like a firestorm, demanding to know what's going on. Mom's ranting continues even while she frantically jabs her index finger on the keypad of the landline, calling Mike's house.

It's 3 a.m. when Mr. Sutton arrives to pick up Mike. "I don't even recall leaving home," Mike finally speaks when his father asks why he left their house.

Mike's teeth stop chattering as he shares his best recollection of the story. He still has both hands wrapped firmly around his warm mug, and he's sipping on his third cup.

"And I don't know how long I stood out there. I can't believe I went outside in my underwear," he says, staring at my bathrobe on his body. "The only thing I remember was lying on my bed, reading my part for Marshall Herrick, wearing sweatpants and a hoodie, and the next thing I remember is being pushed up the driveway. It was as if I had been awakened from a heavy sleep, still groggy, when I realized I was being led into the Bulmers' house by Jonas."

Everyone looks at me as soon as Mike says my name.

I share my recollection of the event for the third time since sitting at the kitchen table. But when I get to the part about how Mike psychotically stared at me, I explain it as a look of exhaustion before I guided him into the house. I didn't mention anything about Mike's maniacal laughter ... or what I saw gyrating up the street.

It's nearly 5 o'clock in the morning before Mr. Sutton walks Mike home. I didn't accompany Mom and Dad when they lead them to the front door, for fear of what might be waiting in the yard.

4.

Mom said I could stay home, but I don't want to miss the festivities for my last Halloween at Mayville Middle. But, more importantly, I need to talk with Anthony. I missed walking with him to school this morning because we were running late in the house. I finally find Anthony at lunch time.

The faculty has decorated the cafeteria walls with paper cut-outs and orange and black streamers dangling from the ceiling. Every table has Halloween props on it. A green-tinted witch with a wide grin stands on our designated table.

I sit to face Anthony, but before I can say anything, the witch's crackling voice startles me. Her hips sway, and her hands jiggle her broom. It's the first time I've ever seen an animatronic made specifically for Halloween, so naturally I react unaware.

Anthony chuckles. "Yeah, she got me too."

The animatronic signs off with a crackling "Happy Halloween!"

I share last night's events with Anthony, leaving in the creepy details I held back from my parents and Mike's Dad. I wait for Anthony to laugh at me, expecting him to brush it off as Mike being Mike. I even prepare myself for him clowning me, saying what I shared would had been something Mike would say. However, what came from his lips floored me.

"Jonas, Mike's weirdness is becoming too much. He's just cramping our style, man. I mean, the football players and *even a few hot girls* had invited me to some parties tonight. And they said I could bring you. I mean, they specifically said, 'And that Jonas friend of yours.' Band geeks go to these things, so you must be on their radar, dude. But Mike ..."

He savagely rips off a corner part of his square pizza with his teeth, as if that alone speaks his disrespectful thoughts about Mike. Which it did; I can't respond to his actions without showing any level of offensiveness. I only witness his taste buds savoring his scorn feelings about our childhood friend.

Anthony finishes the bite and his thoughts. "Maybe ... we could hang tonight, just you and me, bro. I know we usually chill together with Mike for Halloween and all, but perhaps we just go to these parties instead trick-or-treating tonight. Mike might even need to lay back tonight anyhow, after what you told me."

I'm lost for words over what I just heard. Sure, Mike is in his own world, but that's always been Mike. His awkwardness had never "cramped our style" before, why would it now? He'll still be him at these parties like how he has been at school and on our adventures. People know how he is.

I must had show my hurt because Anthony's expression reads as if I'm ready to cuss him out.

"Or," he continues, still chewing but setting his slice down to rise his hands in defense, "maybe we could go by his house after school to check on him. Maybe watch a movie with him. Then, we leave for home and can get ourselves ready for an awesome, grown folk Halloween night."

Anthony's insensitive plan unsettles in my heart throughout the rest of the school day, but we meet at the front lobby when the last bell rang and saunter to Mike's place with few exchange of words. Anthony and I take turns knocking on the front door a few times before Anthony tries the doorknob. It twists, the door creaks open, and we exchange baffled looks before letting ourselves into Mike's house.

We roam room to room, our voice's echo off the walls in the otherwise still home when calling for Mike. Shadows loom throughout the murky corridors and the eerie silence. We enter the open kitchen, feeling some relief due to the direct sunlight shining through the double-hung windows. We only enjoy the warmth and comfort for a moment before something swooshes between us.

"You two came!" Mike proclaims, circling the kitchen island. "That must mean you want to go trick-or-treating!"

Anthony and I swap more concerning glances over Mike's excitement before Anthony ask timidly: "Trick-or-treating? You still up for it, man? I mean, Jonas told me about your wild night, bud."

Mike nods, smacking his forehead and temples. His eyes are as huge as they were last night but not as bloodshot.

Mike halts before us, tapping his fingertips before his torso. "Let's go trick-or-treating!"
Anthony mouth drops, and I wordlessly stutter.

Mike makes eye contact with me, and I could not resist cringing from his dilated pupils. "Just wait until you two see my costume. You're going to *freak*!"

•   •   •

Mike was right about freaking out. I take several steps back from him after Anthony opens his front door. The dark hues from the sunset don't help the vibe.

"Man, what's this?" I try to contain my discomfort.

Anthony and I had decided to go to the parties after leaving Mike's place in complete horror of Mike's behavior. It was as if he wasn't … Mike, even for Mike. Him popping up like this was a disturbing surprise.

"You like it?" Mike asks with glee as he bops up Anthony's front steps. "I made it myself." Obviously is what I thought, but kept to myself.

Leather chaps cover an old pair of Mike's jeans. He sports a brown vest over a red-checkered shirt. The adhesive isn't holding the thick black moustache, so it's crooked above Mike's sweaty upper lip. The creepy costume is capped with a brimmed brown cowboy hat—which is too big for Mike's head.

I glance at Anthony. He isn't budging from the doorway, as if too worried to let Mike into his house. I scramble for something to say to end the awkward silence. Anthony beat me to it, shaking his head. "You've lost your mind, Mike."

I'm struggling to say something intelligent. "I think … town hall has stations at this year's Halloween party for trick-or-treaters. Practically everyone's going there. I heard people talking about it in school today. We could join our parents and get some candy there tonight."

"Let's just go do that, guys," Anthony agrees. "Too many people are bugging us about trick-or-treating being for little kids anyhow. Let's just go downtown with the adults and chill tonight."

"Yeah," I say, waving my glove with the fake blades on the fingertips. "We can change into something more … comfortable and just go chill—"

"No!" Mike shouts. How he yell is like how he got upset when we suggested for him to stay home instead going trick-ot-treating. "We took an oath, and we're sticking to it. If you guys aren't with me, I'll go by myself."

He grips his candy bag with both hands, as if for dear life, and stares at the ground, feet marching in place on the cement step. Tears form in his eyes. He repeats, in more so of a murmur than a holler his same last four words.

Anthony finally releases the doorknob and raises his hands up. "It's cool. It's cool, Mikey." Anthony puts a hand on Mike's shoulder. "Let's go trick-or-treating."

It's funny to see to a guy trying to look tough in a karate gi while patting a wannabe cowboy. I want to taunt them, but realize this isn't the time. I need to remember to tease them later … if there is a later with the three of us together after this night.

"Hey." I use my thumb to point behind me. "How about we go check out that new neighborhood, Finnern Terrance?"

Mike's gloomy demeanor instantly shifts to exhilaration. He darts between us and disappears into Anthony's kitchen. "Yeah, let's do that. Let's go!" I mean for it to be a suggestion to change the mood, but he makes the decision for us, without any discussion. But I think Anthony and I are worried he'd stay true to trick-or-treating alone if we don't join him.

"Let's just make this quick," I whisper for only Anthony to hear. "This shouldn't take too long. We'll hit a few of the houses and then walk Mike home to hang with him there until his Dad gets home from downtown."

"Nah." Anthony says, waving the idea off with a hand gesture. "After trick-or-treating for ten minutes, I'm going straight to Molly's party regardless where we're at. You can come if you want …" he points his thumb behind him, "or hang with that freak loser."

Anthony heads toward the back of his house, not bothering to check behind him me or my scrunched face.

5.

We traverse through the bare trees and decaying shrubs behind Macon Street. The sun has vanished, and we rely on the faint twilight to guide us through the depths of the decomposing brush. The wind rustles the dead leaves, and pierces my thin red-and-green-striped sweater.

We have a clear view of the highway, and we can see headlights of vehicles traveling downtown. The view of U-Lasso-U-Pull is decent … and so is Cowboy Bill, with the decorative décor of haystacks and uncarved, oversized pumpkins Old Man Larry piles around the animatronic every Halloween.

To our right, Madam Bedingfield's colonial house peeps through the bare and bent tree limbs. Madam Bedingfield lives alone and has no family to visit her, so she's always peppy when handing out the best trick-or-treating candy around. It's our tradition to start at her house, before our usual route along Macon Street, but since we are checking out the new development, we decide to hit Madam Bedingfield's upon returning to our neighborhood.

We're walking in the dark by the time we reach the edge of Finnern Terrance.

The sprawling three-story Victorian-style houses mesmerize us. The Homeowners

Association wanted to do Finnern Terrance's first Halloween right—with tasteful decorations thoughtfully placed on well-maintained lawns. The community is engaged—many new faces are becoming acquainted with the long-standing residents of Mayville. One of the houses even has a youthful adult dressed as a scarecrow, hopping from a stand and chasing trick-or-treaters after they get their candy.

My chest swells with warm delight. Mike and Anthony have wide grins on their faces as well. Mike's wearing his signature goofy smile, indicating he's back to normal. We exchange head nods of approval and proceed into the neighborhood.

As veterans of the trick-or-treating game, we know big homes usually mean great candy. We map out our path. A couple parents give us sideways glances, implying we have aged out of trick-or-treating. We probably look like some hoodlums conspiring mischievousness. But we don't care.

We finally choose a cul-de-sac and bound up the driveway of the first house on the left. Our excitement adds a spring to our step, but our internal alarms abruptly stop us in our tracks. Some of our peers are escorting younger trick-or-treaters—stuck with sibling duty for the night. Without younger siblings to provide cover, are we standing out? But with everything that has happened over the past twenty-four hours or so, I couldn't care less what anyone thought right now. And I can tell Anthony and Mike are in the Halloween vein with me. The Mayville Trio is functioning as a team for the first time since Spring.

I initiate the running. Mike lets out a whoop and joins me in jogging. Anthony, easily the best athlete among us, blows past us and he's the first one to the door.

·   ·   ·

By the time we complete the Finnern Terrance, it's chilly out. Many families have wrapped up their trick-or-treating for the night. We depart the development and journey back through the dormant shrubs toward Macon Street.

"Hold up," Mike says, trailing Anthony and I.

We turn to find he has stopped walking.

"We can't forget Old Madam Bedingfield's."

The thought of protesting floods my thoughts, but I stay silent. I exchange looks with Anthony, and I know we are thinking the same thing:

It didn't take long for us to spot Madam Bedingfield's still lit-up home. Headlights from the steady stream of traffic illuminates her yard, helping her display her outdated plastic pumpkins with happy faces and ridiculous witches flashing a snaggletooth. The rusty gate creaks as Mike pushes it open. I follow behind him, and Anthony lags along.

Tiny raindrops pelt my costume and bare skin. It's a light rain, and it shouldn't run the makeup on the trick-or-treaters' faces.

A car loaded with teen-agers speeds down the roadway with laughter bellowing from the open windows, and it passes by the gate for U-Lasso-U-Pull. It races out of sight as quickly as it came into view. My eyes fixate on the animatronic sitting behind the haystack and pumpkins in front of the junkyard's gate.

Cowboy Bill twirls his lasso in a hazy glow through the mist. With each cycle, the lights radiate brighter. The quicker the rope-light spins, the more Cowboy Bill's eyes and teeth shimmer with platinum radiances.

That's when it occurs to me that in all these years living in Mayville, Cowboy Bill's lasso has never moved before. The robot only lifts the rope in the air but never twirls it. But now, the rope is circling just above his massive hat. While keeping the balance of the twirling rope above his head, Cowboy Bill lifts his knee—something else he has never done before.

The mist thickens, clouds have blanketed the stars in the sky, and my view is hindered by the headlights fighting through the raindrops, but I'm sure about what I just saw. My field of vision is shrinking, but it looks like Cowboy Bill's other arm is bending, and he's starting a clogging routine in his boots. In what has to be the spookiest moment of my life, he pops his neck and faces me with a sneer as wide as his eyes.

Bill lifts his left hand and waves to me, smiling through his matted mustache. He has massive pearly teeth. He starts dancing.

I want to start dancing, too.

"Jonas, dude!" I hear Mike's voice from Victorian's front steps, while Anthony gets his goodies from the madam.

"You want some more candy or what? She's giving out king-size candy bars this year."

Preoccupied, I look back down the road.

Cowboy Bill has returned to his repetitive moves, and the lasso is motionless again as he sways.

Anthony and Mike are checking their stash when I pass them, bound for the Madam's porch steps.

Madam Bedingfield's porchlight casts a shadow on her pale, wrinkled complexion. Draped over her thin frame is a lacy black dress, and her white hair sits in a tight bun above her frail head. "Treat or treat." Her bony fingers tremble as she drops a Kit Kat King bar in my bulging bag.

I thank her graciously and wheel around to join Mike and Anthony down the walkway, and just as I'm about to step off the porch, a skeletal hand clasps my wrist.

"You saw him, didn't you, child?" Madam Bedingfield whispers. The gaze from her dark coal eyes peer into mine. "I saw you staring that way." She glances toward the junkyard, then locks eyes with me again. I want to lie but the way she's looking into my eyes … I know better.

"I've watched him every Halloween night for nearly 50 years." The stench from her breath invades my nostrils, making my stomach curl. "Don't let Bill cast his spell on you, child. If he dance up to you, he'll sink those teeth into you. Then, he'll forever control you. It happened to a boy in the 40s, but his parents covered it up with that autism spell that just came out then. But us children knew. Don't let him get you and your friends, tonight; he only goes for the babies."

I ease my arm from her grip. "Yes ma'am."

I'm not sure what else to say, but I nervously thank her again for the candy, and jump off her porch to join Anthony and Mike before she could say any more.

6.

Our bags are practically filled to the brim with an assortment of every kind of candy under the sun, but there's enough room to hit the few familiar houses we've been visiting together since our first trick-or-treat outing on Macon Street back before first grade. Neighbors tell us they've been waiting on us when we get to their front doors and, while dropping the candy into our bags, urge us to say hey to our parents for them.

We reach the end of the road and it's getting late for Mayville; one by one, front porch lights and being turned off. It seems like some of them were waiting up for us before calling it a night. By the time we get back to the road after our final stop at Mr. McNeill's house—he always passes out fun-size Snickers—the street's completely dark, except for the neglected jack-o-lanterns left lit on a few porches.

The mist has turned into a steady downpour.

We are only a few dozen steps from the intersection, so there's no way to resist giving it a glance. Across the highway from Macon Street, Cowboy Bill remains lit and in motion. The change of weather hasn't disturbed the hay and pumpkins. The rain pours while we stand watching the animatronic.

What Madam Bedingfield shared with me floods my thoughts.

"He seems more … lively than usual tonight, huh?" Anthony says.

As if his words were the que, the situation unravels quicker than my concentration can keep up.

Cowboy Bill starts to twirl his lasso and raises up into a hip-swirling dance, keeping time with his lasso of lights. His movement triggers my blood to run cold, yet also boils my body fluids to start dancing with him. I'm waiting for someone to scream, or dart into Mr. McNeill's house without knocking. But I sense none of us can't resist taking our eyes off him.

Anthony breaks the silence with nervous laughter. "He doesn't seem so bad. Hey, I heard about your dance party last night, Mikey. Do you think you can keep up with those moves—holy bat shit, Mike!"

I check to see what has startled Anthony and discover Mike performing his new-found dance moves, similar to what he did the night before. Mike is wearing that same creepy smile, too—his resemblance of Jack in The Shining is uncanny. Anthony reaches out to pat Mike on the shoulder but jumps back when Mike jerks his head around to face Anthony with blood-shot eyes. Mike looks like he's possessed … and I'm pretty sure he is.

I've never felt this scared and I'm not sure what to do. I'm thankful Anthony is here.

Mike's constantly contorting his arms and legs with moves I've never seen before. He popped his head forward to lock eyes with the dancing cowboy.

Confused, I look up and down Macon Street for an adult to rescue us. Nobody's outside, just like last night. Even Anthony's loud cussing or Mike's wicked laughter don't bring people from their houses. We are on our own.

Anthony calls out to the Lord.

The rain limits my vision, but the haystack just got knocked over and one of the pumpkins rolled into the street, while the other slammed into the junkyard gate.

Cowboy Bill is no longer on his perch, and he's ducked out of sight.

I scan the area and quickly discover Cowboy Bill next to the stop sign, twirling those lights above his brimmed lid. A grin spreads from cheek to cheek across Bill's face, and his moonlit eyes are locked on Mike.

Mike keeps their eye contact as well, like he's under the spell.

I look at creepy Bill, then back at my friend. They are doing the exact same dance moves.

"Oh, shit!" Anthony shouts, adjusting himself near Mike. "Okay, Jonas … We need to get Mike out of here, now!"

I nod, and we both grab one of Mike's arms and do our damnedest to keep a firm grip on our wiggling buddy as we carry him up the street. Anthony's athletic training and my marching practices with a sousaphone are paying off, because we don't struggle in the least to haul our plus-size friend up Macon Street. The rain has turned into a heavy thunderstorm with lightning bolts by the time we reach my yard.

We're almost to my front door when Mike kicks one of Mom's jack-o-lantern off the stoop.

The melon's rolling coincides with the thunder. Anthony is trying to snap Mike out of his trance while I struggle with my house keys. I'm shaking from sheer terror and struggle to slide my house key into the lock. Anthony yells for me to focus, but the storm's lightning is making it hard to see what I'm doing.

I look back and my fears are realized. Bill has followed us home and he's closing quickly. He looks angry and he's huge—at least 10 feet tall and massively thick.

With all of this going on, why do I feel the urge to dance? Has he cast a spell on me, too? Self preservation kicks in. If we leave Mike for him to bite, maybe he will leave me alone.

"He wants Mike," I yell over the storm and me giggling my keys. "So let him have him"

"What?" Anthony shrieks. "No way!"

My eyes are burning from the sweat and raindrops. My thoughts are jumbled, and I'm struggling to form words. "He just wants to bite Mike, Anthony."

The monster's chest is puffed out and his biceps are bulging … I'm paralyzed with fear. I literally feel like I can't move.

"Bite him?" Anthony screams at me. "The hell does that even mean, Jonas? We can't just leave our friend out here for that … monster! That mother-freaking beast coming this way and that isn't something we … give me those damn keys!"

I feel the keys snatch from my hand. I numbly zone on to Mike rather than the creature, grasping his arm again to help recompose my nerves, and listening to the jingle of keys entering the handle. I hear the door open just as Anthony screams: "Oh, shit, he's practically on top of us!"

I release Mike as soon as we enter my living room, bolting the door behind us. The lamps are off, but the kitchen is shedding dim light in the living room. When Anthony lets our troubled friend go, Mike's frantic dancing resumes and he seems more agitated than before.

Then Mike starts wheezing.

"Oh, hell," I say through exhaustion. "Mike's asthma."

I frisk my buddy to find his inhaler while Anthony looks for Bill through the front window. I locate, with relief, the pump in a back pocket while I'm assessing Mike's condition.

"This thing looks freaky as hell," Anthony says. "What does it—holy cow crap!"

Mike stops dancing.

"What?" I ask, trying to administer the inhaler to Mike.

"Bill has stopped dancing," Anthony says. "He took a giant leap and was back behind the trees, Jonas! Just one long jump, at least 20-something feet. How's that physically possible?"

I give Mike a few more doses of the inhaler before putting it back in his pocket, then joining Anthony for a scout from the window.

There's Bill, staring at us motionless with the rain pouring down and the occasional lightning bolt illuminating the sky. Through the steady rainfall, I can see the once-metal fingers are now flesh-toned and his lasso is burlap. It all looks real.

Mike, to no surprise, is acting super creepy. He's now a statue with a scowl on his face, standing exactly the way Bill is.

"What do we do now?" Anthony asks. "I can't go home with Bill the Freak out there in the pouring rain, and I don't know about you but I don't want to fall asleep under the same roof with Mikey in an ungodly trance. What are we going to do?"

I shrug in defeat, and then a movement in the yard catches my attention. But it's not from the section of the thing. It's on the other side of the yard.

Finn steps onto the grass, leading Rebecca Little by the hand.

"Oh, no, no, no," I implore aloud, but to no one in particular.

I pound on the glass, and Anthony does the same, both of us shouting. My throat starts to burn from the yelling.

They continue across the lawn, deep in conversation and oblivious to our ruckus—and to what lurks at the other end of the yard.

Bill hasn't moved from his spot but he's now looking in Finn's direction.

Bill's facial details are now visible in the moonlight, and he's watching Finn and Rebecca like a hawk about to pounce on his prey. His face has morphed into a ruddy, flesh tone, but he's mostly pale like a corpse and he doesn't blink. He pants like a thirsty hound.

I'm trembling, and I can't stop picturing what the Madam said about Bill biting that kid. Finn remains smitten and toned out the world around him and Rebecca Little … including us pounding the window for dear life due to the violent lightning storm and pouring rain. "Anthony, what can we do? He's going to attack them any second!"

I step backward toward the door, terrified to open it and reluctant to take my eyes off what's happening out there. I take two steps back when I bump into something plump. Mike's blocking my path. His eyes are blood red and he's glaring into mine.

I struggle to get around him, with a plan to fling open the door and yell at Finn and Rebecca to sprint inside. Mike doesn't budge, but I'm determined. I grasp the front door knob, but it doesn't turn. I'm shaking it in a panic before getting it unlocked and yanking it open. I screech Finn's name. They look at me as if I've lost my mind, and I've asked myself the same thing.

"What in the flipping hell is wrong with you, freaky band boy?" Finn snarls, acting especially tough and mean to impress his female friend.

I kick over the last of Mom's favorite carved-out pumpkins as I leap over the front porch steps and it's in a hundred pieces on the walkway. I'm in front of Finn and Rebecca in a matter of seconds, frantically scanning the perimeter.

But Bill's nowhere in sight.

The rain has died.

My watch beeps; it's midnight.

"Where did he go?" The panic constricts my throat, and it's hard to breathe, much less talk.

"Where did who go, Jonas?" Finn asks with a baffled look. He can now see the sheer terror in my eyes.

"Cowboy Bill."

There was a pregnant pause before Finn and Rebecca burst into laughter.

"I tried to tell you what a weirdo my brother is," Finn says to Rebecca, as they continue to the house.

Anthony remains in the window, mouth hanging and his face washed out. His eyes follow me as I enter behind my brother and his guest.

"Woah, did you three go on a drinking binge or smoke some weed?" Finn chuckles, as I plop down and lean back in the recliner. "Maybe I'll have to hang out with you guys next Halloween, unless something better comes along."

I don't follow what my brother is talking about at first, but then I see Mike laid out on the couch, snoring. Finn and Rebecca head off to the kitchen, giving Anthony and I a chance to talk about it.

"No way," Anthony says, mystified at Mike's sudden tranquility. "When the hell did his big ass pass out?" Anthony and I look at each other and the same thought instantly cross our minds. We run outside into the middle of Macon Street and look down the end of the road.

There he is, the lit-up electronic cowboy swaying in his repetitive motion across the roadway in front of Old Man Larry's U-Lasso-U-Pull Junkyard.

Headlights turn onto Macon Street from the intersection, blocking our view of Cowboy Bill. I recognize them as the lights of my parents' Dodge Omni. The hardened look on my mother's face doesn't even faze me as they drive around

Anthony and me. I remain fixated on the mechanical man we call Cowboy Bill.

The haystack that Old Man Larry places in front of Cowboy Bill on every Halloween remains shredded at his boots and the oversized pumpkins are demolished—one squashed in the street, and the other torn in two by the gate. I give Anthony one more glace at him with his hands on his knees And we both start laughing with what remaining energy we have left.

He and I know the three of us will forever be teased for being seen trick-or-treating as eighth-graders. Anthony and I will just laugh it off, like how we're trying to do with tonight at this moment. I'm sure Mike won't remember any of it, like last night. And that's good, because he would share it with any and everyone at Mayville Middle, only making things worse.

However, Anthony and I won't say a word to anyone. This will be the secret that keeps us connected between the head nods in passing one another through the high school halls, our eye contacts across the cafeteria and during assemblies amongst our newfound classmates, and along the yard lines during the football games on Friday nights. He and I will keep the legend of the dancing cowboy between us for the years to come and the years after.

CUE BALL

I notice them.

They're not doing anything to stand out. Just sitting in the shadows of the far back corner in Rocco's Pub and Grill, at the only table without a jack-o-lantern. If they're trying to discreet, they're not doing a good job.

I can't deny it, their rugged looks attract my eye as soon as I walked this relic of an establishment. In the mass of patrons dressed as sexy royalty, hunky cowboys or some vague reference to pop culture or online memes, these two are the only patrons not wearing a Halloween costume, so that's not helping their lowkey chill session—unless their theme is 90's gangster rap, or something. I miss the 90's; better concepts than today, from the looks of the other wacked get-ups.

"Cid!" Kim bellows over the blaring band playing the Monster Mash—she has the kind of pipes you can hear across a football stadium on a Homecoming Friday night.

I wave at her and Corey by the bar and begin my struggle through the congested pub. I shift in random directions to avoid colliding with an Egyptian Queen, a Greek God and a Jolly Green Giant.

I reach the end of the bar, only seven stools from the newlywed couple, before guy dressed as a big baby steps toward the bar and into my path. I quickly realize there's no way around this portly, and nearly nude fella. My eyes travel along the remaining ten feet to discover Kim laughing at my situation, and I smile with her.

I scan the scene again, soaking in the festive vibes, and find the two guys in the corner overtly glaring at me. I couldn't resist staring back. Tension constricts my brow; did they watch me maneuver through the crowd, enjoying my struggles?

The bigger of the two skulks in the dimmest crevices of the corner, but I can't miss his thick features, as if he did something like construction for a living. His partner is thinner and fitter, with a chiseled jawline ... and just looks more human than his beastly partner. The silhouettes of their wide-eyed sockets illuminate a bright gray.

The Big Baby thanks the long-standing bartender, James, and clears the way for me to join Corey and Kim.

Kim gives me a look-down after our hug. "I'm digging the scarecrow get-up."

I thank her and compliment her flower child attire. I share fist bumps with Corey and inform him that I dig his bright-retro yellow zoot suit—I can't the bright-ass thing. I guess they couldn't agree on a decade, so they dressed stag.

Kim slides two shots my way. "You need to catch up."

I grab one without hesitation or asking what it is. "I haven't seen Rocco's this packed since the Gamecocks' baseball team became two-time National Champions."

Kim agrees. "So many new faces, too. Congaree River is growing."

The history residents of our backwoods hometown haven't been the most assorted, so I do take note of the majority tonight appear to have some level multi-cultural background. The subconscious acknowledgement compels me to glance toward the two unfamiliar guys in the corner once more. I've never seen them in here before tonight. How do they know this place?

There's a lit jack-o-lantern resting between them now, as if it had loomed from the musty pub air. A candlelight flickers through its slanted eyes and jagged teeth, casting a hazy glow on the guys' features. The construction worker's eyes remain huge and dark. A snarl puckers out of his untamed beard, and a deep scar outlines his right jawline. The handsome, more fit one obviously takes care of his smooth, caramel skin and maintains a clean goatee. If it weren't for the teardrop tattoo under his left eye, he could try for a model—like that would even matter today. I redirect my focus to the toast with Kim and Corey.

"To Halloween!" Kim cheers. Corey and I echo the toast, and that's when I throw back my first shot with a shiver: Tequila. Corey excuses himself, and Kim turns to James behind the bar to order more alcohol. I down the second shot without any trouble and read the banner spread above the bar: ROCCO'S PUB AND GRILL 30th ANNIVERSARY.

"That's right," I say in reference to the banner, to no one in particular. "Rocco *did* open his bar on Halloween."

Behind the bar, the wall is adorned with countless written messages from the many patrons wishing the pub and Rocco a happy anniversary. Children helped decorate the wall with handmade cards, thanking Rocco for his contributions to Congaree River Elementary. Mixed with the thank-you cards are collages of faded polaroid pictures and computer print-outs reflecting years past. I travel down the bar, enjoying the timeline, and find a picture of Kim and me during our teenage years hugging Rocco.

Rocco's Pub and Grill has always been my and Kim's hangout; we used to sneak in underage—back when it was called Rocco's Bar. After about three months of constantly kicking our sneaky adolescent asses out of his place, Rocco decided to put us to work rather than report us to Chief Crisp or our parents. Kim and I remained long-term employees throughout our high school years, working along side James, until completing our undergrad studies—me at USC and Kim attending Midlands Tech—and officially joining the working world.

Rocco grew into a father figure for me, ever since my parents discovered my all-male porn mags. To this day, Mom and Dad are still fixated on my sexuality rather than recognizing my accomplishments as a college graduate and case manager for the Department of Corrections— granted, not a glamorous job, but we all must start somewhere.

The musk of a fresh, yet spicy fragrance overwhelms my nostrils, and a raspy voice barks an order for two beers while wedged next to me and breaks my daydreaming. "That looks like you."

I shudder from his heated breath hitting my neck and shoulder. I calm my discomfort, making sure my face muscles feel relaxed before looking to my right.

The first thing I notice is the teardrop under this guy's left eye. The thumping of my accelerating heartbeat drowns out the tempo from the music. I swallow air. I catch a chill again, but it wasn't from the liquor this time. He flashes a soft smile from those pillow-soft lips centering his groomed goatee.

He grins at me a moment longer before nodding at one of the displayed collages. "Is that you, man, right?" His voice is silky, yet husky.

What the hell is he talking about?

"Oh!" My face flushes. "You mean, in the picture? Yes. Yes, it is ... it's me. Younger."

The man glares at me, as if I embarrassed him by correcting one of his mistakes. His eyes grow dark, malevolent.

He then bursts into laughter. His overbearing chuckles would be awkward if the entire damn bar wasn't overhearing with the live music and crowds partying. I force a bland giggle. His expression goes flat two seconds after my fake titter, and I abruptly stop laughing. He lightly lifts one side of his grimace and releases a breathed snicker. Okay, this prick is screwing with me. Or flirting with me?

James serves his order, and the model hands him a ten-dollar bill, telling James to keep the change. He gives me one more—much more welcoming—head nod and smile. I reciprocate before he quickly turns to stroll back to the corner table.

I can't pull my gaze from watching his strut. My heart flutters, but the excitement isn't just from checking him out. I fear if I take my eyes off him for even a second before glancing back, he'd no longer be in sight. The idea of him disappearing without a trace makes my heart pound into my chest bones.

He obviously makes it to the table, hands one of the longnecks to the construction worker, and takes his seat while talking.

What the hell is wrong with me!? The dude just came up here for some drinks. He was just being friendly toward me. And here I am acting paranoid.

I've been trying to work on the eccentric thoughts since it's been noticed in therapy how my job had got me to this point of worry and distrust with society. Not everyone is evil. I created a mantra for myself: Not everyone has some hidden agenda, Cidney, man.

"Cidney!" Kim snaps her fingers in my face, then follows my gaze to discover what I've been ogling. "Oh, don't want to interrupt you being fast again?"

I want to tell her what's been happening since I arrived, but she will think I'm being silly … paranoid.

I shrug. "Don't be jealous because you're married."

Kim amusingly huffs. "Right. Like I don't look. And believe me, Corey has no shame in gawking. He tells me when he's girl-watching."

As if invoked, Corey appears from nowhere and kisses Kim on the cheek while collecting his drink.

• • •

My green six ball bounces just to the right of the side pocket.

"Damn it!" I don't know why I even play pool against Corey, with his cheating ass.

Corey chuckles. "I told you before, Cid: You can't beat me, son."

I sulk playfully to a stool. "You swindle, Corey."

Corey lifts his right hand from the cue stick and makes a stop signal. "Don't hate cause I got mad skills." He bends over the billiard table, lining the stick with the cue ball. "And don't give me that 'because you're black' bullshit, like you do when I whoop your ass in cards."

I purse my lips. "That's why I always want you as my spades partner—"

Something solid taps the side of my foot. I glance down to find a white cue ball next to my shoe. I check the table to discover Corey has just struck our cue ball, making a brash *smack*.

"Hey," a familiar honied, yet smoky voice calls out.

I follow the call and the surprise catches in the air in my throat.

The two guys from the back corner are now occupying the pool table next to ours. The burly construction worker stands at the farthest end from me, as if trying to stay hidden in the shadows from the hanging lights.

The model points below me. "Could you get that for me, pal?"

I check the cue ball on the floor again, then glance at Corey, who's watching me with uneven eyebrows—slightly and restlessly leaning on his billiard stick while waiting for me to help the guys out so I can take my shot.

"Oh, yeah," I say with my vocal cords wavering. I scoop it up and hand it to him.

"Thanks, brah." His fingertips brush my palm as he takes the cue ball from my hand.

His smooth skin instantly boils my blood. I have to blink to interrupt the room from spinning. His thankful smile is bigger than I'd anticipated, as if it had some deeper, intimate message behind it. Did he do that on purpose? He is actually catching some feeling over me? I keep it cool with a nod: "No problem."

The model winks at me with his smirk.

"Your turn, partner," Corey reminds me from afar.

The model's cold eyes hold my attention an extra second before looking at his own game. It's as if he's allowing me permission to return to my party. I meander back to the pool table.

I lean against the tabletop to pocket the red number three ball into the far-right corner. As I circle the table to size up my solid orange ball, a jerky movement in the distance catches my eye.

Their attention was on their own game, not me.

I need to stop tripping. Not everyone has hidden agendas, Cidney.

"Cid, any time, pal." Corey taps the handle of his cue stick impatiently against the bare floor. "I know the guys after us have no chill, and I don't want to beat someone's ass all because you're moving too damn slow."

I roll my eyes at him but appreciate his sarcasm interrupting my thoughts. I focus back on my playing and pocket the five ball in the center pocket. Corey taunts me with how I must be taking notes from him. I rise from the table and brush his words off with a sly grin.

I survey the remaining balls before returning to the other side of the table for my two ball. I visually measure the distance between the ball and a corner pocket, pull back the stick a few times and a blaring *crack* bellows through the pool hall, causing my nerves to jolt just before I give a stiff, short thrust. The solid blue ball rolls to a stop centimeters short of the pocket. I look from my tabletop to meet the eyes of the model at the next table … giving a blank glare at me while stuck in mid-play beneath the dim pub chandelier. He doesn't move. He doesn't even blink is almond-shape eyes.

There's a gentle shove from my right.

Corey sucks in air. "Oh, tough break, partńer. Now, step aside so I can school you some more."

I back to the nearby half wall just as Kim joins us with a round of drinks.

"How's it going?" She asks.

I rest my pool stick next to me and use my other hand to mimic a duck's flapping beak before collecting the drink she hands to me.

Kim laughs. "Oh, poor Cid. You know Corey is a serious player."

"That's right," Corey chimes. He thumbs his silk neon yellow collar shirt and then tips his matching brim hat. "Nothing but a player, Cat Mama."

Kim flips her hair and tosses her head back to laugh some more. "That's right, Pimp Daddy." She walks over to give Corey his drink and a smooch.

Something hits my foot again. I know what it is before I look down: the white cue ball.

I ease up my head to find both of them standing on the far side of their billiard table. The model leans in, flexing his muscular arms against the tabletop. The construction worker holds his cue stick vertically to his side like a combatant guard. The dim glow from the hanging lights shadows their grave expressions.

I want to signal Kim, but I see her and Corey in the corner of my eye making out and not paying the would around them any attetion.

The guys remain motionless, just waiting in silence for me to move with no verbal direction, as if I know what their demanding glares are requesting.

And I obey.

"Here you go." The weak words barely leave my throat as I hand over the ball.

Neither one budges.

Every ounce of blood in my body cascades to my feet. Despite all the bodies in the pub's game room, a sudden chill hit my bare nerve endings like needles poking my skin. My eardrums pop, and a ringing tone invades my head. Spots form before my eyes.

The model reaches for the ball and holds it with me rather than gathering from my grasp. I feel his fingertips grazing my own skin.

"Cid!"

I call back: "I hear you, Corey. Chill." I hold the patron's eyes.

He tugs the ball from my grasp. "Thanks, again ... Cid."

The room spins from the sound of the stranger's smooth voice uttering my name as if the word is a bag of bricks weighing down his tone.

I don't remember rejoining Kim and Corey. I don't remember playing my turn, even though I hear Corey picking on me about missing again. Corey makes his move on the table while I return to my stool.

Kim slides next to me. "What was that all about?"

I can only respond with "You know I can't play pool—"

"No, Cid. You and that guy at the other pool table. Isn't that the one your were eyeing back at the bar?"

I'm relieved that someone had noticed what's been happened, yet I flinch at her awareness. Kim's face changes from jovial to concern. She parts her lips, but then closes them speechless. She wants to ask, but don't know where to start. I part my lip to inform her.

"Game!"

My bones almost jump out of my skin; Kim flinches from my reaction.

Corey hops around the table. "You owe me that drink, man!"

• • •

"Was Atkins not a plum dumb fool, Cid?" Corey asks, slurring his words.

I couldn't hold back my prison jargon. "Ten-four, L-T." He and I laugh and clink bottles.

"Boykins and Pierce weren't playing that day with the inmate," Corey said, referencing Antonio Atkins' threats while the two correctional officers detained and escorted him from my office.

I hate negative talk about inmate clients, but, being a correctional officer, Corey couldn't care less about respecting inmates, nor how his brothers in blue treated the inmate. I continually hear from the incarcerated about how inhumane the C.O.'s treat them; it's part of my job as a correctional case manager to provide counseling to inmates. I've had to report some of the confessions to my supervisors—I have bills, too.

"But you can't deny it." Corey's words become firm and clear. "You were thankful that day for what they had to do."

I nod.

"If we didn't get there in time," Corey continues, "who knows what Atkins would've done to you."

The thought of whether or not I'd be sitting here enjoying a drink with my friends crosses my mind, and then darker images of what could've happened to me in my office that day flood over those thoughts. I flick my wrist and glance at my watch as a distraction; the hands read past three in the morning. No wonder the party crowd has died down. I scan the room—no sight of those two guys. It must be down to us three, plus Rocco and James behind the bar. Even those two guys appeared to vanish soon after Kim noticed their unusual behavior toward me … wish I relaxed toward the cute model guy. But they were lurking and creepy, but alcohol does effect people differently.

"Well," Corey continues, "good thing Assistant Superintendent Maid and Captain Meadows placed him in max security. No one has to worry about his crazy ass now."

Kim usually hates our shop talk, but I see the curiosity on her face. "Why did the prisoner come at you like that, Cid?"

I lift the beer bottle to my lips. "No one knows."

"Atkins is in for life," Corey adds. "Sometimes those do stupid shit because they have nothing to lose."

"That just doesn't make sense, though ..." Kim shifts in her chair. "Well, he's in max security, meaning he won't bother you anymore, right?"

I haven't taken a sip yet. "Pretty much."

Corey belches before laughing. "Yeah, I always love when they yell 'I'm going to fuck you all up!' while they're being escorted to the hole."

I finish my beer instead of reacting to his comment.

I worked with Atkins for about nine years before his permanent assignment in max, and I'm the only one that'd ever been able to counsel him for that long. But, even with my stretch of working with Atkins, all correctional case managers know any style of rehabilitation treatment is only entertainment to Atkins; he toyed with us about the therapy. Nevertheless, I had enough time to learn about how he survived childhood in the streets, the details of how his double-murder of two state troopers was initiation into the Blood Moons and what got him incarcerated, and how high he climbed the gang's chain of command while behind bars.

Also, I've worked in the field long enough to know gang leaders usually don't make idle threats. That glare he gave when being escorted from my office still haunts my dreams, with that crescent moon tattoo on his left cheek.

My unsettling thoughts cause me to baulk when Rocco puts his arms around the shoulders of Corey and me. "Isn't it past you boys' bedtime?"

We all laugh, and I doubt anyone recognizes my uneasiness.

Kim leans into Corey, like a slushy oozing down someone's shoulder. "Baby, let's go home."

I tell the couple I'll stay to help Rocco and James close up. I join in with the seeping and pour out the remaining alcohol before tossing the cups into the trash.

James says he really just needs to sweep and throw away the pumpkins. He gives me an empty plastic bin outlined with a trash bag to help him gather the jack-o-lanterns on the tables. He starts at the front while I begin in the center of the pub. I scoot the tub along the floor toward the back, dumping the carved melons into it after making sure the candles have died. I stumble to the last round table in the dark corner, and it looks neglected as if no one had sat there all night. I'm shocked at the revelation until it occurs to me that this is where the two freaks sat practically all night, stalking me, even after their pool game.

The jack-o-lantern isn't on the table anymore.

Rocco, James and I wrap up cleaning before he lets me out of the front door—like old times. Behind me, the familiar clicking of the front door locking and the illumination behind me from Rocco's Pub and Grill goes out after I take a few steps onto the sidewalk. The only lights in the area now are the dim orange phosphorescent streetlights spread widely throughout the mini-strip-mall's vacant parking lot.

The breeze leads the Halloween afterhours into the All Saint's Day early morning, and the alcohol in my stomach and pores isn't helping me stay warm. I place my hands into my jacket pockets, searching for my Impala's keys, but also appreciating what little heat they provide. I struggle with inserting the right key into my Impala's driver door as my hand shivers.

"Hey."

My icy fingers drop the keys from the shock of hearing a random voice yelling.

"Hey, man."

I look in the direction the words come from.

The construction work and model stand by a late-70's Caprice under a flickering orange streetlight that's failing to brighten the lot's section. The car's backend faces me diagonally, about two rows in front of me and five spaces to my left. The trunk is open.

I can't see anything in the trunk because the wide lid blocks the streetlight, allowing on darkness. However, I can't miss how the construction worker continues to remain inconspicuous behind the open cover on the side opposite of me.

An eerie lit jack-o-lantern sits on the car's top. One with sinister eyes and jagged teeth The model stands three feet from the exposed trunk.

"Hey, man. Come here for a second."

My nerves join my stomach acid in swooshing the alcohol about my body.

"Brah," he continues beckoning me. He gestures with his right hand. "Can you come over for a second?"

The construction worker doesn't seem to even blink—not that I can really see any details that far. The ground feels like it's spinning beneath my feet, and I have to grab my car hood to keep my balance. I look back at Rocco's Pub and Grill; it's pitch black.

He sounds more and more distant the longer I stand. "Hey, man. Come here."

I wave my hand at them dismissively. "No, man. I'm good."

I'm not good. I need to get my drunk ass into my car right now.

"Huh?" He gives me a look as if I hurt his feelings.

What the hell do these two want from me?

He steps into the streetlight, and I can't help admiring his looks. "I got something to show you." I identify his scowl as the one from when I'd first arrived at Rocco's.

I refuse the invite with my hands again. "Nah, bro. Thanks, but I don't do that stuff."

"Do that *stuff*?" He looks offended now. "What you talking about?" His tone becomes edgy and demanding. "Man, shit … Just come here for a minute."

The one behind the trunk remains as still as a statue.

The model's calling me with one finger directing me toward him. His face shows the apathetic grin I recognize at the pool tables.

"Come here." His tone is grave.

His icy tone makes my blood run cold. He waits for me to be civil, like I'd demonstrated when returning their cue ball.

However, I'm too drunk and scared to give a damn. If it's not drugs, then what could it be? Maybe I should be polite and go check it out, considering he's my type and he's been flirting with me all night.

But my instincts makes me holler, "No."

The two look annoyed. The one behind the trunk lid flinches, as if my word slap him. I start to consider all the things that could go wrong in this situation. I control my voice. "I'm okay. Have a good night."

The adrenaline sobers me up enough to quickly pick up my keyring from the pavement and insert the correct key into the door lock.

Before the guy could say anything else—or start coming at me—I unlock the door, climb into my car, and push the button a few times to make sure all my doors are locked. I insert the key into the ignition and turn it. The engine sputters before dying.

"Come on!" I hiss into the dashboard.

I turn the key once more while pressing the gas pedal. The engine sputters again but does so for only about two seconds before turning over. I never thought I'd ever fall in love with the sound of a running car and the smell of exhaust, but that's how I feel at this moment.

I put the Impala into Drive and roll forward. The car struggles with the acceleration but it goes. I keep my eyes forward, pressing the accelerator to make my car rushes across the empty parking spots. I align with the red traffic light at the lot exit. The lights facing me remain red while the opposite streetlights begin to gradually shift from green to yellow. I look into the rearview mirror, impatiently waiting for the too-slow yellow to go red.

They remain standing under the streetlight. Their bodies both face in my direction. A gust of wind rocks their car, and the candle in the jack-o-lantern extinguishes and slams their trunk lid. They remain stone-faced, unaffected by the closed backend.

The green hue flashes, and I turn left, not looking back.

.   .   .

My ringing phone irritates the headache pounding in my skull. I can't pry open my eyelids at first because the mid morning sun rays are too blinding. I blindly smack all over my nightstand before my fingertips hit the familiar smooth glass of my phone screen.

Oh, shit! It's you, Cid!" Corey's voice is far too loud.

I go to answer him sarcastically, but I only cough out a "Yep." The breath from my lungs scratches against my raw vocal cords. I need some water.

"Thank God you answered."

I make a baffling grumble in the receiver.

"You haven't heard, man?"

I throw my legs over the edge of my bed— they're stiff and heavy, like a deceased pet that's been through taxidermy. "Heard what, Corey?"

"The murders of some public safety officers that were discovered last night."

The unsettling information forces my eyes wide open. "The hell you say?"

"Yeah, it's some fucked up shit! It's—Just turn on the news."

I quickly do so and hear the report as the screen comes to life: "Last night's Halloween became genuinely frightening indeed when some early morning joggers in Congaree River Park discovered four decapitated heads. Congaree River Police report the heads were arranged facing one another in a circle, with a broken shape drawn into the dirt between the heads. Police aren't sharing any details about a potential motive, but all victims were employees from the Broad River Correctional Facility. Their bodies are yet to be found."

The news report displays pictures of the slain, with their names captioned below: Officer James Boykins, Officer Ridley Pierce, Captain William Meadows, and Assistant Warden Veronica Maid.

The screen shows a drawing in the middle of markers where their heads were found is the drawing of a disfigured crescent moon with liquid dripping from the bottom tip. Just like the tattoo on Atkins' cheek. Just like the tear beneath the left eye of the good-looking model at Rocco's.

SACRED HOME

I poured round four in response to Jessie's last question. I usually don't drink in front of her, but why give a damn now? Took her as long to run out of the house as it took me to gulp the rum in one swallow. My eyes flinched under the shot glass as she slammed the door, rattling the foundations of her childhood home. I kept staring through the bottom of the stained glass, watching the flame dancing through the eyes and mouth of Jessie's personal jack-o-lantern. She's always carved me a jack-o-lantern every Halloween since high school. Big Bill Broonzy oozed from the living room stereo, through the foyer speakers, and into the dining room. I poured drink number five.

My father drank himself to death. Not sure, but I think it was because he couldn't handle his temperament and womanizing any longer after I moved on to college. With Mom passing at a young age, introducing myself to some of the many of Dad's female guests satisfied the curiosities I had for the other sex as a teen. Still, witnessing this man being irresponsible as a parent and a demon of a human towards women affected me. Either a boy's first idol and a daughter's first hero, one's father is children's first window into society. All I learned from him is how to avoid human connection.

My undergrad years at the University of South Carolina in Columbia are still a complete blur, yet I remember practicing the routine the old man taught me: drink to function and abuse women in a world of personal illusions. I don't know how I graduated with a rocketing GPA, but I somehow got accepted into USC's graduate program for school counseling.

I met Lisa during her studies in the program for music education. She stayed with me through hell and high water, and we married after we both graduated. I promised Lisa and our therapist I would stop drinking. I promised myself I would at least monitor the addiction, and drink no more than three glasses of whiskey or rum a day—and only when Lisa wasn't home. The three or four glasses were better than killing a whole bottle in one sitting. I enjoyed cutting back, and not drinking myself to the point of hallucinations anymore.

It took the birth of the twins, Jessie and Jimmy, for me to realize what I needed to do: be a better father than my own. I got treatment for the alcohol, with Lisa by my side, through therapy, the AA meetings, exercising, turning down party invites and sexual advances from others ... everything for my family.

I can only snicker at myself now.

Jessie's jack-o-lantern watched me pour my sixth glass. The low rumble of thunder pierced through the music and lured me to glance out the double-hung window in mid-gulp. A cloud eased before the moonlight and blanketed the backyard. The dogwood tree and pond vanished from clear sight. It appeared as if a black curtain has closed a stage without the performers being aware the show was over.

Lightning flooded the backyard, and the tree's knots looked as if they were sneering at me. The lightning subdued when the thunder returned, but the silhouette of the tree still lingered in a grayish hue when the rest of the backyard faded back to black. The simmering ash glowed along the trunk, as if some of the lightning's residue had rubbed onto it.

I heard the humming seeping through the dark backyard.

These roses are going to look beautiful ...

I didn't give it a second thought whether or not to respond to the whisper. "Yes, they will be, but never as beautiful as you, Lisa."

Don't patronize me!

"Oh, no ma'am!"

Mmmhmm ...

I thought I would never hear her soft voice again.

The tree's silhouette began to luster silver.

When are you getting out here ...

The ocher gloss radiated, and the golden arches climbed up the trunk's wrinkles, turning the dogwood an amber tone. The golden lights stretched onto the limbs and bled into the veins of the remaining leaves and fizzled more vegetation into life.

The amber hues sparkled among the pond's reflection. The rays overflowed from the waters and covered the back yard. It was a majestic sunrise.

Then she emerged from behind the rose bed, and we made eye contact.

It's such a beautiful morning. Join me out here ...

Nature's colors bounced off of her, like a halo illuminating from an angel. Her garden clothes glimmered so bright they faded into a pearl-tone tunic. Her radiance, with the backyard's gleam, nearly blinded me.

Lisa knelt in her backyard garden of flowers in front of the dogwood tree, digging into the ground.

I wanted to reach through the window and touch her. I wanted to believe it was her outside.

Instead, I choked on my words: "It's only beautiful because you're out there ..."

She wiped her brow with the back of her right arm, then looked up. When she smiled at me through the window, the tears flowed. I attempted to stand from the chair, but my head started spinning. The room wouldn't stop twirling around me in any attempt to step forward, and I was knocked back into the chair from the intoxicated dizziness.

You need to get out here before it burns out.

"I will ..."

Seriously, before the storm arrives ...

"I'm ... I'm so sorry, Lisa ..."

She looked from her flowers, eyes wide, as if those four words pierced through her chest.

Do you hear that?

I did. It was faint, but I heard the piano playing behind me. She smiled wide.

That's our son ...

Lisa went back to her flower bed, humming to the piano playing. Each rose petal Lisa caressed milked a black ooze.

The first drops hit the window. They continued, each raindrop making the morning glow fade, as if God was gradually dimming the sun's rays. When the drops hit the flower petals, the roses and tulips trembled and shrieked as they shriveled deep into the cores of their stamens. The pigments bled red and violet. Crimson dyes soaked into Lisa's tunic, as if she was being randomly stabbed. But she remained, attending the rose bed as if nothing unnatural was happening around her. The shower enlarged while the remaining standing flowers finally screeched in agony, as if each raindrop malevolently stabbed them, and withered away.

Fear of loneliness surfaced in my heart once again. When I rose, my eardrums became clouted from the screaming of the flowers mixing with the profound thunder. The auditory chaos overwhelmed me to the point I fell back into my chair during another attempt to stand. Only movement I could do now was grab my ears in attempts to dilute the pain. I screamed for Lisa, and my words intensified the vibration in my head. Lisa continued to work on the dying flowers, oblivious to my cries.

The raindrops drained the golden auras out the tree. The leaves rolled down the trunk and melted onto the ground while the backyard turned dark. The yelling of the flowers died into the thrashing of the rain ramming into the outside walls and windows. As if the storm was saving the best agony for last, I watched Lisa fade into the black. I sat on the edge of the chair, hoping my prayers for her to come back to me were heard. Only the tree reemerged from the chaotic scene.

But the piano playing continued to trickle through the storm.

A quick flash flooded the house with some roaring thunder, and my body finally rose with no problems. I waited for silence to follow when the thunder settled, but the composition remained alive and pulsating. The urge to search for the source of the piano music became overwhelming. I finished off the whiskey bottle before getting up from the dining room table.

I got as far as the wall separating the dining room from the foyer when my legs became too heavy with terror to travel into the next room. I fought them, but my knees threatened to drop me in my spot in defense. I quickly placed my back to the wall before gravity overcame my equilibrium.

The entry to the foyer was only five inches from my right arm. All I had to do was swing my drunk-ass around the door frame. And I could do this. Looking up the flight of stairs is what paralyzed me.

Either to learn where the music came from or denying that I knew where the music came from, the frightening thought of discovering the source of the music drained all of the remaining energy in my core to the point where the dining room began to spin. The jack-o-lantern bobbed while chuckling at me. I shut my eyes and held my breath. The hum of the keys continued to vibrate my spine through the wall, which didn't ease the queasiness. I released the air in my chest, eased around the doorway, and forced myself into the foyer. I remained dizzy when I opened my eyes.

Only a pitch black empty hallway at the top of the stairs stared back at me.

Lightning flashed across the second floor, and everything at the top step stood as still as my heart: the hall table, my wife's floral spread, and the oval wall mirror. The attic door reflected in the mirror remained closed.

It was just the sound that moved. The music poured angry and somber through the creases of the attic door. The harder I heard the ivory keys being played, the heavier the door pulsated with the forte tempo. The blood in my temples began to thump with the rhythm.

I recognized the music being in a minor key. Not that I was a musician or anything.

Lisa and Jimmy were the musicians of the family.

Lisa taught music education at the middle school that also housed the high school where I worked as a school counselor. She gave private piano lessons in her "workroom" in the far right room upstairs. In that room, Lisa practiced performances and pieces with her cello.

Jimmy was following in his mother's footsteps. He studied mostly music in school, but also had a thing for psychology and sociology during his junior and senior years. I miss the heavy, deep conversations Jimmy and I had before Jimmy went off to college. Jimmy had a rough time deciding on his major— between music and counseling—when he began college with Jessie. Jimmy was only nineteen then: He never got to decide.

Crackling static made me snap my head toward the living room. The MP3 player had switched to a recording of one of Lisa's recitals. The allegro beat came from the wireless speakers near the stairs. No other music came from anywhere else in the house. The piano music had been from the stereo system.

I laughed hard, adding more pain on my already strained ab muscles. "You've drunk yourself crazy, again, buddy."

I returned to the dining room table to finish off the bottle, only to be reminded from the empty bottle I finished before I when searching for a ghost. I got a bottle of vodka from the minibar to pour my next glass when I heard the hinges of the swinging kitchen door creak. I spun around, dropping the bottle. I felt it roll next to my left foot as I watched the kitchen door. It looked like it was gently moving. I wasn't sure. The movement could've been the dancing candlelight from the jack-o-lantern.

"Of, course," I heard myself say aloud. "You're alone in this house. It's the damn liquor fucking with your head, again. You need to stop drinking for the night." I bent to collect the bottle and sat it with me at the table before grabbing my glass to start pouring.

The house had only been emptied recently. Normally, Jessie came once a week but never stayed long because of her studies, she would say, even though I knew it was tough on her as well. The police came by on occasion, still asking questions and stirring the place somewhat. But I lived alone now with hardly any visitors since the funeral.

I emptied the rest of the vodka before placing the glass on the dining table. I stood there, certain something came from upstairs, but the music from the stereo kept interfering with the clarity. I felt my feet tumbling over one another as I clumsily bounded into the living room.

There are times when I swear I hear movement downstairs while I'm reading in bed upstairs, or footsteps above me while I'm watching TV in the living room or working in my downstairs study. I knew no one lurked around the house corners while I migrated between rooms. I'm always reminding myself I'm just lonely and the familiarity of the place being full of active bodies plays tricks on my mind.

I reached for the tuner to turn down the music when cold air ran down my back. I was able to gain full balance when I rose onto my toes. I twisted the volume tuner in the opposite direction than intended. The orchestra amplified toward the ceiling and rattled through the living room. I turned to find the dark foyer vacant. I searched the living room and foyer once more before turning the music down completely and listened for the sound upstairs: Just the rain.

I grabbed the front of my shirt, feeling my heart thumping in my chest. My throat tightened when I swallowed stale, dry air. I planted myself in my recliner so I could contain my thoughts and emotions, which were spinning as fast as the room—sitting felt good because the alcohol interfered with balance.

The kids and Lisa got me the recliner for Father's Day about thirteen years ago. When school was in session, Lisa and I stayed busy, hardly seeing each other. When we were all home, Lisa made sure we all ate dinner at the dining table. When Lisa was working late for some school function and it was my turn to prep dinner, I'd just order a pizza and we'd eat in the living room—the children on the floor watching some annoying kid's program and me with a book in the chair. They said Mom made them still eat at the table when I worked late and they loved when I had to "make" dinner.

When Jessie and her boyfriend of some years now came to the house during the beginning of this October to scavenge through the home to "help me rid some stuff," I refused to let Jessie include the recliner in the house memorabilia being donated to charity. Jessie argued it was ragged and promised to buy me a new one this coming Christmas, but I sat in the chair in protest while the movers hauled the rest. Stubborn Jessie got the hint from her more stubborn father and left the house without the chair.

It sounded like knocking on the front door is mixing with the music's tempo and the rain's rhythm. I tried to ignore the knocking, but it didn't cease. Having Jessie there much earlier was enough guests for one night. Damn

… it may be trick or treaters. With the steady pounding on the wooden door, I couldn't ignore it any longer.

I rose and eased to the front door with gentle footsteps. I was hoping my intoxication wouldn't get the best of my motor skills. I pressed my hands on the front door, easing to the peephole when another knock echoed in the foyer. As I reached for the door knob, the loudest knock yet rattled the foyer. It was as if the sound lifted me off the floor. But this time the noise came behind me.

I turned toward my study— the door was closed door at the end of the hall. The long walk down the hall to the study had no light, only the occasional streetlamp reflection coming through a window and bouncing off the hardwood floor. My right elbow banged against the doorknob of the hallway's half bathroom, but the alcohol numbing my body dulled the pain. Just as I reached the back end of the hall, another knock came distinctly from behind the wooden study door. I didn't hesitate when I reached for the knob.

The wind from the open window behind the desk rattled the blinds, causing them to knock against the window pane. I must have opened it to enjoy the autumn breeze before Jessie came to the house and forgot to close it. My chuckles eased my nerves enough to go close the window. I felt the chilly rain on my arms as I closed the opening. I grabbed the blind cord when the corner of my eye caught a shape emerging between the dogwood tree and lake. I skipped a step behind me. The blinds slid downward diagonally, leaving the backyard visible through the lower left corner of the window. The figure remained perfectly still.

"Asshole!" I heard my voice tremble. "Get the hell out my yard!"

This thing didn't budge. I continued to yell at whoever it was, but the figure remained unfazed by my rants. I struggled to get to my cabinet on the other side of the desk. The room felt like it was rotating. I flung open the cabinet doors, and rummaged through the papers until I felt the cold metal. I pulled the revolver from the cabinet. Bullets fell to the floor as I tried to load the weapon. I struggled to jam three bullets into the chamber. Feeling dizzy, I lunged toward my desk. I slammed my gun onto the mahogany finish, but my grip remained firm. Clammy, I fought back the bile rushing up toward my mouth. After I swallowed the rancid bitterness, I used the edge of the desk as a guide to make my way back to the window.

I raised my revolver in the air, screaming for the son of a bitch to get the hell out my backyard when I noticed something in his hand. Through blurred vision I could swear the guy was waving a gun in the air as well. I cased my gun and secured it in my waistline. The man did the same thing. I stepped to the left; he stepped to the right. I moved to the right and he moved to his left. I leaned toward the window to get a clearer view of the guy.

That's when I realized I was staring at my reflection in the window. The light from the study hid my features in the window.

I groaned, a mixture of relief and embarrassment. I went to the minibar in the study, placed the gun on the bar, and poured bourbon to the rim of the first glass I could grab. I looked out the window to watch the rain ripple in the pond and finished the drink in one haggard swig.

There are so many memories with the pond: we played near it, the kids learned to swim in it, Lisa practiced her cello out there, the picnics ... I scanned the study. My hazy vision was still adjusting to the room, but I found the family picture right before my glass on the desk. It was the most recent photo of the entire family in the backyard shortly before Jessie and Jimmy went to college. I remember that day very well. The twins were still home the summer before moving into the dorms and they wanted to spend a day in the backyard like their younger years before parading off to college and the beginning of the rest of their lives. I found the idea rather wasteful but went with the flow. Lisa embraced the idea. Lisa made her famous homemade pimento cheese sandwiches that were for "special occasions." The family spread a quilt along the shadow line of the dogwoods on a warm June Sunday afternoon. The tree tire swung across the pond in the background. Lisa and I sipped wine while the children had sweet tea. Jessie rested the camera on the picnic basket and placed it on a timer so she could get into the picture with the family. The week they took the picture was exactly a year before Lisa passed and three months after Jimmy caught his father in the workroom with a college kid. It disturbed me how unaffected Jimmy remained the entire time.

I allowed myself to get lost in the memories with the classical music from the living room being a gentle soundtrack for the photo. I placed the photo back on the desk and went to pour another glass of bourbon. Just as I lifted the glass to my lips, the realization froze me. I had turned down the volume before coming into the study.

I eased myself to the doorway of the study and peered down the eerie hallway. The sounds were haunting, anchored by piano music. Each key pressed had a hallowed and deep tone that shivered down my esophagus.

The shiver climbed up my back and into my throat. The fear bubbled into rage.

I walked down the unlit hallway, missing the half bath door handle this trip. I got to the edge of the stairs. I was looking in the living room to make sure the radio remained off when the music echoed behind me. I spun toward the staircase too quickly, and had to grab the railing. I nursed myself along the railing and made it to the bottom step. I stared at the attic door through the mirror, and it felt like I could touch the waves of music oozing out the cracks of the door. The music was oddly soothing, but sometimes sent chills through my bones. I felt the breeze of the music tickle the back of my neck. I involuntarily grasped for my throat while I felt my heartbeat keep time with the tempo of the piano. Air escaped my lungs. I gasped for breath, and had to relax my mind. I eventually caught my breath again, but still felt tightness in my chest.

I eased my hand on the railing, hoping to not disturb the phantom musician. My feet made every ascending step graciously, but I could faintly hear the squeak of my sneakers. After three steps I stopped and the melodic noise continued. Every step closer, the music pounded faster. Nervous perspiration dripped from my forehead out of dread for what I would discover, allowing some of the alcohol to escape my pores. When I reached the middle step, the playing became so intense it nearly knocked me backwards. The music changed not only tempo but scale. Something darker, more haunting, came from the attic. My eardrums clattered with the walls. I proceeded despite the pressure and fear. When I reached the attic door, the music stopped. I paused there, thinking the door might burst off its hinges. Nothing happened except the spinning of the hallway. I had to lean into the door to still my head when the pounding on the keys scared me back to the steps. It stopped before I could descend from the top step, so I turned back toward the door. My heart banged against my chest bones with each thump. I wanted to run at that moment. Forget all this drum nonsense. Yet, I was determined to learn who played the piano.

I struggled with the doorknob. Sometimes the handle had to be jiggled to loosen the latch. It took several jiggles before I finally got the handle to turn. The hinges creaked as I pried opened the door. I looked into the dark and lightning abruptly filled the attic with visibility. I rubbed my hand on the wooden wall until I felt the switch. Some light filled the room, but it was a smoky haze. The smell of mothballs, mildew and dirt flooded my nostrils, adding to the nausea from the liquor. I thought I shouldn't go into the attic, but before I realized it, I stood in the center or the room. It was as if something drug me up the wooden steps and slid me over the wobbly floorboards. But here I stood, about eight feet from the piano.

The piano wasn't always in the attic. It was removed from her workroom not too long after Lisa died from ovarian cancer. She was in remission for a few years, but it snuck up on her again and she was rushed to the hospital with sudden, sharp pain. The doctors wanted her to stay in the hospital, but Lisa told them she'd rather die at the home she took years to create with the family she loved. Lisa spent most of her final days in her workroom, pounding scores she composed or old pieces she practiced. She migrated to her workroom a lot to play the piano. She practiced her lesson plans, personal piano compositions and cello recital performances. It got tough for her to sit for long in the room, but she said the view of the pond, dogwoods, and her flower garden below eased the suffering. Jimmy continued to go into his mother's workroom to practice his work when she passed. Sometimes, he kept the door open, and I would sneak peeks of him following in his mother's footsteps. Those were the only moments when the grieving tears formed in my eyes. Keeping the secret of the affair between Jimmy and me only shredded my filthy heart more. When Jimmy walked in on me with that college intern in Lisa's workroom that afternoon ...

My affair with the intern from my school office was immature, heartless and selfish. The reality that it would become very risky only trickled in the back of my mind after the third time I felt myself in the girl. I knew everyone's routines, thus, when the house was empty, but my paranoia and guilt had me reviewing everyone's schedule. Lisa went to rehearse with her own orchestra right after rehearsing with the middle school band, keeping her away from home until after nine. The twins were active in school, so they wouldn't be home until in the evenings. Of course I was uneasy during the first month of my scandalous rendezvouses in the home. The shame led me to drink heavy again. I loved Lisa more than my own life, but her distance was evident and my self-centered urges needed satisfying. I didn't know her illness returned. No one did; she hid her struggles in her studies and work. It was month four when I began to get sloppy with hiding the affair with the intern. It was nearing the end of the school year, and I wanted to give the intern a personal "thank you for all the hard work" she had put in. I was piss blind drunk when I led her by the hand to Lisa's workroom. I dropped my pants and boxers to my ankles and sat down, and she didn't hesitate to straddle me. My hand and ass slid in our saturated sweat on the piano bench. My God we were so fucking loud between our pants and pounding on the piano keys. I don't know how long Jimmy stood in the doorway watching his father penetrate a girl just a few years older than him, and we made a second of eye contact before he ran off. I finished quicker than planned with in the intern.

I had the piano moved into the attic after Lisa and Jimmy's death. I wanted the thing to be removed from the house when the movers came to get some of the furniture. I didn't want the piano anymore, but Jessie refused to let go of something that meant so much to her brother and her mother.

Now, here I stood, gulping the last of my bourbon and walking to the tainted piano. The neglected instrument was covered in months worth of dust. I kept studying it, knowing logically this thing could not have made any of the noise I've been hearing all night. I laughed at my drunken ignorance. Just as I went to turn from the piano, I glanced at the bench. A butt print disturbed the settled dust on the bench, as if someone was just sitting there. I scanned the ivories and found fresh fingerprints scattered along the keys. My blood ran cold. I started to run the hell out the attic when the attic door slammed and the lights flickered out.

I stood in the dark. The only sounds I heard at that moment were the boards creaking below my feet. Then came the heavy breathing from the bottom of the steps. I was too far from the stairs to know for sure, but I sensed someone—or something—stood at the attic door. I resisted running down the stairs, refusing to give it any satisfaction at my horrified expense. If I survived the day I caught my son kissing and groping a much older man's groin in the exact room his mother spent her final days, on the exact same bench my son caught me screwing a girl half my age, then I could survive whatever else Hell had in store for me.

"Come on!" I said. "I'm right here, you bastard! I've been waiting for you to arrive! You've been here since the first day I fucked that girl! I felt you watching me then! Did you enjoy watching me fuck her!? You've been here since then! For months!—around the corners, lurking in the shadows like a spineless scarecrow … Why act shy now, you sick bastard!?"

Lightning filled the room for a second; making the room darker when it subsided. I felt the run, bourbon and vodka bubble from my stomach into my throat.

"Did you tell my son to come to the room that day?!" The alcohol climbed my throat, and I gargled my words. "To catch me with that intern!? My wife couldn't make love to me, anymore! I am a man; I need what I need!"

The sweltering attic spun around me. I reached to find something to grasp. Instead, I clutched my stomach before vomiting on the attic floor.

At first, the only noises were my heaves and spitting. The thunder settled and I regained control of my breathing. What I heard next made the hairs on the back of my neck stand: The A below middle C pulsated from the piano. I rose as the notes descended from the A: the G, the F, the E, D ... all natural. It was the A minor scale. I knew this because this was the scale Lisa used to write her final score about her battle with cancer. She told me it was like cheating on her love for music to play like an amateur by using a scale without any sharps or flats. Her energy and concentration diminished due to the cancer spreading, and she couldn't focus past the F Major Scale. Lisa played the piece professionally yet privately when she shared with me her final composition. I got the handheld to record her final piece. She said she ended the last four cords in C Major progression because she wanted to compose how she was victorious in winning the war in spite of the cancer trying to take her spirit. Lisa said that she would fight until she was ready to go. Her final performance was a month before her died.

The keys kept descending in A minor. I didn't realize I had spun toward the piano again. It was too dark to see what stroked the keys, but I saw the space before the piano much murkier than the natural darkness in the attic. I was hypnotized by the playing, and when it stopped That's when I felt its glare. I knew whatever was there had turned to face me. I couldn't see a damn thing, but I knew my fear alone fueled what monstrous grin sneered at me.

Lightning flashed, and I saw it for just a second. I could've handled a demon from hell. I could've handled some ungodly being with razor-sharp talons ready to claw my eyes and heart out in a clean sweep. I prayed for what horror haunted me all these months to finally approach me and end my torture and self-pity. I had been ready to end it all after everything. But when the lightning flashed, Jimmy glared into my eyes with that same blank stare he had when I took his last breath with my own hands.

The scream ripped its way up my throat and out my mouth.

The lights flickered while I ran down the attic stairs. I tried to turn the doorknob, but it wouldn't budge. My instincts told to shake the doorknob. I did so frantically, trying to loosen the latch. I turned my head and saw my son on the top step watching me struggle with the door with the softest grin, as if he was amused by my torment. I had to look away from Jimmy. The doorknob remained jammed. I looked back up the stairs: My son was on the middle step. My pulse thumped in my ears. I looked back at the stuck doorknob. I wanted to look anywhere except back up the stairs, but the hot foul breath along my neck forced me to look once more. I shook the doorknob harder while squinting my eyes for a better look.

Jimmy was only two steps behind me.

I saw the blood vessels in my son's dim eyes. They were as profound as the day I watched them go bloodshot during the final moments my hands were wrapped around my son's neck. Jimmy tried to scream for me to stop punching the man on the floor, but by the fourth blow the guy died instantly while help pounding in his face. Jimmy tried to run out the workroom, but I grabbed him and threw him on the floor. I jumped on Jimmy's chest and wrapped my hands around his throat, screaming *why this room of all rooms!? You little shit had to demoralize your mother's room with your filth and greed!* Jimmy didn't blink. I will never forget watching the last of light dim from my son's eyes.

I fell through the doorway when it finally opened. I crawled to the top step of the second floor stairs and used the railing to lift my body. I almost lost my balance down the stairs, but I made it to the first floor only after tripping over the third step. I felt my shin pulsate when I cradled it. I turned to look up the stairs. The attic door remained wide open. Nothing stood inside its frame. I struggled to stand, leaning on the wall.

The kitchen's swinging door opened. I didn't flinch when Lisa stepped into the dining room. She stared at me with her blue angelic eyes. Seeing her made me cry.

"I'm so sorry," I said. "I couldn't control myself. Jimmy was gay. And he held my affair within him for so long. He never told you, did he?"

Lisa remained motionless, staring at me.

"When I caught him with that man, his last words were to keep his love life a secret like he kept mine a secret. My affair from *you*, Lisa! I couldn't resist. It was too much." I drop to my knees. "You should've told me you were in remission! I hit the bottle hard after that ... hell!—before that ... Been drinking more since you died. I'm lost without you.

"I blamed him for making your workroom dirty. It was me! I brought my filthy affair into your final resting room way before Jimmy brought his. He followed my steps just as he followed yours! Just like how I followed my father's ..."

The stairs creaked. I looked up to find Jimmy glaring from the center of the flight.

"I'm so sorry, son," I cried out, fighting more alcohol building up my body. "I lost my mind. I couldn't live with the guilt. And then she died before knowing the truth. I could never get myself to tell her. Why didn't you!? If you just told her, my guilt would have never lived in a bottle.

"I can only blame myself. She was so good to me. You were a good son ... I am sorry. Please, forgive me ..."

The knock on the front door made me jump and scream. A collection of knocks followed. Then I heard my name coming from behind the door. Through the door window I saw two heads. I knew who they were. I looked back up the stairs to find it vacant. I looked into the dining room. Lisa was gone. I opened to find two police officers and my daughter Jessie standing on the stoop. I couldn't look any of them in the eyes.

"The bodies are in the pond in the back."

. . .

The storm had died to a drizzle when more circled outside the house. A uniformed cop stayed inside to watch me. Jessie stood near the steps and glared at me through tear-stained eyes. I sat in the recliner staring at the carpet. I could really use another drink.

It was the whiskey that got me to tell Jessie everything. That and the prolonged guilt eating my insides worse than the alcohol. I shared my affair with the intern and how her twin brother caught me in their mother's workroom with the intern. I explained how we kept the affair between one another even after their mother's death. I also shared how I caught Jimmy in their mother's workroom with an older man—the officials informed me it was some graduate assistant of one of his instructors that had disappeared basically the same time Jimmy had been reported missing by Jessie—and how I killed them both and dumped the bodies in the pond. I told her about lying to everyone that her brother ran off with this man rather than telling the truth. I didn't have to tell her that I started drinking again.

I rose from the recliner. Jessie flinched toward the front door. The police officer moved in my direction. I raised my hands and said I had to use the restroom. The cop looked reluctant but let me go. My own daughter ran behind the stair railings before I passed her and stared down at the wood flooring in the foyer while I crossed her. I wanted to hug her, tell her I loved her, to apologize for everything, but I knew she would resist. I just sighed into tears as I strolled in the direction of the foyer half bathroom.

But I wasn't really going to the half bathroom. My destination was the mini bar in the study. Everything I wanted at that moment rested there. First, I make another drink there before whatever happens next.

THE RETRACTOR

Gwyneth couldn't believe she was standing in line again for the rollercoaster that traumatized her, lingering by the wooden cutout of carnival's icon Sticks the Scarecrow having his gloved hand showing how high five-foot two is from the ground. Brick and Amy had talked her into it, taking advantage of her giddiness now that mid-term exams were over. She blamed the Mega-Blaster Pop; the thirty-two ounces of syrupy goodness provided the best high she'd had all week, dulling the edges after the grind of taking on one exam after another. The fuzzy buzz blended well with the ambient noise—which included thunderous train rails, flashing bulbs, and animated shrills, mixed with the electronic drone you hear at every carnival. Gwyneth could never have pictured herself standing in this line again, but that was before Brick asked with high cheek bones and through his chiseled jaw and with his movie-star blue eyes.

Gwyneth developed a crush on Brick the instant she witnessed from her bedroom window as he helped unload the U-Haul into the house across the street five years earlier. She recalled others at school had been calling him Brick rather than Owen since eighth grade because he already had rippling muscles before they hit high school. Those six-pack abs only harden over the years between training to become this year's varsity team's star receiver in football and featured diver for the swim team each winter. The results were the body every teenage girl dreams to brag about dating.

After going through an ugly-duckling stage, Gwyneth had owned blossoming into a beauty. At the moment, though, her confidence was running low. She stared back into the black-painted, triangle-shaped eyes of her petite jack-o-lantern while clutching it for comfort with both hands. *So, here you are. You're once again in line for The Retractor.*

The only other time Gwyneth had ever stood in line for any roller coaster was for this exact one. She'd attended the fair with her mother, father, and much-older brother for her eighth birthday. The three of them were nearly tall enough to reach up and ring the bell at the top of the Test Your Strength Game, no anvil required. Gwyneth, however, didn't get the giant gene like the rest of the family, and knew she wouldn't meet the height requirement to ride the coaster. Yet, her family was getting on, and she didn't want to be the one who made her mom or dad miss any of the fun on her birthday.

To avoid spoiling the good time, Gwyneth scooted underneath the annoying carnival guests who'd pushed past the carnie and onto the roller coaster's queue. The operator was distracted while checking the safety bars, too busy staring at the rack on the young lady in Car 7, and he overlooked Gwyneth being well short of filling up her shoulder strap in Cart 8. The flashback to the moments when she nearly tumbled out the roller coaster cart during the sudden acceleration down Hill Two made Gwyneth shiver with anticipation. She tightened her jacket in an attempt to feel more secure.

You promised yourself never another roller coaster as long as you live because you wanted to live*!*

"Oh, Gwyneth," Amy said, interrupting the horrific memory. "Don't get cold feet on us *now*."

"Yeah!" Brick chimed in, bouncing on the balls of his feet. "We're nearly next. Can't back out now."

Oh can't I?

Gwyneth wanted to turn and run, but she was frozen from fear. Besides that, she didn't want to let Brick down. The roller coaster rattled overhead, vibrating her bones and escalating her nerves. The same terror that kept her frozen in line was the exact same feeling she had when she woke from her nightmare nine years ago. She remembers falling from her bed, thinking she had tumbled from the cart in her nightmare, and awaking drenched in sweat. Now, she was about to relive the nightmare. The reality of it was overwhelming.

"No." Gwyneth choked on her words, keeping focus on her tiny jack-o-lantern. "No cold feet."

Brick and Amy both giggled, dismissing her fear, while all three inched forward. Gwyneth was aware Amy, a budding beauty in her own right, had a long-standing crush on Brick, too, but guessing out of respect for her best friend, Amy never acted on it. She was honoring the "I saw him first" rule that applies to close friendships. Gwyneth didn't have the courage to act on her feelings for Brick, but she promised herself the day would come.

However, her reluctance must had been apparent, because Amy had been more … *friendly* toward Brick than usual since they got to the carnival. In fact, it was Amy's suggestion to go on the Retractor … the best friend that knew Gwyneth's experience.

She sighed. *You got this, Gwyneth …*

Click, click, click, click came the sound from the tunnel to their right, and seconds later the coaster carts came to a rest at the boarding station. Brick could barely contain himself while Amy shuffled closer to him. Gwyneth's heart jumped into her throat and skipped a beat, knowing they were the next ones to ride. She squeezed her pumpkin tighter.

The rails swung open, and the carnie, dressed as a scarecrow, directed the next crop of riders in line to board the coaster.

Brick rested both hands on Gwyneth's shoulders as he bounced in place behind her, giving her a rush that washed away her concern for a brief moment. "It's on now!" he shouted.

Amy enthusiastically hopped into the front part of the No. 8 car, like a frog onto a floating lily pad. The vibrating rails compounded the intensity of Gwyneth's tremble, and her prized pumpkin slipped out of her grasp.

The seeds and tangled guts exploded upon landing. Chunky melon shards covered the walkway. The black eyes survived and an orange forehead glared at her: *This is going to be you, Gwyneth.*

She drew stares while sulking over the shattered jack-o-lantern. The scarecrow carnie cussed under his breath, stewing about having to clean up the fruit. Those next to ride hastily pushed past her, climbing into the cars.

Gwyneth looked back one last time at her ruined jack-o-lantern and stepped toward the Retractor because of her friends' shoving.

The bold-painted number eight on the side of the coaster gave Gwyneth pause. She felt Brick's nudge from behind, but anxiety kept her frozen in place. She saw from the corner of her eye people strapping on their safety devices. She knew this was too much, and she couldn't do it. Her stomach started churning, and she was just about to follow the original plan to turn and run.

But that's when she felt Brick's hand take hers, and their fingers interlocking together. Her fear fell away, and all she could think about was how good it felt to hold the hand of the guy she wanted more than any other.

"I got you," Brick whispered in hers right ear. "You got this."

His fresh breath tickled her neck, and butterflies took flight in her stomach. Gwyneth was practically floating from the joy of Brick's touch, and he wasn't letting go. Before she knew it, Gwyneth was in the seat behind Amy, still holding Brick's hand. She looked up to find Brick smiling warmly at her. She couldn't help but wonder if this was the start of something between them. He never showed her this side before.

"You can do this," Brick said. "You're not eight anymore, Gwyneth. You're seventeen now, and this is the year of new beginnings."

He squeezed her hand and they exchanged smiles while the coaster began its first climb. Hill One wasn't as steep; that wasn't what petrified her. It was Hill Two.

The wind whipped her hair around as they hung a sharp right turn. Then the roller coaster quickly halted, jerking her toward the back of Amy's head. Gwyneth couldn't help but instinctively squeeze her eyes shut. The reaction wasn't because she thought she was going to smack into Amy's head, it was the pull in her gut as the coaster climbed Hill Two. She tightened her grip on Brick's hand, and he gave her a squeeze back to acknowledge it.

Gwyneth felt gravity weigh her down as if she had boulders strapped to her back. Her jaw hurt from grinding her teeth. Her heartbeat pulsed through her veins as she clasped a death grip on the safety bar. Her blood ran colder than the chill in the air. Gwyneth knew they would top the hill in a matter of seconds.

She felt panic when Brick pulled his grip from hers, only to be renewed with comfort when he wrapped his arm around her shoulder and pulled her into his muscular chest. His smooth skin touching her bare shoulder sent a warm rush through her body. She could have lived in that moment forever.

"Gwyneth," Brick said. "You might want to open your eyes now. I really don't think you want to miss this."

Gwyneth felt a mix of courage and fear: Her instincts told her to not look, but it was over-ridden by her trust in Brick.

When her eyes popped open, she couldn't believe the sight.

She paid no attention to how The Retractor held car number eight in the sky, because she was witnessing the most beautiful sunset ever. It was as if the artist she was studying in art class, Kano Eitoku, had painted it with nature's water-colors, just for her and Brick to have this romantic moment. That's when Brick leaned in and gave her a long kiss.

Amy looked back and stared for a second … but then gave a soft, assuring smile. The anxiety Gwyneth felt about this ride for the past nine years was now gone for good. *I got this.* she thought. She smiles back at her best friend, then to her new boyfriend.

"I got this."

LET HER SLEEP

Those of us who live along the Carolina coast know better than to even utter her name. Admittedly, storytelling is a common practice with us, but we don't ever talk about the Boo Hag. The hoodoo novices are the only ones who can explain her fate without consequences, for they've been blessed to stabilize the netherworld's darkness with the world's natural light. Others are forewarned to let her sleep or she'd mess with you when you sleep. Whether it's a child's scary mirror game kids do during a sleepover, or a scholar's exploration while writing her thesis, meddling in the Boo Hag's business will only bring pure hell to all involved.

I've been raised to understand the repercussions of those not consecrated. I want to share this experience as a cautionary tale of what'll happen to anyone foolish enough to think the Boo Hag's just a Gullah ghost story.

If you're bold and choose read on, I advise you to keep the story to yourself; the Boo Hag's always listening ... and vengeful.

•   •   •

Thursday, October 28, 2010

Grandmama Abba has started serving fish and collard greens at the dining table when we hear the front door creak open and slam shut. Right after, Antwan strides into the kitchen. Looking exhausted, he drags himself to the table and takes the available chair, exhaling through pursed lips. He doesn't bother making a plate, most likely due to another grinding day of cooking and serving guests at the hotel.

My only child, Seble, hasn't even taken her first bite when she starts in with the questions. "Anything cool happen today, 'Twan?"

I shovel some rice from the pot. "Seble, let your cousin settle before you bug him. The man worked all day."

Abba points at Seble's plate with a serving spoon. "You best be fixin' on them groceries, Gran' than bumping those gums."

Antwan chuckles. "She's good, y'all. It was the same old, anyhow, Baby Girl. Tourists visiting Charleston, tie-wearing businessmen carrying brief cases for mini-meetings, younger folks wanting to know about Gullah history ..."

I snicker. "You didn't have to talk all Geechee again, did you, son?"

Antwan succumbs to the supper's rich aroma and leans across the table for a hand-made biscuit from the sweetgrass basket. "No, sir, Uncle Ray."

I've always referred to my nephew as "son." I raised him after my brother and his wife had passed when he was six. I've kept Antwan on track in school, given him guidance on girls, and helped him steer clear of hoodlum-life choices throughout grade school, but he wasn't a challenge to raise. Antwan had goals in mind early. He grew, from learning Abba's old-style recipes, to a culinary apprentice at Trident Technical College, and now he's one of the best-known lead chefs on the Carolina coast. If he's not at the hotel working, he's traveling from Savannah to Charlotte and other places in-between doing catering jobs.

"Were there some people looking for ghosts, again?" Seble asks, with her mouth full.

Abba pops the side of Seble's plate with a fork. "You know better! Swalluh, Gran'."

Antwan spreads some marmalade on his biscuit. "Not this time, Seble. There are four students staying at the hotel for the weekend. They're doing some research about the Boo Hag."

An unsettling silence ensues, and everyone stops eating.

My breathing shallows from shock that the boy was foolish enough to speak her name. Seble's mouth drops open, exposing chewed corn and rice. Abba's hands are trembling, and the beans from her spoon spill onto the table. Abba begins uttering in her native tongue. I lean over and place my hand on her shoulder, asking if she's okay.

Abba's head twitches slightly before ceases chanting. "Oh yes, baby."

She rests the spoon on her plate before caressing my hand to release her. She gathers her wits by cleaning the scattered food and rests the napkin on her plate. Her demeanor stiffens, and her index finger is only centimeters from her grandson's nose.

"Antwan Somerset, you tell them white babies to best leave be if they know what's good. And you know what's best for this family to not say aloud." Abba points at Seble and then to the hallway. "Gran', go on and grab my shawl and roots to bless this house, baby."

• • •

Antwan joins me in the den after Abba and Seble settle for the night—a habit he developed in his youth. The only difference tonight was he came into the room sweaty and with haint blue splotches on his arms and clothing. I arrange myself in my recliner with today's *Post and Courier*, and he sits in his usual spot on the sofa near my lounger. The evening's ritual begins as it has for many years: he shares his day; I talk shit about how crazy and stupid the world's getting based on the headlines; and we give one another a hard time=--tonight, I had one up on him with Mama's demand.

Antwan eases his laughter to ask, "Why'd you think Grams reacted like that, Uncle Ray?"

I'd been waiting for him to bring it up but shrug at Antwan's question, not looking up from the newspaper.

Seble and I finished dinner in silence after my mother's cautionary words. She had chanted while swirling that fowl smelling lit herbs about all the entrances into the home, demanding for my nephew to put a fresh coat of blue along the window panes and door frames. Antwan's quivering eyes appeared wounded. I'd exchanged stares with Antwan, hinting to let it go and do what his grandma asked of him.

I've not seen Abba worked up like that in some time. She's the old school type. I have scars from childhood on the back of my calves from the switchins' to show the cost of upsetting my mother. I feared what Abba would do if my stubborn nephew kept persisting about what we know to not mention. So, of course, he comes to his favorite uncle with the questions.

"How'd she even know they were white—"

I interrupt him. "Because only white folks are foolish enough to go stirring up shit they have no business messing with in the first place, 'Twan. I bet it was some girl you were trying to impress, again, anyhow."

Antwan whistles. "Shit, Unk, you know me … There was a blonde-headed girl, asking the questions."

"Did you get her name even?"

"Amber. Fine as hell, with her country-thick self. Should had seen her, Uncle Ray."

He makes me blurt a belly laugh, but at the same time irritating the dull ache in my right shoulder—an old high school football injury. "Boy, stay clear from them white witches."

Antwan waves both hands. "Naw. It's not like that, Unk. Her blue eyes and soft smile are from goods. That fair skin, too ... But there's some truth to it, right?" His question throws me. "The stories. I see the neighbors still painting their front doors blue, too"—he lifts his hand to display some droplets of paint on his fingers—"and hanging sweetgrass trinkets on their porches ..."

I shoot my eyes back to the newspaper. "It's just our elders settled in their superstitions. Most know none of that mess is real, but they still do it out of habit from how they were raised. You gonna holler at that girl?"

Antwan laughs, throwing his head back and easing deeper into the sofa. His brow and lips soften as he interlocks his fingers behind his head. He stretches his scarecrow legs and gets lost in his thoughts. Mentioning the girl got him thinking about her and not anything else—mission accomplished.

"What do you know about the Boo Hag, Uncle Ray?"

I thought wrong. "Son, where's all this nonsense coming from? You know better than to get mixed up with the tourists. And you know better than to talk that mess."

Antwan readjusts on the couch, sitting up and studying the floor. "They're not tourists, Uncle Ray. They're grad students." To me there's little difference, unlike my nephew, apparently. "They're from the psych department at USC Columbia. They said they'd came across the Boo

Hag while reading up on sleep paralysis for a thesis and came for the weekend to do research on the folklore."

I react with a deep sigh. "I've done told you and Seble both all the same stuff Abba had passed to me from her grandparents—the Boo Hag's an evil Geechee witch from slave days and she possesses men in their sleep. Some have said they can't raise up from their sleep because she sits on their chest. That's all *anyone* knows." I'm hoping my uninterested flat tone gives Antwan the hint to finally drop the subject. But I also add, "And you know we're all raised to let her sleep."

"It's just Amber—that's the blonde-headed girl—and the jock-looking fella, Brian I think's the white boy's name, were telling me about how serious this research is for some neuropsychological periodical." His college words get a raised brow out of me. "And I get that, Uncle Ray. Your graduate work isn't like some book report or an experiment for the science fair in high school. Your reputation and success is on the line with your final graduate project. I went all out for my dishes I college and look where that hard work got me! They're doing the same with their thesis—" Antwan sees my attention's back on the paper, and he mumbles, "They asked where they could get some authentic research. I know the hotel's little gift shop wouldn't have anything good. If I could let them look at that book Abba reads to the trick-or-treaters—"

I can't believe my ears. "You'd be a damn fool if you did that!" I slam the newspaper on the ottoman. Antwan stiffens his back and sits up straight. I peer over my glasses and into my nephew's eyes. "Now, listen, son. I might not be all into the history of that hoodoo mess like your grandma, but the stories our ancestors passed down throughout the years are haunting enough for me to leave what needs to be left alone. I'm happy to see the younger generations wanting to be ... progressive and all that jumbo, but the best *research* you can share with them youngsters is what smart people would do: visit the local library and take one of those Gullah tours." I ease back into the recliner, gathering the now crumpled paper and my composure. "Hell! Tell them to hang around for Abba's storytelling at the hotel this Sunday evening. That'd be best for them." I give Antwan a final glower. "And for you too, son."

•.....•.....•

Friday, October 29, 2010
Antwan comes home around the same time as last night. When he joins the table, he slumps in his chair and stares at the gravy-stained tablecloth. When Seble asks, he shares that today was "busy but good" and not another word.

"Nothing wrong with a hardworking man," Abba praises, keeping her focus on the yams.

Antwan doesn't respond. He's been raised better than to ignore his elders. I waited for her to chastise his insolence, but I think Abba reads the same ass-whooped expression as I do and leaves the boy be.

Seble jabbers about her day, sharing how her teacher had the class create paper-mâché jack-o-lanterns. She gripes about how that's what little kids do, not fifth graders, but she eventually gives into admitting how she enjoyed the activity.

I smile and giggle to pretend I'm interested in her story, but my mind is on my nephew. I hope that blonde didn't crush his ego.

•   •   •

I take my usual place in the den, catching up on the daily headlines. The sun has set and the ladies of the house have settled for the night. I figured my nephew called it an early night since he excused himself shortly after joining us at the kitchen nook; I settle in for some solitude, and tune into history and highlights of South Carolina playing against Tennessee as their game is tomorrow.

I'm deep into the stats and analysis when Antwan peers around the entranceway, leaning his body against the border. I keep watching the screen but monitor him from the corner of my eye. His face is constricted with worry, the same as it was when he came home. He studies the floor, outlining the pattern with his foot like a child. He shifts his weight off the doorframe and sluggishly makes his way to the sofa.

I keep my eyes on the television. "You good, son?"

Antwan leans forward but doesn't pull his focus from the dated carpet. "Sure, Unk." His breath catches his words in a sigh and he fidgets his fingers. "So, those students were in the dining area before Hera and I arrived this morning to set up for breakfast, right? Hera, being the best assistant any chef could ask for, did her thing and asked if they'd like anything to drink while we're still prepping. They responded they were good but then were quick to share with Hera how they'd been hyped since before the sun rose, mapping out the parts of Charleston they wanted to visit and shit. Without warning, they quickly dove into tapping Hera's knowledge of Gullah shit, right? She played all naïve and what not. When the rest of my crew clocked in, the students drilled them pretty much the same way. The staff was friendly, but I saw the discomfort on their faces when the students mentioned the Boo Hag. Only a handful had shared what they knew, but you know, I have employees not much older than the college kids themselves, so there wasn't much they could really tell the kids."

My attention had shifted to my nephew, waiting for him to get to why he'd been moping around the house all evening.

Antwan senses my impatience. "Yeah … So, Hera told me they keep bugging our staff to get me. I laughed and asked why they would want to talk with me? Hera said someone had told them about how Abba plays a hoodoo priestess and reads from her book every Halloween. When Hera told them I was too busy at the moment, the students got all demanding, refusing to pay the bill until they spoke with me. So, I finally came out of the kitchen and ask how were their meals. They said everything was fine but then were quick to jump into asking about Abba and the Geechee witch."

Antwan pauses, as if his thoughts are holding back his tongue.

Leaning forward, I eagerly await his response. "'Twan, did you tell them what we spoke of last—"

"I did!" He's still avoiding eye contact, but darts his eyes in my direction, suggesting he took heed of my warning.

My nephew clears his throat. "I didn't mean to snap at you, Unk. But I told them about going to the library or taking one of those city tours. They seemed to love the suggestion, calling it *raw* or some shit. They were unfazed, and I didn't know how to react at all, Unk. Mr. Baseball Scholarship Brian informed me that he and Amber had booked some tours for today, while the other two—Emily and Trevor—were hitting the libraries along the bay area. Emily held up an advertisement with those neon pink nails about Sister Annalise—"

I sit up straight. "Oh, Lord! Please say they didn't ... Where'd they even get such trash?"

Antwan lifts his hands into the air, shaking his head. "The Emily girl said they found it on the lobby bulletin board while they were checking in yesterday. She said she tried reaching out to her but had no luck with the number on the flyer, so they were going to look her up at the library."

"Oh, hell ... Did you tell them not to go seeking out that bull shit!?"

"Yes sir, I told them."

My concern for these kids heightens. "Sister Annalise knows better than to mess around with them tourists with her nonsense. You'd figured she and that no-good brother of hers, Stanton, would lay low with the cops' radar on them since the TV news exposed them—"

"Did them babies go out there?" Abba's soft, scratchy voice made both Antwan and I shift in our seats. She glides gracefully into the room from the hallway, wrapped in her shawl.

"Mama," I gruffly say, "how long you been standing there? You know you should be in bed—"

"Did you tell them children to stay away from that demon enchantress?" Abba's big heart worries for the kids' well-being, rather than to pay any mind to my concerns for her own health.

Antwan swallows air. "I'm ... I'm not sure, Abba—"

"What you mean, child?" Abba spat her words like daggers. "How can you not be sure if you told them? Do we not tell you children to forewarn her spooks on the playground? Do we not tell you babies to tell your mates?"

Antwan furrows his brow at me and opens his palms toward the sky.

I snigger and divert my eyes back on the sports news.

"I mean, I never saw them again after this morning, ma'am," he stutters. "So I didn't have a chance to really talk with them like that. I asked Felisha at the front desk if she'd seen them come through the lobby before I left the hotel, but she hadn't ..." Antwan trails, thinking that'd suffice for his grandmother.

Abba tightens the cloak around her. "That Sista 'Leese's no good. She and her brother are dirty fiends. When you see them babies tomorrow, Gran', you best tell them Abba forbids it and they'd abide if they know what's good for their souls."

Antwan acknowledges his grandmother.

Abba turns and flounces toward the darkened hallway. "Pray them babies be safe in their beds."

· · ·

Saturday, October 30, 2010
Antwan still isn't home when we start fixin' the shrimp and cabbage with the corned beef. Antwan often works overtime at the hotel, so it isn't beyond the norm. Abba gets a little huffy, but ultimately she always falls back on her motto: "there's nothing wrong with a hardworking man."

There are many reasons why Antwan might have to stay late. Usually, he stays longer when tourist season is booming, and Halloween in Charleston draws a lot of out-of-town folks interested in the cemetery tours, carriage rides and other festivities. The students at College of Charleston have become highly active with the season, too. Maybe some company rented the conference room for an Autumn jubilee. We just go about our night, as he does with his.

I thank Abba for another great meal with a forehead kiss and migrate to the den with Seble at my heels. I haven't even situated myself into the recliner with my paper when she asks about Antwan. I answer with how she needs to go help her grandmother clear the table rather than meddling in someone's business. She quickly responds: "it's already done."

I'm quicker to say: "Then go clean your room."

She stands in the doorway a little longer with crossed arms, and I cannot help but be reminded of her deadbeat mama—the hard glare and all. With a firm tone I remind her: "I've already told you once." She huffs and stomps off.

I finally get into my reading while listening to Seble deliberately making a ruckus and thumping on the bedroom walls. I should get up and whoop her, but think better of it—at least she isn't bugging me about why Antwan isn't home yet.

• • •

It's my third time reading through the headlines about the Carolina-Tennessee game on the screen when Antwan enters the house. He mechanically nods but keeps looking forward as he drags himself toward the kitchen. He stays in the back long enough for me to gently fold the paper and rest it on the nearby ottoman—irritating the arthritis in the shoulder.

He returns with two longnecks. He's unfastened a few of the top buttons on his chef tunic, releasing the stench from the grease-stained, sweat-drenched undershirt. Antwan hands one of the bottles to me with a wilted wrist. His grave and muddled expression doesn't meet my concerned gaze.

I gladly accept the Budweiser. My nerves could use it.

Antwan plops down on the couch and sinks in, resting his head against the back cushion. His glassy eyes are fixed on the ceiling while he twists off the bottle top. He takes three big gulps. "The police visited the hotel today."

The hairs on the back of my neck stand, and I edge closer toward him. I try to arrange questions in my head, but there's so much to ask and I'm overwhelmed. I take a swig and decide it's best if I just hear him out.

Antwan lowers the beer from his lips. "The students didn't talk when they came down for breakfast this morning. I checked them out when I helped Hera restock the condiment bar. They looked as if they hadn't slept; they had bags under their bloodshot eyes. They slumped over their plates, pushing food around with their forks, seldom taking a bite. Hera pointed out there were only three of them at the table—the two guys and Amber. I also noticed they had their luggage under the table. They didn't have the brunette with them.

"Hera asked about the Emily girl when she refilled their drinks. The Trevor fella muttered something before rising and staggering out the dining room. The other two remained in their chairs damn near dead. Not too much more came from their table for a good while after that, Unk.

"A ringtone of some country song played beneath their table, but no one answered the phone at first. The guests tried to be all low key when looking in their direction when the cell rang again. The third time disturbed my servers from working. That shit got old, and I came out of the kitchen on ring four, near blanking. But Hera saw me pissed and handled it for me.

"Amber fumbled through her things before getting to the phone. That damn phone started playing that twangy country shit a fifth time before she finally answered it.

"She didn't say anything, hardly holding the cell to her head. She held it like that for so long, and we went back to work. Then she screams 'Oh, god!' and jumped up from the table, knocking her chair backward. She motioned for Brian to follow her. Her crazy-ass commotion got the guests and my staff all freaked out. I couldn't believe the way they jumped up and ran out the dining room like that. I heard a little of Amber's rant as they fled the area—something about Trevor saying Emily isn't waking up. They left their luggage under the table."

Antwan pauses for another sip. "The police came into the hotel like gangbusters not even an hour after the two had split. The detectives demanded to interview *everyone* in the building—guests and staff. The hotel manager, Jason, even had to call last night's graveyard shift to come in; I know they had to be sleeping. No one knew what the hell was going on, and administration weren't sharing shit.

"They weren't done interrogating the dining staff when we started serving lunch. They talked to every cook and every server. It was stressful. I had to constantly remind my crew to maintain their hospitality—some I just let go home after they met with the police because they were too shook to work. Hera told me some of the questions they had asked after she was done, like how the students were acting and why they were in Charleston, but we couldn't really talk too much due to how hectic lunch had gotten. Some people came into the restaurant just being nosey.

"I'd served the last lunch for the day when Rebecka, the assistant manager, came to get me. Rebecka led me by the table where the three had sat this morning. Their totes remained under the table, and no one had bothered to buss the tabletop after they ran from the area—avoiding it like an damn epidemic.

"Rebecka escorted me into the lobby, and my head spun. My workplace—my comfort zone—was infested with cops. Rebecka struggled to open the admin door with her cardkey, and I waited for her near the front desk but couldn't stand still. I couldn't help but to feel scowls reading me up and down, Unk, it felt like they thought I had something to do with … whatever had happened to that white girl—damn racist cops always itching to trap a black man. But never the white boys, right? Even after the church shooting! I mean wasn't it the white boy Trevor that saw the bitch last!? I turned to talk with Felisha behind the front desk to distract me building up rage, but her attention was on something outside the front entrance foyer.

"The paramedics lifted the gurney carrying a covered body into the back of the ambulance. There was a dark red stain in the center of the sheet. When the medics bumped the gurney against the door while raising it up, a hand flopped from under the sheet. The fingernails were neon pink, and I knew right then it was her.

"My body when numb as fuck, and noise in the lobby got all muffled and shit. I chest hurt and forehead all sweaty, Uncle Ray. Rebecka had to get my attention to follow her into the admin area. I was in a funk.

"Two officers stood guard in the business relations reps' office with the other three students; I only knew this because Amy and Jill's work cubby is just two glass dividers blocking a cornered wall. They were quiet, but I could tell they'd been crying for a while now, and their pale, spindly legs were trembling. Amber spotted me, and her face looked terrifying as hell with the running mascara and bloodshot eyes. I nearly ran into the doorframe when entering Jason's office.

"I didn't have much to say during the interview. I told the detectives the students checked into the hotel on Thursday, had dinner the same night, and so on. I felt wrong added how the kids asked about Gullah history, you know, for their research topic and shit, and their sightseeing plans—"

"Did any of the police ... I don't know, flinch, when you mentioned Gullah?"

Antwan shrugs and shakes his head.

"Son, why didn't you tell those detectives the students wanted to visit with Sister Annalise? You know the authorities have been watching her and that brother—"

"Because I ain't no snitch, Uncle Ray!" Antwan's sharp tone takes me by surprise. "The students must have told them anyhow, because they questioned me about those two creeps, being the dirty pigs police are. I kept saying I never have time like that for our guests. Besides, don't you always tell us to mind our own business, Uncle Raymond?"

Even though I'm not sure this applies to anything he has told me so far, Antwan got me there. I cannot deny, and when he sees his words caught this old man's tongue, he softens his tone.

"Anyway, I finished telling them how Amber's screaming scared the piss out of everyone.

"The police and paramedics didn't clear the hotel until an hour before time to serve dinner. It was just … pure insanity, Unk. I was in such a daze, like I was stuck in a nightmare. The hotel didn't feel right all day … Maybe it never will again."

The way Antwan muffled those last five words, it sounded like a child who just lost his best friend.

"When everything had somewhat settled, I was so drained I couldn't do shit. I just sat at one of the dining tables, staring out the nearby window, and hoping I could pull my worked up ass together for dinner. My girl Hera did most of the prep work. Hera checked on me a few times, even brought me some coffee, for a boost before the shift.

"I forced myself to watch the people walking along the sidewalk, all decked out for Saturday night. And I eventually got lost in the action. So much so I saw the girl's reflection in the glass only seconds before the hand gripped my shoulder. I spun quickly, ready for what was about to pop off. It was Amber. I blurted something and clutched the shirt on my chest. I was all jittery and anxious.

"She looked like she'd been raked over hell's coals. She didn't wash the smeared make-up around her eyes, her hair was frizzed and she smelled all musty. I hardly heard her when she'd asked if she could sit.

"And, Unk, I have to confess: my stomach flip-flopped. There was just too much shit going on with this broad at that point, you know? I wanted her as far away from me as possible.

"I put my hands on the table, got up from my chair, and was about to tell her I needed to prep for dinner. Then she cusped her small, clammy hands around mine. I wanted to ditch her, but those teary eyes told me she needed to talk with *someone* about all this … whatever that shit was. I hesitated but eased back to the table before motioning for her to take the chair across from me; you know I can't say no to a female, Unk.

"Amber had shared that the police took Trevor to the station for more interrogation—he's the guy that got up from the table first this morning. Amber said that's why she and Brian were still at the hotel, to wait for the police to release Trevor, when they learned the truth. She grew quiet after that.

"The silence got uncomfortable, and I asked what happened when Trevor got to the room to check on Emily. She slammed her fist on the tabletop, shouting it wasn't him, like I had accused the brother. Uncle, I nearly fell back in the chair, man. This bitch blanked crazy.

"Hera, refilling the condiments on the tables at the time to be nosey, met my wide eyes and was quick to provide the girl with some iced tea, hoping to break the awkwardness. Amber thanked Hera. I glanced at Hera, and she took the cue to join us. Amber didn't seem to notice Hera taking the seat next to her, or just didn't give a damn.

"Amber said she was in the girls' hotel room the entire time before Brian told her Trevor had gone to the dining room before them two. She said Trevor never went into their room during the night. She began to say, 'In fact, I remember seeing him behind the desk in the boys' room in my dream—'"

So much of what Antwan had shared so far is bizarre and vague. There are holes and a lack of clarity in this girl's story. I stay silent in hopes it'll all make sense soon.

"It got quiet for a moment after that. Amber's dry, cracking voice startled Hera and me when she said, 'We visited Sister Annalise today.'"

I shift in the recliner when Antwan says that name.

Antwan keeps ogling at the ceiling. "Amber said it wasn't easy finding her. She said they tried GPS and Google maps but couldn't find any directions. So they decided to take some more tours in the afternoon. Amber said they were so caught up in the tours that it got late when they found a homemade flyer on the ground near where the Bulldog Tours have their kiosk off Anson Street. Amber choked on her tears when she said something like 'Our tour guide was enjoyable, entertaining with rich history, and Trevor pulled out the camcorder to get the info; he recorded everything throughout the night.' She put a tiny camcorder on the table. Hera turned it on, and we started watching the video as Amber went on, providing commentary. Amber said they were so amazed by how knowledgeable the guide sounded.

"Amber said they were determined to get a one-on-one with the tour guide afterward. She said some shit like they were ready to bribe the man if they had to because they were blown away by his knowledge. 'It sounded like he grew up in the era.' Amber said, 'Brian was the bold one who asked if he knew Sister Annalise.' Then she added the man's eyes nearly bulged out of his sockets. Amber said he got animated, proclaiming he actually knew Sista Annalise personally, and he provided them directions to Sista Annalise's house."

I throw up my hands. "Hold up, 'Twan. How'd a tour guide even know Annalise like that?"

My nephew rises his head, holding direct eye contact with me for the first time tonight. "Stanton, Uncle Ray. Brother Stanton was their tour guide."

I lose control of all my muscles, and my body puddles into the recliner, rocking the lounger. "Goddamn."

"Amber told Hera and me some detailed shit, like how the paved roads became gravel pathways when they had reached the swamplands along the outskirts of the coast. She said her and Emily wanted to go back to the hotel when they passed Folly Beach, thinking it was getting too far from the safe zone. But the guys wanted to go on.

"And then Amber told Hera and me that there were some skinned furs and crossbones dangling from low limbs when they turned on a pebbled driveway. I've never heard of that shit before, have you, Uncle Ray?

"Anyway, she said she got more scared when the tall sweetgrass and shrubs were overgrown in the area and they could barely see the road. The

SUV rocked and it bounced her around. She hit her head on the ceiling. She said she had a headache from then on and felt dazed when they pulled up on Sister Annalise's place.

"Now, I have to quote the shit she told Hera and me, because I've never been there. But, Uncle, how she described the place matched what Hera and I saw on the camcorder and embedded I my mind.

"'The cabin stood only two or three feet above the murky trenches,' she began. 'The place just looked like it would tumble into the swamp if one good thunderstorm came through. The weeds were overgrown, mostly covering the surrounding moat.

"'The humidity felt like summer instead of October, and the disgusting bugs clung to our sweaty skin. We had to cross over a flimsy board, one foot in front of the other, to get onto the cabin's porch. The deck panels that we stepped on creaked; I waited in fear for us all to just drop through the porch and into that dirty alligator water below.

"'Brian banged on the front door, made from tree bark, and we waited. We didn't speak—just looked around constantly. Toads and mice were on the porch with us, and I wanted to throw up.

"'No one answered the door, so Brian knocked again. Still no luck. After Brian's fourth or fifth try, Emily and I said we wanted to go back to the hotel. He and Trevor told us to chill again, but Emily said to hell with you two and turned back toward the SUV. That's when the door opened slowly; it sounded like someone wailing in pain.

"'The one-room shack smelled like mildew, sludge, and rusting iron. There wasn't much light coming through the tiny windows and fractured walls, and the dust flying in the air made my sinuses act up. I remember a rocking chair, a cot, and a hearth. I noticed a bucket along an odd opening in the far wall. The rancid odor made me nauseous. And there were so many of these little sweetgrass trinkets and other bizarre objects drooping and twirling from the low ceiling. Creepiest of all were the stuffed foxes, bobcats, and alligator heads all over the place. And I'm sure that was their organs stored in jars filled with this nasty, bloody-looking fluid. Emily yelled "Fuck this shit!" That's when we all turned to leave.

"'I don't remember how everyone reacted, but I know I screamed at the top of my lungs when this stout, wrinkly old lady—hunched over a tree branch for a cane—blocked the only exit. The elderly woman stared us down, one by one with that wide eye and the other one squinted. She didn't seem upset or demand to know why were in her house. Instead she introduced herself as Sister Annalise.'

"Amber said they tried to explain who they were, but Sister Annalise lifted her hand and informed them their Tour Guide had given her a heads up—"

I shake my head and utter, "Those poor kids."

"And, Unk, that old hag looked *fucked up* on that damn video.

"Amber said Sista Annalise offered them seats while she planted herself in the rocking chair. It was hard for them to find anywhere decent to sit.

Amber and Emily used some wooden crates while the guys remained standing—'Trevor wanted to, anyway, for better camera angles,' she said. 'Annalise didn't seem bothered by the filming.' Amber continued with how she and Brian took turns explaining their purpose behind just popping up at Annalise's place like that. When they told her they wanted to know about the Boo Hag, Sista Annalise laughed. And the way she laughed on that video, Unk …" Antwan says, breaking from the story, "I still get chills, Uncle Ray. That crackled wailing rose from the depths of Sista Annalise's bowels. Amber added that a foul-ass odor filled the room as soon as Sister Annalise yowled. Amber swore the cabin shook, and the animals outside bayed and croaked, as if responding to Sister Annalise's howling—the screen did tremble, but I figured it was that Trevor boy being scared and shit ... Amber said when the unnerving disorder finally stopped, Sista Annalise stood from her rocking chair and collected a broom from hooks on the wall.

"Sister Annalise waved the broom in the air and began to tell the story about the house slave, Nea Bell. Sista Annalise said on the video Nea Bell was raped every time her plantation owner threw his late night gatherings with his neighbors. Sista Annalise continued on the camcorder with how Nea Bell had many miscarriages because the wretched wife was jealous and worked her harder than the other slaves. Sista Annalise told them how Nea Bell had the hoodoo doctor in the slave quarters abort some pregnancies, burying the fetuses in the cemetery behind the slaves' worship building. Sister Annalise explained how one infant survived—the daughter of the plantation owner. She said they hid the baby within the slaves, but the plantation owner's wife took notice of the light-skinned child working in the fields. Annalise said when the plantation owner went on one of his business trips, his wife framed Nea Bell, saying she stole food from the pantry. She demanded the Sheriff have Nea Bell lynched in front of all the slaves in the quarters for the crime. Her corpse hung for weeks while the swamp critters ate the meat off her bones. Not long after, her only child's dead body was discovered in what's now the North Edisto River. Sista Annalise said the plantation owner returned home furious as fuck, but he couldn't show how pissed he was in front of his wife, for it would confirm the affair.

"Amber said Annalise got worked up while she shared the story about the owner's nightmares of being ridden around his own property like bucking bronco. She said when he woke from these nightmares, he had trouble getting out of bed at first, feeling like something heavy was sitting on his chest. When he could finally rise from bed, he discovered his hands and knees were scraped and dirty. Amber said the grad students had found some of the owner journal entries about these nightmares up until his final days.

"Amber continued as Hera and I watched on the screen: 'Then, Sista Annalise handed Brian the handmade miniature broom, with a thick bundle of straw at the head. What Sister Annalise told us next freaked us all out even more.' Sista Annalise said on the film that anyone who talks about the Boo Hag will invoke her spirit from the beyond.

She's known to haunt people in their sleep. Then, the kids started rambling off-screen while Amber said 'Brian and I were quick to interject we weren't hunting anyone, just collecting information.' Sista Annalise said it didn't matter: the Boo Hag finds any attention as an invite, and with the hour ringing on the cusp of the unveiling, when the dead walks among the living, the Boo Hag comes out to prowl. Sister Annalise suggested it'd be best if both Brian and Trevor add a strand of straw into the bundle to delay the Boo Hag's torture when she comes.'

"Sista Annalise explained on the screen how Nea Bell developed an obsession with the housework being perfect, due to the abuse of the slave owner's wife. Annalise said something along the lines of how the Boo Hag would be too distracted tallying the straws over and over to make sure the amount of straws matched how many children she had and wouldn't be focused on her rage. Uncle, have you ever heard that? Amber said Sister Annalise told them if Brian and Trevor added more straw to the broom, the Boo Hag would count too many, pluck them out, and would need to start counting all over again to make sure it's the right amount. Usually, by the time she's content with the results, morning light will start rising.

"Amber told Hera and me how Sister Annalise told them that Nea Bell always had to sneak out of the slave quarters before the crack of dawn, when the daily labor over the crops began, so she wouldn't be caught fucking around with the male negroes."

Antwan confirms with a distinct nod when my eyes widen from the image of a petite, blonde-haired, blue-eyed white girl saying "negroes" with her rosy thin lips.

"Amber said that's why the Boo Hag cannot stand the sunlight and only roams the nights. Sista Annalise also suggested for them to keep salt nearby, to trap the Boo Hag, or some weird shit like that.

"Amber added, 'Brian said he was still confused about the broom. I personally was a little baffled about the salt.' Amber said they had so many questions—and I heard the kids rambling on the tape, too—that Sista Annalise became irritated with them, and that was when Hera and I jumped in our seats. Sista Annalise released such a piercing shrieked over their voices that I thought I felt the camcorder quake in my hand. Sista Annalise rambled on how the Boo Hag doesn't like females, especially white girls. Amber muttered, 'Sister Annalise said we remind her of the slave owner's wife.' Amber said that's when Sister Annalise pointed her crooked finger at her and Emily. Then Sista Annalise cackled more, telling them how her and Emily were going to die. That's when the camcorder got all shaky from Trevor holding and running, I heard them all running and panting, trying to get out the house and down that thin-ass plank, Amber said that's when they hauled ass. She said she heard stomping behind them as they ran out the cabin. I heard some heavy footsteps in the distance.

"Amber said they ran as fast as they could back to the SUV, which was a struggle, since nighttime had fallen and the marsh tide made the ground soggy. She said the swamp noises were louder and more aggressive.

"When the Brian guy backed out the yard, the camera pointed at the shack through the windshield. I saw the old hag's profile in her doorway, blocking the firelight from her hearth. Amber said her figure looked contorted.

"She sounded like she was reliving it when she told Hera and me how they got lost in the marsh trying to get out of there. She pointed at the camcorder, saying Trevor got good images of what they saw. That camera picked up some fucked up creepy shit hanging from those trees. I saw how those crossbones looked like skeletons and how those skinned furs shook and lifted their heads, like they were coming back to life. I swear some of the howls we heard from the video came from them. So did Amber and Emily, as we heard from the video. Hera and I both said 'Like hell!' when we heard Trevor and Brian try to reassure Emily and Amber it was the wind carrying the rodents' cries."

Antwan's voice is getting raspy now, but he continues. "Amber said they saw shadowy figures peeking through the sweetgrass. Something charged the vehicle and banged into the SUV, but Brian brushed it off as trees branches.

"It was around midnight when they got back to the hotel. The film showed them going into the lobby when I think the battery died or some shit. Anyway, I handed it back to her, letting Amber know she had to share that with the police. Hara added why hasn't she yet. Amber never answered."

Antwan paused for a moment, reflecting what all he had shared with me. "The graveyard front desk rep Denis told me they all collapsed in the lobby on the sofas and chairs," my nephew eventually continues. "He said when they ran into the hotel, they looked scared for their lives. Denis said Brian held some small ass broom in the air, and they all started laughing uncontrollably. Denis told me he wanted to call security, but they finally drifted to the elevators."

Antwan gulps down the last of his beer.

I figure Antwan had finished his story. "Damn, son, they've been through some shit, huh? Well, sure Abba glad to know they made it safely to their beds—"

Antwan's startled eyes glare at me, as if I forgot something.

And I did.

The girl that never woke from her sleep after all that.

I check the wall clock; the hands read past two in the morning.

It's officially Halloween.

• • •

Sunday, October 31, 2010
"Amber told me she woke at three-something yesterday morning to find Emily not in the other bed." Antwan is determined to fight off his exhaustion to tell me the rest. "When she wobbled into the third-floor hallway to search for her friend, Amber said not every walkway light was on, and she could only use the blue shadows climbing the

walls and the few working hall lights flashing like strobe lights to guide herself along the wall.

"She knocked on the guys' door. She said she remembered knocking three times, but when she stopped, the knocking continued. She said, first, the echoing sounded as if it was coming from down the hall near the elevators. Then, there were three loud bangs from the other side of the guys' hotel room door. Amber said the vibration from the pounding made her shriek and hop back. Then the door pried open.

"Amber said she peeked into room and immediately caught a whiff of an odor that almost made her hurl, as she described it. She said the smell was familiar: woodlands and shit and rancid. The only light in the room was from the moon peeking through the partially closed curtains. She said she eased into the room to find Trevor standing in the far corner, behind the desk, naked. 'That's how I know it couldn't have been him who killed Emily; he was in their room during the entire timeline of—' Amber teared up, unable to share her theory of Trevor's innocence. She put the camcorder on the tabletop to cradle her eyes.

"Amber composed herself. She said she stepped farther into the room, calling Trevor, when something on four legs crossed her path. She said she screamed and jumped back. When her eyes adjusted, she realized it was Brian galloping around the hotel room on his hands and knees, completely nude. She said a fuzzy silhouette was straddling his back, and it slapped Brian's bare ass with the straw end of that damn broom. Amber said she screamed for Trevor to help, but he stood still and quiet in the damn corner. She said her yelling made the shadowy figure to screech a louder crackling laughter—similar to the one they heard before at Sista Annalise's shack, Amber said. The howling halted Brian's prancing. When the ghost slowly looked over its shoulder, Amber could only see beady, green eyes glowing in the dark. It screamed something—Amber recognized it as Gullah dialect—and lunged at her.

"Then Amber said she woke up, flying out of bed. The morning sun was shining through the window. She saw Emily still asleep, so Amber said she showered and departed the hotel room, letting her friend sleep in after the shit they'd been through. She ran into Brian in the hallway. He said Trevor was already downstairs, and Amber said she told him Emily was still asleep as they rode the elevator down to the dining area. There was an awkwardness between them, she shared, because they both knew they were in one another's dream.

"Hera and I sat quietly, thinking she was going to share more, but she went silent. She got to the part we already knew, the part of the story we were in. She didn't need to say any else."

When Antwan said that, his expression was pure terror. "Oh, shit! We need that book, Uncle Ray."

I'm dumbfounded to what he's referencing.

"Abba's book. Don't it hold how to rid the Boo Hag?" I watch Antwan gain his second wind.

He and I both know it does. It's the last existing Gullah scripture in this region. It details how to commune with the animals, the spirituals the slaves used to communicate with one another, the incantations the hoodoo clergy uses—it tells it all, even how to exorcise a demon. Abba's spirituals explain how to banish the Boo Hag to the hallows.

But I refuse to get involved. "That's them white kids' problem. Not ours. We don't want to meddle with that, okay?"

Antwan stands up from the couch. "But, it's now my problem, Uncle Ray. Hera and I are a part of this."

"Son, you're fine. You only heard the white girl tell it. She's the one fucked." I want to believe my own words. I can't bare the thought of my nephew getting caught up in this living nightmare. But he watched the video. Him and Hera both. I hand over the glass bottle. "Take those into the kitchen before Abba throws a fit."

As Antwan carries the empty longnecks to the kitchen, I dwell on whether or not he's going to be okay. My gut bubbles. We know how the legend works.

When he returns, Antwan stands in the den entranceway with a canister of salt.

"'Twan, what the hell are you doing with that, son?"

"When Amber left the table tonight, she grabbed the salt shaker." Antwan's tone sounds confident. "I remember she said Sista Annalise had told them some shit about how salt would protect anyone from the Boo Hag."

I'm too shocked to rebut his ignorance.

Antwan tells me he's going to bed and heads to his bedroom with the salt before I can get out my words.

• • •

I sit at the kitchen table, listening to the morning radio when the front door opens and then slams shut, rattling the windows. Antwan calls from the den. "I left something!"

Abba and I continue with our breakfast while Seble is quick to jump from the table, chasing Antwan. The sunrays catch the shimmering gold from her Egyptian Queen costume. She's screaming her cousin's name through the house.

The radio broadcast continues. "Early this morning, Charleston City Police apprehended the brother and sister duo, Annalise and Stanton Green, for evidence pointing them to the murder of USC student Emily Smith. Police reported they still have Trevor Tyler in custody but most likely will soon release him. We've been following a Channel Five Whistle Blower report for months now because many tourists have complained that the Green siblings have been running a scam. After paying a pricy rate for what Stanton describes as an 'Authentic Gullah Tour,' tourists have been paying extra for the directions to a shack the Greens rented in Kiawah Island, after a convincing story of Annalise Green being an authentic Gullah Witch—"

Antwan enters the kitchen, guiding Seble by her shoulders. He lightly pushes her forward, and Seble climbs into her seat at the table. Seble says she can't wait to visit the hotel after Sunday School. At the same time, they put a finger to their lips, obviously reminding each other to keep a secret—they're always doing that.

He sees Abba and I eyeing him, and says he left part of his Gullah costume for tonight, Antwan shares. He pecks both Abba and Seble with a forehead kiss and gives me a handshake, then interlocking our fingers to pull one another in for a half-hug before anyone can question him. He fights with the back door before exiting.

I sip my coffee and reflect on what all he shared last night.

I didn't go to bed after Antwan retired with the salt canister last night—didn't sleep a wink. I felt the need to stay awake to monitor the house. I doubted anything would pop off but still needed to be sure. The last thing Antwan said before leaving me in the den had me concerned about his well-being. Gullah witchcraft is nothing to mess with, and what he shared and how he acted got me on edge. He knows better than to get wrapped up in tourists' nonsense—

I suddenly recall he said he forgot something and jump up from the table, startling the girls. I dash to the cupboards. The salt is back in its place.

I laugh, and Abba asks me if I've started smoking grass again.

Abba and I finish our ham and eggs while Seble pours another bowl of Captain Crunch. Abba excuses herself, and heads back to her room to prepare her attire for the storytelling at the hotel this evening.

I'm wrapping up dishwashing when Abba returns to the kitchen. "Ma, you look lovely as always in your Gullah priestess—"

"Raymond, have you seen my book?"

Her question throws me off. "You mean your spiritual?"

She nods with haste. "It's not on the bookshelf with the other spell books in my worship room. It's not around my altar—"

"Twan took it to the hotel," Seble shares while staring down at her cereal bowl. "That's why he came back, to get the book." She then covers her mouth. "Oops! Please don't tell 'Twan I told the secret."

• • •

I rush through the hotel lobby and into the dining room. Police officers are everywhere. One tries to tell me I can't enter the hotel right now. I tell the officer it's an emergency, and I need to find my nephew, who works here.

He's one of those hard-ass cops with a crew cut, probably goes to KKK meetings, and the fat-ass reaches for the cuffs he carries on his hip. But the young Sous Chef, Hera, comes to the rescue, pulling me away from the racist pig. "He's with me," she says.

Not even waiting the cop to reply, she guides me into the dining area, where Antwan sits with a tiny, blonde-headed girl who looks a few years younger than him. Between them, Antwan points in Abba's opened book.

I couldn't get to their table fast enough to snatch the book. Antwan quickly removes his finger before I slam the book on it. "What the hell is wrong with you, boy!? Done lost your damn mind."

My sharp tone puts Antwan on alert and frightens the hell out of the girl.

"Uncle Ray, you don't understand—"

"The hell I need to understand, Antwan!"

"No, no, Uncle; I saw it too."

I take a moment to collect my patience before asking, "Saw what, son?"

It's the girl that answers. "The Boo Hag."

She bursts into tears, her hands catching her falling face before her forehead bumps the clothed table.

I take a deep breath and shrug my shoulders to release some of the stress before I shake the shit out of them both. My right shoulder flares up from the tension.

"She stood there." Antwan says, pointing at the dining room entranceway. "It was dawn, and usually Hera and I are the only ones in here. But Hera waited for me at the doorway as I saw the two sitting at this table; Amber and Brian had been in here since three this morning.

"Her and Brian met in the hall, frantic from the nightmares they had awoken from, like the morning before. Amber said the two shared a room, and when she woke at three this morning, someone was sitting on Brian's chest. Amber said it was too dark to see, but the silhouette leaned too close near Brian's face, and there was a light gray hue between their mouths. Amber said she grabbed whatever she could near her and threw it at the figure. The thing looked at her and hissed. Amber said she grabbed the lamp by her bed and lunged at the damn thing! The thing fell off Brain, and Amber grabbed Brain from the bed to get them both out the room.

They got to the elevators, waiting on their call by pushing the button, when there was some stealth movement at the far end of the third floor.

When they glanced, there stood their friend, Emily. She was completely naked and body was bleeding. They took the stairway to the ground floor."

It took a moment, but then I recall Emily is the girl who didn't wake from sleep yesterday morning. "How the hell …"

Antwan takes the book from my hands. He quickly finds the page he needs and points at the earliest Geechee calligraphy. "It says here, Uncle Ray, the Boo Hag wears other females' skins to trick and lure men."

It takes a few seconds for me to register what Antwan's implying. "That's some bullshit."

"And you know I'd agree with you, Unk! But, as I argued with the two about the wives' tale when they ran into the dining room here, screaming for dear life, there the other girl stood." He points toward the dining room entrance. "I saw it with my own two eyes, Emily was butt-ass naked. Her body was smeared with blood, and some of it seeping from her eyes and ears. Her eyes looked detached, like they were behind another layer of flesh."

The blonde-headed girl looks up from her hands, with tears streaming down her face. "Brian, being the dumb, macho athlete he's always been, charges at Emily—" She abruptly stops herself. "That Boo Hag! He gets right on the thing and grabs it by the shoulder. Some of the loose skin tears off in his fingers and his eyes bulge; he tries to scream but nothing comes out. Brian's so freaked out by what's happening that he cannot react in time when the Boo Hag grabs his throat, squeezes, and lifts him into the air …" She bursts into loud sobs.

Antwan motions to his Sous Chef, who stands by me. "That's when Hera did what she did."

"I remember my grandma and Ms. Abba saying how salt burns the Boo Hag's skin," Hera says. "I grab one of the shakers from the table, twist off the cap, and throw that shit in the bitch's face."

Typically, pretty, young girls using profanity really irks me, but this isn't one of those times.

"The creature drops Brian," Antwan says. "The brother is rolling on the floor and gasping for air. That's when we all grab the salt shakers from the tables—"

I look around, just now noticing all the salt shakers and minerals scatter on the floor.

"And the thing runs off, squealing like a sow in the slaughter," Hera adds.

"The police found Emily's carcass in the ally, body been skinned," Amber says somberly; it's tough to make out her words. "Ambulances rushed Brian to the hospital. After being quick to arrive, they got the air going to his lungs." The white girl abruptly stops talking.

They say no more; there's nothing else to say, really. I take a seat at their table.

Dawn peers over the historical slave market building across the street and through the hotel windows. The light seems more intense than usual this Halloween morning. Some children are already wearing their costumes and carrying their jack-o-lantern candy pales while roaming the streets with their families.

I glance at Abba's open spirituals. The sketch of a bare, titty-sagging, old hag with wart-covered skin glares from the page; it feels like those beady, green eyes are trying to pierce my soul. Knowing this isn't the first time seeing those unforgettable eyes flares discomfort in my shoulder.

My right shoulder was already bad from football, and it will always ache from that morning when I kept ramming it into the backdoor of the kitchen to answer my brother Nate's blood-curdling screams for help. He was no longer yelling when the door finally splintered. Dawn thinly blanketed the horizon over the sweetgrass beyond the backyard, and it was enough light for me to identify Nate's hunched, naked body. I scrambled to get to him, cradling my older brother in my arms and shouting his name over and over while praying this was just a bad dream.

At first, I thought I was hearing an echo. But then the crackling voice grew more shrill each time it shouted Nate's name. The frightening awareness hushed me. Only ten steps from us, in the marsh, those same beady, green eyes were watching me crying over my brother's lifeless body. I struggled through tears to watch the desiccated hag vanish into the thick bogs. The only thing that remained was the smoke from the sun burning her exposed skin. Just before the shrubbery, bundled on the ground like a soiled blanket, lay the skin of Nate's late wife—

I lean across Antwan and shut Abba's book.

WHAT TERRIFIED ME

Seeing my cousin outside my bedroom window dressed as a scarecrow for Halloween and cradling a jack-o-lantern only hours after we admitted him didn't scare me. What terrified me was that my apartment is on the eleventh story with no balcony.

GIRLS' NIGHT IN

Author's Note: "Diet," pronounced "yee-et," is a female Vietnamese name, meaning "Conquer" or "Destroyer."

The Calm Before

I

The knocking startles me awake.

The first image I come to is a female who looks too old to portray a teenage girl, tumbling into the corner of some tiny, dank-looking room. The black mascara to match her cat outfit is running down her cheeks from the uncontrollable crying. She remains on her knees and claws for dear life at the walls, as if she could dig herself away from whatever's terrorizing her.

The flat screen mounted over the den's fireplace shifts scenes to the creature pounding its oversized fists against a wooden doorframe. The girl's annoying sobs pierce through the monster's bashing and the anxiety forces me to bury my face into the throw pillow on the couch. I blindly slap the coffee table top for the remote. I knock my paperback onto the floor, hearing it plop onto the floor, before locating the device to lower the volume. The burning logs crackle from the fireplace.

The knocks blare over the now softened cinematic noise. They're more distinct from the dated horror movie's soundtrack, as if coming from inside the house.

I groggily thrust my petite frame into a sitting position on the couch, still re-orienting myself. I secure the shawl around my shoulders, survey the ranch-style living area, and squint at the digital clock perched on the shelf. The quartz neon-blue dashes arrange the time—5:37—with the tiny black dot near the number seven indicating dusk is approaching.

Three more staccato knocks are heavy enough to rattle the glass in the windows. I stare into the kitchen, thinking the sound must be coming from the back door.

"Amy? Is that you?" My voice crackles from a combination of sleepiness and discomfort.

There's no response.

I clear my throat. "Did you forget your house key again?"

Still no answer.

If it was Amy or Rea at the back door, they would've yelled my name to let them in by now.

I wave my hands in front of my face and shake my head repeatedly: "Stop freaking yourself out, Diet*. It might just be the Groceries-on-the-Go order."

I collect my nerves and rise from the couch, securing the shawl around my shoulders. I keep my eyes forward, waiting for any surprises and wait for my bare feet to let me know when I've reached the kitchen's wood floor. The knot in my stomach tightens with each step. I reach the room's center but cannot force myself to go any farther. The icy floor radiates chills through my body.

In the mudroom, Charlie's perched on the top floor of his cat condo, watching the outdoors through the tinted window. His head swooshes for a look through the glass window of the back door, keeping his radar on whatever he's stalking—his tail twitching with excitement.

No one's standing in the carport on the other side of the back door. That's a relief, until the knocking resumes. I nearly jump out of my skin. I quickly dart my eyes to the commotion at my left. It's one of the million daily notifications I get vibrating my cell phone on the marble-topped island in the kitchen.

Resting my hand on my chest, I exhale a deep breath through my mouth. "You *really* need to quit creeping yourself out, Diet. It's like Dr. Ambaum said: *You should always feel safe in your own home.*"

I say it out loud, as if Amy is sitting on the sofa, getting a thrill at my fear's expense: *Oh, Diet, you'll always be that timid, little, transfer Asian school girl.*

I quickly turn my head and bark: "Shut up, Amy!" before realizing I'm staring at an empty recliner. I have to be fair to myself in the healing process, but I still feel silly being spooked by a message notification. I can hear Amy's sarcastic response in my head, as if she's standing behind the island: *Mm Humm.*

The screen continues to flash while I collect my phone, and I unlock the phone before reading the text message: *HEY, DIET! YOUR GROCERIES-ON-THE-GO SHOPPER AARON IS APPROX 15 MINUTES FROM YOUR LOCATION.*

The heavy feeling in my chest is lightened by internal glee.

I always get stupid giddy every time I use this new grocery-shopping app. Rea laughs at me whenever I tickle myself over the simplest things—but I've learned to laugh at myself with her these days rather than feel embarrassed. If she saw me now, she'd praise me for having fun.

I quickly glance at the security camera monitors tucked in the far corner of the kitchen counter. I don't see anyone near the outside doors. No one knocked. It was just my cell phone rattling from text alerts.

I hear Amy's voice in my mind, and that noise she makes when she clicks her tongue behind her teeth seems to echo right behind my head. I force a smile rather than yelling at nothing again and grab the folded five-dollar bill from the kitchen island.

After stroking the chin of my feline friend—Amy never cared for Charlie, but I had to bring him from Mom and Dad's—I push the garage door opener mounted on the mudroom wall. The door rises about three feet from the cement before screeching to a halt.

I huff. "We really need to tell the landlord about the stupid garage door again."

I hear Amy's voice as if she's standing behind me in the mudroom: *I thought you already did that. What's the holdup?*

I turn, regardless how it might look. "I did email him ... twice! What've your lazy ass done at it?"

All remains silent. No one is there.

"That's what I thought, Amy."

I push the button again to raise the door. This time the door functions properly. I make my way around my silver Chevy Caprice and pause at the edge of the carport. I scan to the left and then the right of the backyard. My mind's convince everything's clear, but my legs are immobile.

The breeze influences me to tighten the hand-stitched shawl my Great Aunt Chau passed onto me during my I visit to Saigon with my grandparents when I was much younger. I remember how I couldn't had been happier to return to the states after those five days of boredom with no guilt, but now I cradle myself with this wrap, envious of the simple life she chose. She didn't hesitate to roam her streets, no less her own backyard.

The golden sunset rests in the horizon, and I can hear the creek trickling down the hill. No one's looming in the shadows or behind any shrubbery. Okay, just to satisfy my paranoia, I'm going to check the front of the house.

But I still remain frozen.

If Amy was home, she'd stand at the back door, rolling in laughter at my expense. I can hear her nasally titter echoing through the vacant two-car garage now. That witch.

Dr. Ambaum's therapeutic words from our last session resonate in my head once more, her German accent as thick as ever: *"You need to work with yourself to accept that the majority of the time someone isn't waiting for you in the dark, Diet. Develop coping skills to help you walk past the dark shadows of the world. Practice by walking through your house at night without any lights on. You know where the light switches are, and you can always turn them on when you need to. Wonder your backyard, even, and trust your instincts in the dark. You can always use the flashlight on your cell phone if you're not ready for pitch dark just yet."*

I fumble through my phone's screen settings to locate the flashlight command. I tap the screen, and it works without any glitches. I scan the yard once more; there's still no one looming in the shadows. I use my phone light to guide me along the paved driveway that curves in front of the house.

I reach an area where there's just a sliver of sunlight touching the cracked cement, and I turn off the phone light. Amy's personal ringtone blares from the speaker, and I nearly drop my phone.

I stare at the incandescent-digital picture of the two of us posing like a couple of goof-balls during a high school cheerleading retreat. We're now in our final year of college, and I still have this outdated image of me with my signature adolescent pigtails and Amy with her provocative wild-teen long hair in a ribbon. I'll be sure to take a new picture of us tonight while we're enduring horror movies and pounding popcorn … and cocktails.

"Hey, girl," I answer. "When will you be home? Tonight's goodies are on the way—"

"Hey, Diet," Amy chirps in my ear. "Yeah, about tonight—"

I know when Amy uses her chirpy tone she's about to change *everyone's* plans.

"—I know you, Rea, and I talked about chilling at the house tonight," Amy continues, "but Landon *finally* texted me back."

I shake my head with disapproval, but fight back my feelings and force out the supportive, positive tone: "Oh, exciting."

"And he says there's this *huge* Halloween party everyone's going to off campus tonight. He asked me to go … *maybe* we all could go do that instead."

I know which "party" she's referencing. Kappa Alpha Epsilon is hosting their annual Octoberfest fundraiser mixer. And, technically, the Greek village does rest just beyond the university, but their houses are within a couple blocks of campus.

The wind picks up velocity and rustles the falling dried leaves along the driveway. The airstream ushers in storm clouds, which blocks the sunset. There's no sunlight along the driveway now, and my insides start forming a knot.

"I don't know, Amy ..." My chest tightens and I cringe right after I share my words—not sure due to anxiety of going out or trying to tell Amy no..

"Oh, come on, Diet," Amy pleads in her high-pitch whine. "We've always partied it up *every* Halloween night since high school. And we can hang with Landon and his friends. He has some really cute friends."

"Who? Never mind, Amy."

I want to rant: *Yeah, Amy, like we did with some other boys* before *a "cute friends"* ...

Instead, I mutter, "I know it's tradition, but ... I'm just not feeling it this year, you know?"

"I hear you, Diet." Amy shifts into her manipulative psych-major tone now. "But it's our *last* year in college! You can't let what happened to you dominate your final year. I really think being cooped up tonight wouldn't be good for you. We went all out this year with our fairy-tale costumes. It'd suck if we didn't go out to show them off. You cannot let what happened control your life. And I want you to meet Landon." Amy's advice might seem genuine if she didn't wiggle her personal goals into her suggestion.

I half-heartedly agree. "But there'll be other Halloweens to wear them."

The silence on the phone line urges me to continue working on setting boundaries, as Dr. Ambaum has encouraged me to practice.

"It's just … everything has *finally* calmed down, you know? No more interrogations with the lawyers that pervert's rich daddy hired. No more detectives drilling me to find any holes in my statement. No more reporters interviewing me with their insensitive questions." I'm running out of breath.

Amy remains quiet on the other end while I suck in air.

"I just want a mellow night to help me forget it all, Amy."

"And what's a better distraction than a party?" Amy responds, returning to her self-centered voice. "Jeez, you and your issues, Diet." Her harsh words made my abs tremble, like how that boy's cold knife blade did that night. The scar burns.

"Don't be a wet rag about this now, girl," Amy continues. "You didn't want to do the Labor Day Drive Party on campus, but I had to drag you to that. You didn't want to go with me to that Welcome Back Bash—"

While Amy continues to ramble about me being boring—simple—and the "benefits" of me going out, I reflect on some of Dr. Ambaum's advice: *"Diet, if you're not feeling confident and strong with practicing your coping skills, then that's your gut telling you not to place yourself in an uncomfortable situation. Set your boundaries with yourself and others. Be firm with your opinions. Your friends will support your decisions regardless."*

"—you've come so far from being that introvert from high school," Amy continues with her shallow psycho-babble. "Your mass communications studies have helped you with networking, this is no time to regress—"

"Amy, no!"

Not sure if that was a healthy way to set boundaries, but the quiet in my ear indicates Amy gets it.

"I'm sorry," I begin, breaking the stillness. "I'm—"

"Stop," Amy interrupts with a forceful tone. "Just, stop."

I don't think I've ever heard her sound so sincere before. I'm not sure how to take this tone.

"I should be apologizing, not you, Diet. I don't even know what I was trying to do just now. With the prick meeting bond and the trial not being until December— You have been through something traumatic and still experiencing it. I'm just letting some stupid, foolish crush I've developed this semester control any reasoning and compassion I have within me. I'm the worst friend ever."

I see headlights coming around the street corner. "No, no. I mean, if you want to go on, Amy—"

"No, Diet! We planned on having a girls' night in tonight, and we're going to have a girls' night in tonight. You, Rea and me … and Mr. Helmsworth, of course."

We both giggle.

"Don't forget Skeet Ulrich," I add to the list of horror hotties.

Amy groans lightly. "Yes, yes. How could I forget your little nineties killer crush? You and them bad boys, Diet."

I didn't really know how to take that last statement. The tone did sound light, but still …

"No one is thinking you're weak or making fun of what happened to you. Remember, you have strong supports. Amy and Rea are there for you."

A Honda rolls onto Anderson Court.

"Hey, the snacks just got here, Amy."

"Huh?"

"Yeah. I used that Groceries-on-the-Go app, you know? The one the girl in sociology class told me about."

The delivery guy parks and the trunk pops open. In sync with the trunk, the driver's side door swings open, and a guy with a dirty-blond crewcut and a five-o'clock shadow gets out. The polo shirt and kakis are slim fitting on him … *very* fitting.

"Oh, wow," I mutter into the receiver. "Girl, if you were here to see this delivery boy, you'd forget all about that Landon guy."

"Oh," Amy swoons. "What does he look like?"

"You remember the quarterback Adam Sharp on the varsity team ..."

"Oh, dang it! I always miss the eye candy." I know the guy can hear Amy's loud-ass mouth. "We'll have to order something else when I get home to make him come back."

The guy nods and smiles, and I blush, knowing he heard that. He closes the door and starts his way to the trunk.

I turn from him. "Well, he looks like he just graduated from high school, Amy. But anyway, let me wrap up here."

"Okay, Diet. I need to get back to counting the teals, anyway. And I'm still wearing my Bo-Peep costume. You better have your Riding Hood getup on when I get home."

I couldn't help but to chuckle. "Can't wait."

We say our goodbyes, and I hang up.

II

"I have a delivery for a 'Diet,'" he says, raising his voice to question the unusual name. "Never heard that as a name before. Did you parents love diet sodas or something?"

"No," I say with a bland smile, "but I wish I got a dollar for every time someone has asked me that. It's pronounced "Yee-et, as in yet, but stretch out the 'y.'"

"Oh, okay," he chuckles. "I thought someone was pulling a prank on me when I first saw the name on the order."

"That'd be a weak joke," I say.

He grins politely while rising the trunk lid higher. His dimples are adorable with that thin smile.

I pocket my phone before collecting some of the grocery bags from him. He's a little cutie, for sure. Really, more Amy's type though. Yet, I swear, seeing him closer—that chiseled chin and the blond hair—he looks familiar to me. But I can hear Rea laughing at me, as if she was standing right beside me: *You know these freshmen babies look alike every year, girl. Trying to be all Mr. Man now that they ain't high-school boys anymore.*

I shimmy my shoulders loose some. "Thank you … Aaron."

His baby-blue eyes swiftly glance up from the trunk, and he smirks again—amused by me trying out his name.

I withhold my schoolgirl giggle, feeling the internalized joy easing my baffled—paranoid—thoughts.

Rea amusingly huffs in my head, but it's loud enough, almost as if she's right beside me.

His raised eyebrows over the trunk lid interrupt my thoughts. I feel my face grow hot. *Oh, shit! He spotted me staring.* I quickly register that his expression is regarding the plump pumpkin he now cradles. I try to ignore the awkward sensation of the autumn breeze against my flushed cheeks.

"Hyped for tonight?" He asks with is half-grin.

His expression remains stern, but him holding the melon has his muscles flexing through the snug shirt. I dart my eyes to the cracked cement below.

"It's for the trick-or-treaters." I know my face grows warmer, knowing he won't by that for a second. "Anyway, thanks for bring the groceries … oh, wait!"

I dive my hand into my pocket to get his tip, but my hip-hop phone tone bellows from my jeans and throws me off task. I remove it while trying to maintain control of my bags. Rea's name and a picture of us from our snowtubing trip in the mountains right after our junior-year fall-semester finals flashes among the screen.

"Oh, I'm sorry," I say while trying to collect the pumpkin under my already full arms.

He maintains his grip on the pumpkin, and we inadvertently touch. His smooth skin makes me tingle, bit it's mixed with my feeling of vulnerability. "How can I help?" he asks.

I hesitate, and get caught for a second looking into his deep blue eyes. "You're a sweetheart to ask, but I'm used to juggling a lot at once—physically and metaphorically."

Just then, I almost drop my phone and the part of the pumpkin I had. Dr. Ambaum's words echo in my mind again, as if she emerged on the other side of his car: *Not everyone is out to get you, Diet.* Then, it's as if Rea had just appeared from nowhere and stood right beside me when I hear her voice in my head: *Girl, you better let this cute white boy help you! You don't see chivalry too much these days, and he's just doing his job.*

"Well, actually, if you wouldn't mind …"

He gets a fresh grip on the pumpkin. I confirm with a smile while I answer the phone.

"Diet, what's this?" Rea literally blasts in my ear through the receiver. "Amy texts, telling me to wear my princess costume for tonight after all, but then sends me a picture of some white boy named Landon? I mean, he's cute and all—in that Prince Henry sorta way—but I was ready for a relaxing night with my girls in my P.J.'s … This month has been taxing on us *all*, with midterms and everything." How she says "everything" was respectful and friendly. "We're still just chilling at y'all's place tonight, right?"

I assure Rea our plans haven't changed and share my delivery had just arrived for confirmation, while I lead the delivery boy down the driveway, around to the back of the house, and through the carport for easier access to the kitchen. I express how baffled I am about Amy sending Rea a picture of some unknown guy right after we had agreed to stay home tonight.

Charlie's no longer lounging on the roof deck of his cat condo when we enter. The delivery boy surveys the open area, and I point to the nook table that divides the kitchen and den while still reassuring Rea. He nods and crosses the kitchen to rest the oblong fruit on the tabletop. I twirl from facing him and walk to the sink while I chat with my friend about the movies I have lined up for us.

"So, yeah, Rea. We're still chilling tonight, for the millionth time—" I swish back to make eye contact with Aaron.

My heart stops beating and a knot tightens in my stomach when I realize I cannot pull my eye contact away from his beautiful baby blues. His muscular chest grows more intense through the shirt fabric with every breath he inhales. I tighten the shawl around my shoulders and snug the phone close to my ear.

I can hear my own quivering voice in my head now. I feel detached and a sense of panic rushes through my body. *Please, not again ...*

I keep talking with Rea to prolong the phone call, but I'm running out of things to say. But suddenly it's like she had just entered the kitchen from the mudroom. Then Dr. Ambaum stands by the swing door that connects the dining room. I envision them approaching me, and I hear them in my head.

Diet, girlfriend, you got this.

Diet, manage your anxiety with your coping skills. He doesn't know you. Not everyone knows what had happened, and not everyone has hidden agendas.

Aaron takes a step toward me. His Tanjuns squeak against the wood floor as he struts. My hand goes numb.

Dr. Ambaum remains firm, like a guardian. *When all else fails—*

Rea steps backward with her strong foot, facing her open palms in his direction. *Back kick his narrow ass with that Kill Bill shit sensei taught us, best friend!*

I gain control of my rapid heartbeat with several breaths. The two images fade.

Aaron flashes his sparkly grin. He knows he's a looker. "Thank you for your business, ma'am. Have a happy Halloween. Don't let any monsters get ya." He waves from over his shoulder as he crosses into the mudroom.

I thank him once more while hearing the actual Rea babbling into my left ear. I follow the grocer with some haste as he opens the back door and enters the carport. I hastily bolt the door and push the button to close the garage the moment his feet hit the driveway. He's seems sweet enough, but I should have never let him in the house without Amy here. I press my back onto the door's full-body glass and breathe a huge sigh of relief. Charlie's sitting in the center of the kitchen, his void eyes narrowed on me.

How could I put myself in that predicament? I'm not ready. I can't do this—

"Diet? *Diet*?"

I lift the phone to my ear and answer Rea.

"You okay, best friend?"

I trot back to the kitchen sink and watch the grocer through the window above the faucet. My gaze follows every step as he navigates up the driveway. He disappears into the night and I take another deep breath to calm my nerves.

I hear Dr. Ambaum's words from my last therapy session: *"Your post-traumatic stress will be on high alert in the beginning, Diet. Some situations will trigger your emotions from that night. You know the symptoms: shortness of breath, tunnel vision, numbness, night sweats, heart palpitations. Don't rush your recovery. And be hard on yourself, child. Give yourself the time to heal organically. Nurture yourself, and your inner strength will blossom again and flourish more vibrant than before."*

"Yeah," I answer Rea. "Just watching the delivery boy leave and everything. Cute little booty. I told Amy all about the hottie, and she wanted to transport here, like Star Trek. If she saw his fine self, she'd forget about that Landon guy. And when she hears he came into the house, she'll go gaga jealous. She would've put it out there for this baby, having him forget he's on the clock."

"Child," Rea drawls. "Amy's too fast for her own good, she could get a track scholarship with her speed." We both get a chuckle out of that. We love Amy, but, as Rea tells it, we know deep down she only cares about the "D." "I'm surprised she's still all about a girls' night in—"

"Well …"

"She didn't." Rea's tone flattens; she knows what happened without me going any further. "Amy honestly wanted to still go out tonight, after what you went through?

"Her jealous ass wants to slut it up every strange boy she meets, but doesn't express any concern about you being home alone there with him. But that's *your* friend—"

There's a pause. "Hold up. Was that boy in house with you, Diet?" She runs her words together when asking.

Those last words invoked an image of Rea standing in the dinning room corner now with her cockeye glare, arms crossed. I summarize all that just happened, including my anxiety and me confirming he had left the premises. I'm talking in the phone but feel like I'm explaining everything to the imaginary Rea right before me.

Real Rea speaks in my ear. "Girl, that's bold." Imaginary Rea nods to agree with real Rea before fading from sight. "I know we've been kicking butt in the self-defense class and all, but remember sensei saying for us to stay vigilant at all times, to not let our guard down at any moment."

"Relax. That baby looks like he *just* graduated from high school, freshman in college at most. I don't know why I even get myself worked up." I could imagine Amy nodding with my last statement.

"I do. Diet, people crazy. And your and Amy's house is the only one on that cul-de-sac. So you're kinda secluded. And, I mean you just went through—"

"Rea, really. It was fine. I'm okay."

"Okay, okay. Just looking after your well-being, girl. But you're grown. Anyway, I'm on the way."

I shrug even though I know Rea can't see me; imaginary Rea hadn't re-appeared. "Amy insists we wear our costumes tonight."

Rea groans. "Fine. I'll get cute then."

We laugh and say bye before hanging up.

I'm steady looking out the front dining room window, half expecting delivery boy's Honda Accord to roll back down Anderson Street. I shake my head and walk through the vacant, darkened living room and into the den.

My line of sight finds the collage of pictures on the fireplace mantel, just below the mounted television. The digital frame displays a slideshow of pictures with Amy, Rea and me through the past three and a half years: at the Christina Aguilera concert; all the winter and spring break trips; that summer in India ... The smile it conjures stretches the strained muscles in my cheeks and around my mouth; broadening my lips into a great feeling. The internal warmth and the fire below me relaxes the rest of my body.

Amy did have another valid point; this *is* our last year to celebrate Halloween together.

Actually, this is the last *semester* together, period. Rea will be going to Africa in late January to finish her undergraduate studies in archeology and sociology and then begin her graduate work. Amy's been searching for townhomes in the New England area before her first trimester in the counseling graduate program next fall. And I'm still shocked the Southern National News Station offered me an apprenticeship for the summer, before any graduate programs have even accepted me.

Our time to have fun is winding down too quickly, and I can't let what happened to me define these last few months with my best friends. When they both arrive, I'll suggest we go out after all.

Just nowhere near campus.

III

I trudge down the hallway, passing Amy's room on the right, and spot her Bo Peep costume elegantly spread across her bed. I continue through my bedroom and enter my en-suite. Thunder rumbles in the near distance.

I slowly shed my clothes, killing time to let the bath water warm up. I empty my pants pockets and remove the folded five-dollar bill.

"Shit! I meant to give this to the Groceries-on-the-Go guy."

Feeling guilty for not tipping him, I drop the money in the adorable pastel seashell soap tray I bought during our sophomore spring break in Cancun.

I connect my phone to the speaker-adaptor cradle, hit Random, and the music from my playlist floods the bathroom. I switch the water to run from the faucet to the shower head and step into the stall.

Dragging the soapy sponge behind my neck is a tension relief. I guide the sponge down my torso, moving tenderly where the scumbag thrust his boney hip into my side. The purplish-gray bruise healed days ago, but I still flinch when anything brushes along my thigh; it's still sensitive to the touch.

The discomforting tingle invokes images of being inside Graystone Dorm Building. I cringe at the blurry visions of everything shifting from me being in the shower, to being at the frat house that night, to that bastard shoving me on the gazebo pew in the backyard.

I cradle the sponge on my chest, only to trigger the burning sensation in the exact location where the blade penetrated my skin—Dr. Ambaum called it a "psychosomatic response" to the anxiety from the flashbacks.

"Just take deep breaths, Diet, and say to yourself, 'That was in the past. This is where I am now. I am no longer trapped in that situation. I refuse to be a victim. I survived, and I'm thriving. I'm a stronger woman now.' Then start the mantra we just created together: One, two, I'm making it through—"

He used his hip and knees to keep my lower body pinned on the wooden bench. I could feel the growing bulge in his cargo pants.

"Three, four, I'll take no more—"

I repeatedly slapped his chest, and I'll never forget the drunken laugher at my feeble attempt to get him off me. He only needed one of his massive hands to bind my frail wrists. The muscles in my arms grew too weak to fight anymore. The sudden sluggish rush over my body made my eyelids and arms grow heavier, and I wouldn't be able to resist the desire to just lie there much longer, as if I was ready to fall asleep. The darkness spun around me, and the vodka shots bubbled in my stomach. The stench of his beer breath overwhelmed my nostrils, making me gag.

"Five, six, they're the ones that need fixed—"

His pupils dilated while he traced my breasts with the tip of the pocketknife. I could feel the throb in his pants being thrusted against my pelvis. I continued to scream with what strength I could muster within me, but the music was just too loud. His grin widened and eyes darkened when his blade popped another button off my blouse.

The cool blade contrasted the burning pain when he penetrated the flesh between my breastplate. I squeezed my eyelids shut and turned away to avoid the brunt of his stank breath.

A few other guys had stumbled into the backyard to help one of their buds who couldn't handle his booze. The perv covered my mouth when I used all my might to cry.

"Seven, eight, I control my own fate—"

I bit his fingers and shouted more; he slapped me super hard across the face and called me a stupid bitch. But I kept screaming. I had gotten those college guys' attention.

"Nine, ten ..."

Afterward, in the campus police station, I experienced first-hand what others had been complaining about with the university's security. The officers reminded me of *The Stepford Wives*, but *Robocop* editions. They had steroid-built bodies, pretty, chiseled clean-shaven faces, and perfect hair—and they all acted like they were wasting their time with another whiny college girl rather than addressing the actual dangers lurking in the night. Their personalities were stiff, like *Invasion of the Body Snatchers*, throughout what felt like more like an interrogation than an interview.

Their questions made it obvious they were siding with the rich frat boy—I think a few knew him, even—asking me such inapposite questions, like if I'd ever participated in extreme sexual behavior—"like BDSM, ma'am?". I became confused and nauseous from their exhausting and irrelevant questions. Sitting there, holding my bandaged sprained wrist against my stab-wounded chest, they almost had me convinced I led the freak on—

"Don't focus on that, Diet. Revert to your friends, your support. Rea and Amy will help you get through this. They will always be there for you, right?"

The station kept trying Amy's number for the longest, but got Rea after the first ring.

I don't recall much when Rea got me from the station and drove me home at four that morning. She helped me into and out of the shower. She laid on the bed with me, holding my hand until I fell asleep.

I don't think Amy ever came home that night. But the next morning she got all loud when she found Rea in my bed, saying she always suspected we were lovers.

IV

I slap myself across the face, forcing my eyes to open, and demand for the music to be cranked up. The notes sink into my head, and I'm singing so loudly, I'm sure the neighbors could hear me, if there were any.

The images remain the same, whether my eyes are opened or closed. I feel weak, and have to catch myself before collapsing on the shower floor, but I hear Rea's voice right next to me like I did that night—early morning—in the shower: *Come on, girl. I got you.* I can feel her warm embrace as I get steady on my feet. Amy's standing in the doorway, looking smug at us, like her drunk ass did that morning.

I exit the stall and head straight to the medicine cabinet to pop a Xanax. I stare into the vanity mirror, waiting for the pill to kick in. I wipe some of the steam from the mirror and recognize my eyes shaking in the reflection.

Dr. Ambaum stands to my left. Rea is at my right.

"Diet, you need to stop this," I say aloud.

I hear Rea saying, *"For real, girl."*

Dr. Ambaum says, *"You're not a victim, anymore."*

Amy's reflection from the doorway chimes in: *"Yeah, we're going to have fun tonight. It's time to party like rock stars."*

I'm distracted by three knocks coming from a bedroom window. I look back at the mirror. All three women have vanished.

I wrap a towel around my torso and scurry to my desk in my bedroom. I active my laptop and tap the screen through the security camera images. No one's standing at the front door or in the carport at the back door. The side of the house, where I heard the knocking on my window, is also clear.

I'm still home alone.

Amy and Rea's voices sound as if they're standing right behind me, though, when I hear them say in unison: "*Stop this, Diet!*"

"Stop this, Diet," I say aloud.

The Wind

I

The lace at the bottom of my Riding Hood skirt swooshes as I pace around the kitchen. When I place my glass of merlot on the island and retrieve a carving knife from a drawer by the sink, I catch myself staring at my reflection in the blade. The burning on my chest returns, but I bury it. I lay the knife down between the pumpkin and the pile of newspapers on the nook table.

I'm flinging open a cabinet to get a bowl for the popcorn when the front doorbell rings.

The microwave clock reads 7:42. I'm not expecting Rea for at least another 15 minutes, and she's never early for anything. The doorbell chimes again, resonating throughout the house. I check the security monitor on my tablet from the counter corner and see someone standing in the dark at the front door, with a flimsy costume flapping in the wind—I don't have the front porch light on.

"Oh! Trick-or-treaters."

I grab the ceramic scarecrow bowl that I loaded up with bite-sized candy bars. I step into the dark foyer from the unlit living room and I'm reaching for the light switch when I realize there isn't anyone standing in front of the glass door. Confused, I look around. I move my fingers to another switch and turn on the porch light instead of the hall light for a better look.

There's still no one at the front door.

I turn off the outside light and remain in the dark holding the bowl of candy, baffled.

About that time, three distinct knocks echo from the mudroom.

I look through the front door again, expecting someone to jump from the side, but three more bangs travel from the back of the house. My blood flow quickens, causing miniature spots before my vision. I leave the candy on the table before gingerly making my way toward the mudroom.

I stop in the middle of the kitchen when I discover there's no one outside the mudroom's tinted windows. My heart races, and I cross my trembling arms to rub the goosebumps.

Dumbfounded by the sudden commotion and debating internally on whether or not to pop another pill, I didn't realize I had entered the carport until the crisp draft cut through the thin leggings. The breeze had gusted from underneath the rising garage door—I must have pushed the button mindlessly while I was deep in thought. The driveway and backyard are vacant. I walk to the edge of the grass to see no Honda parked on the street. Storm clouds have arrived.

I lock the deadbolt behind me and plan to close the carport door, but a steady noise from down the hallway interrupts my train of thought.

The sound grows louder as I gradually venture down the dark hallway. I check Amy's room again; her outfit remains resting on the comforter. That's when I realize the sound's coming from my bedroom. I ease closer to the light radiating from my bedroom and illuminating the dark hall. It takes all the bravery I have to enter my bedroom.

The music is coming from my bathroom. I know what it is immediately; I've left my cell running. I look at the security cameras' displays from the still-opened laptop on my desk. It's still quiet around the house.

I disconnect my phone from the bathroom speaker, then wirelessly transfer the music from my cellular onto the flat screen in the den, hoping it'll help me relax. The phone vibrates in my hand, and I nearly jump out of my skin. It's Rea.

"You need to stop freaking yourself out, Diet," I mutter before answering the phone.

The Rain

I

The garage door rises like a stage curtain, introducing one of tonight's fairytale heroines gracefully exiting her Mini Cooper. Rea's slimming Elsa dress twinkles in the street light above the garage door. To top off her look, a sparkling tiara surrounds her hair-bun. She grabs her sky-blue clutch from the passenger seat, and a twelve-pack of wine coolers. Still not done, she retrieves a bottle of silver tequila from a brown paper bag, knowing I cannot drink beer anymore—

my best friend knows me so well. It starts to rain lightly by the time she reaches the carport.

Rea follows me into the house after we hug. We exchange pleasantries about each other's attire. Rea drops off the drinks in the fridge after cracking one for herself. I close the carport door before collecting my glass of wine from the kitchen island and join her to prep the pumpkin.

We banter while I slide the butcher knife into the fruit.

Rea swigs her drink. "Are you sure you're okay? You sounded a little shook when I called for you to let me in."

As I wash my hands in the sink, I share the story of the ringing doorbell and knocking before her second phone call.

"Maybe it was just trick-or-treaters tricking *you*," Rea teases. She lifts the knife and spins the tip on the newspaper. "Or maybe it's the cute delivery boy coming back," she says with a sly grin.

I deny the likelihood and snicker. "I even opened the carport door to see if anyone was standing in the driveway, which doesn't make sense considering the knocking was from inside the carport—"

I turn to look back out the tinted windows and notice Rea had stopped carving the last triangle eye.

"Diet, what's wrong?"

I find Rea's eyes sternly staring at me.

"Rea, I had to open the carport for you."

Rea nods with a bewildering smirk.

"I opened the garage door before then but

don't recall shutting it after searching outside because the music from my bathroom distracted me."

Rea's freshly plucked brows furrow. The silence in the kitchen pulsates the longer it lasts.

There's sudden commotion coming from the hallway. Rea and I both shriek before seeing it's just Charlie running into the den. We both grab our chests as the feline settles himself.

Rea shakes her head, and her expression returns to normalcy. "That damn cat … Nonsense, girl. You just pushed the button before going to check on the music." Rea must have read my rebutting expression, because she adds, "Diet, stop freaking yourself out. You've been hitting that button daily for the past few years now. You just didn't realize you'd done it before walking to the back because it's second nature for you."

Did I? I have no recollection of pushing the button. But Rea makes a strong a point—and Amy's going to be the counselor instead of Rea?

I shrug it off. "Maybe so."

I suggest we wait for Amy to get home before starting one of the movies. Rea agrees, and we finish the jack-o-lantern before we head to the sofa with our freshly poured drinks. I tap my phone screen to send online amateur home videos of Halloween pranks to the Smart TV.

Rea grabs a paperback from the floor. "*Survival Techniques and Practices*? Really, Diet? The self-defense class isn't enough?" She flings it onto the coffee table.

Having Rea over always makes me feel better, even when she's making fun of me in her kind-hearted way. We enjoy our drinks, chatting up memories and sharing laughter.

"This is good," Rea adds. "I haven't heard you laugh like that in a while."

My grin softens. "Yeah? Well, what happened was horrible. But I'm also realizing it could have been a lot worse, and—."

"And he got caught," Rea adds.

"But some of the reports and statistics we print for the Safety Awareness section in the school paper show how often these assholes get away with it."

Rea's taken aback by the foul language.

I jovially jab her with my elbow. "Please ... I bet you talk a lot worse when you're with Kenneth."

Rea looks to the ceiling. "True."

"Hey. I thought about going out later on tonight—"

"Do you always leave your money lying around, Diet?"

Rea's random question catches me off guard. I look at what Rea's talking about, the folded-up five-dollar bill next to my margarita.

"Oh. That was for the delivery guy, but I forgot to tip him when you were—Wait."

Rea stops in mid-sip.

"How did that ... I left that in the bathroom."

"Huh?"

"That five-dollar bill! I left it on the counter in the bathroom, Rea. I emptied my pockets before I got in the shower, and I placed it in that stupid seashell soap dish I bought in Cancun."

"Oh, you still have that tacky thing, Diet!? That was a good trip, though."

"How did it get out here?"

I jump off the couch and rush down the hallway. I'm tapping the empty soap plate where the money once laid when Rea enters my bathroom with her wine cooler. Despite the shrieking and giggling from the flat screen in the distance, the silence between Rea and me is unsettling.

II

"Diet," Rea finally says, breaking the silence. "You're talking nonsense. You must've taken it in there with you without remembering, like not recalling the carport. Or maybe you dropped it off in the den when you thought you put it in the soap dish. Which is cool. I do things like that all the time, girl." Before I could protest, Rea mutters, "Stop trying to scare me, best friend. Save that shit for Amy."

I follow Rea down the hallway while she tries her best to reassure me. We enter the den to find the five-dollar bill isn't on the coffee table anymore. I freeze while Rea is spinning and ranting about where it has gone.

My text-alert notification goes off. I scan the coffee table to find that my phone isn't there anymore either. Another notification chimes. Rea and I both search the kitchen.

My phone vibrates next to the unfolded five-dollar bill on the kitchen island.

"What the hell?" Rea asks, as she taps on the money.

I grab my phone. The text from a private number reads, *BOO*.

Three heavy knocks rattle the front door, and we both jump and yell. We stand still, staring at the open walkway between the den and foyer. Three more knocks reverberate from the front door. I check the monitors from the tablet on the kitchen counter. I go to the far corner and yelp at what's on the screen.

Rea stands behind me. "Oh, hell no!"

An off-white latex mask is staring directly into the front door monitor. Two lidless bloodshot eyes had been painted just above a plump red nose. The digital enhancement reveals how the red-coated paint on the sneering lips has been chipping for a while now. Gusts blow the frizzy Coachella-toned hair. The figure's wearing what looks like a yellow, baggy, polka dot jumpsuit made out of nylon. He waves at us.

Rea sucks her teeth. "It's probably just a trick-or-treater." I can tell Rea's trying to keep a calm voice. She takes a quick sip of her wine cooler right behind her words. Suddenly Rea darts toward the front of the house. "You got me hollering and acting like I'm crazy, girl. You've left the front door light on for Amy and me, so they think you're giving out candy. Stop scaring me, Diet."

I remain frozen while she disappears into the unlit foyer. I hear the front door creaking open. Then nothing more. My blood pressure rises as I hastily trot in Rea's direction.

I find Rea's alcoholic beverage on the table where the candy dish once laid. I remain in the entranceway between the den and foyer, watching

Rea pace on the same front stoop where the clown figure once stood ... but she's alone outside, holding the ceramic scarecrow bowl. Plump raindrops steadily pound the marble slabs.

"Rea, did you turn on the porch light?"

"No." She raises the candy dish. "It was already on. The trick-or-treater saw the porch light and came for some candy—"

"We usually remember the details in the most unusual, extreme moments, Diet. It's part of our survival instinct. Let nothing else steer you away. Men are made stronger but women have better intuition. So follow your gut. You know better."

Dr. Ambaum's last three words are stern and vibrate in my mind.

"Okay, I distinctly remember turning off the porch light earlier, Rea—"

Rea points toward the cul-de-sac. "Isn't that Amy's Bug?"

I ease to the doorway to discover the familiar red Volkswagen Beetle with the pink and green Sorority Greek letters on the front car plate shimmering under the streetlight. Lightning crackles and the thunder soon follows.

"See, it's just Amy being ... Amy." Rea projects loudly enough for me to hear her aggravated tone while she looks left and right in the front yard. "Okay, Amy! We know you're out here trying to be spook-tacluar. Ha, ha. Nice Halloween prank. You got us good. *I* even jumped. It's time to come in now. We're already started drinking and we're ready to binge watch our sexy-men horror movies."

The driveway lights around the side of the house flicker. Rea stops spinning in the grass to face the electrical activity. Rea glows during every lightning display in the shadowed night. The unsettling light show disturbs the alcoholic bubbles in my stomach enough to float to my head. Everything before me spins, and I hold the back of my hand across my forehead.

"Rea, the outside light switch is in the mudroom." I cannot tell if I'm projecting my voice or only hearing my words in my head. "You have to manually turn on the driveway lights from inside the house."

Rea puts her free fist on her hip, still holding the bowl. "Told you it was Amy. She went around to the back and snuck in through the carport. She knows we have to go look in the mudroom to see who's doing that, and she's going to jump out from somewhere in that tacky clown outfit …" Rea's expression shows no amusement as she starts toward the front door.

I dart through the house and halt in the middle of the kitchen. The mudroom is vacant. I shift my attention to the back door: The bolt remains locked. I look out the sink window and it's pitch dark, until a lightning bolt illuminates the sky. I can make out the outline of Rea's Cooper in the flashes. But no trick-or-treaters in some creepy clown costume. No Amy. Nobody.

I turn, thinking Rea had followed me into the house, but I am all alone in the kitchen. I ease to the foyer, calling for Rea and Amy both. The front door remains wide open, but I don't find anyone in the yard—only shards of the scarecrow bowl and candy spread across the damp front stoop.

The farther I step toward the mess, the quicker my heart pumps. I tip-toe over the shattered ceramic and chocolate and into the grass.

Neither Rea nor Amy are in sight. I look back at Amy's parked car for no reason in particular. My heart pounds in my chest—it feels like it could burst at any moment. The wind whips the rain, the lightning highlights Amy's vehicle, and the thunder claps.

Heavy Precipitation

I

"Whenever you find yourself having the same emotions and thoughts as during the sexual assault, remember to call on your coping skills."

I take a deep breath, hold it, count to ten, and slowly exhale. Gray translucent vapor drifts from my lips and evaporates into the stormy night.

"Okay, guys. This isn't funny. You know this isn't a good time to be pranking me."

The dewy grass dampens my black slippers. Raindrops hit my chest and trickle over the scar.

"Okay, forget it. I'm not in the mood."

I close and lock the front door behind me. I meander to the kitchen, stewing about how much those two are really pissing me off. I don't notice the knocking at first. It's the movement in my periphery that catches my attention.

There's a clown is staring through the backdoor glass. I know it's too tinted on the other side to see inside the house, but it raises a fist, as if realizing I had noticed. The clown remains motionless, fist still in the air. I remain frozen, but my mind reels with what to do—my cell phone. I turn toward the kitchen island.

A sharp yelp slips out of my mouth and I freeze again. The clown leans close to the glass with the hope of seeing inside. It's like we're in a staring contest. Then, three more distinct knocks rattle the door. It rests its knuckles on the glass and stays frozen. I get lost in the silhouette's catatonic stance and when it slams its pale forehead into the glass door, I jump and shriek.

It sways, dragging its rubbery forehead along the glass. I convulse, allowing another cry to claw up my throat. The being remains still, then grabs the doorknob and jiggles it with force. I dash for the kitchen island.

My cell phone isn't on the countertop anymore. Only the five-dollar bill remains.

My knees go weak. The rattling stops, but it's followed by two fists pounding on the door, shaking the glass in the doorframe. I scream for help as my body crumbles onto the kitchen floor. Every time the lightning flashes, I can decipher every blood-red detail on its face. I close my eyes, hoping this is just a bad dream, but I still hear the pounding.

But Dr. Abraum forms from the smoky gray clouds within my closed eyelids. She's so vivid, in a slim, black, long shirt and a white blouse. Her usual long hair resting over her shoulders has been wrapped in a tight bun, and she isn't wearing her thick-framed glasses.

"Eventually, you will *need to learn how to fight, Diet—physically and mentally."* Her tone

isn't what you'd expect from a therapist, but more like from a sister or a close friend. Rea and Amy come into view as Dr. Ambaum continues her monologue. *"People today are not getting better. As a psychologist, I fear for humanity's future. But you, Diet, you're strong and genuine. People like you need to know how to fight the monsters in this world. I suggest some self-defense classes, maybe kickboxing. It'll help you feel safer, confident and more at peace. Your doubt with authority will become irrelevant because you'll learn how to defend yourself."*

The self-confidence I have developed from the classes Rea and I've been taking the past few weeks fuels my adrenaline. I move my dominant foot behind me and open my palms before facing away from my torso. I never take my eyes off the freak.

"I'm ready, you dick."

II

Lightning flickers. I'm no longer staring at the disturbing face.

I stand there, waiting for the creep to return to the door. Instead, I hear a lot of noise coming from the back of the house.

I keep my defense on alert while inching toward the hallway. The random videos continue to play from the television. I continue down my path.

The doorbell rings again. Then knocking on the backdoor echoes down the hallway. The two are not in sync, making my thoughts spin. I grab the sides of my head.

"Stop it!"

But the knocking and ringing doorbell don't stop.

Images from that night at the frat house flood my brain. I start to sweat profusely. I'm reliving what happened. I can feel his weight pressing against my frail frame. I can smell his alcohol breath.

"Rea! Amy! Where are you?"

They do not emerge. Neither does Dr. Ambaum. Not in the area. Not from my mind. I'm alone.

The sour odor grosses me out as he snickers in my face.

This isn't happening. This is not happening again!

I begin to hyperventilate. The perv laughs, and I feel his erection growing. The banging on the door and the ringing of the doorbell is uneven with the perv's laughter.

I turn my face away from his hot breath.

A figure steps from the fog of the streets. It's those college guys, the ones that helped their wasted friend, that rescued me. I scream for help.

It's no male that had emerged.

It's Dr. Natasha Ambaum emerging from the murky background. *"Diet, that scared girl was you in the past."* Rea forms behind her as Dr. Ambaum continues. *"Remind yourself where you are now. You're no longer in a helpless situation."* Amy emerges from the fog next, and Dr. Ambaum stands firmer. *"Do not remain a victim. You've survived before, and thriving now toward becoming a stronger woman."*

Tears form, but I nod, then close my eyes.

Dr. Ambaum's voice is clear in the darkness. *"Count with me, Diet. One, two, I'm making it through—"*

The doorbell chimes over and over in the background.

"Three, four, I'll take no more—"

My heartbeat is slowing down as I become more relaxed.

"Five, six, they're the ones that need fixed—"

The screaming from the living room television makes the horror more real. But I remain focused on my breathing.

"Seven, eight, I control my own fate—"

My nerves are now calm. I'm still behind the frat house in my mind, alone with that fraternity freak all over me. I build the inner strength and shove the rapist off me. He disappears into the shadows.

I open my eyes and release a deep breath. I'm back in the kitchen. The banging and ringing of the doorbell continue, but I have control of my emotions … and this situation.

I rise from the wooden floor. I finish the countdown alone and strong.

"Nine, ten, never again."

The Thunderstorm

I

I collect the knife by the jack-o-lantern and ignore the pumpkin remnants that rolled off the blade and down my forearm. Eerie music, followed by kids' bloodcurdling screams, overwhelm the acoustics in the house.

As I stride between the kitchen and den, I spot a silhouette floating in the far side of the unlit living room, blending into the foyer's shadows. I pull the knife inward. I have a tight grip on the handle with the blade's back end along my forearm, and I glide my feet, weak one always before the strong one, through the den ready.

A latex hand clasps the frame before I reach the foyer entranceway, and I make out the rainbow-dyed frizzy hair, then a bloodshot, scowling eye. Finally, half of the blood-red lips sneer beneath the leering eye. The evil clown taps its fingers on the doorframe. There's shrilling behind me from the television.

I ready the knife. "Bring it, asshole!"

The figure cowers into the foyer, and the alarm system indicates the front door is ajar. By the time I reach the foyer, the front door's wide open, exposing the wailing storm outside. The clown's waving at me from the middle of the yard. I remain focused, watching a few more hand gestures before it freezes.

I don't flinch; my dominant leg supports me as my right arm is tucked into my side with the knife. I stare down those soul-less painted eyes while he snarls through jagged teeth.

Suddenly, the creepy clown charges at me.

My heart's racing, but I stay in stance.

The lights in the house go out, and the clown stops on the stoop. I re-adjust my feet, and the figure slams the door closed. Thunder follows the sound of the slammed door. Lightning flickers throughout the dark house. My adrenaline tells me to run to the bedroom and lock myself in the bathroom.

But I remain at the front door.

The clown's face is pressed against the glass. He just stares, as if it he knows I'm in the dark foyer. The storm violently shakes the trees across the street.

There's a noise behind me. I turn, but nothing's there.

The clown is still glaring through the window. I creep toward the door and lock it.

The noise in the kitchen continues, and I inch toward it as quietly as I can. I enter the den to find no one in sight. I slide along the in-wall door that partitions the den and foyer. I ease myself along in the dark. I reach the doorway entrance between the den and front living room to close the glass doors separating the living room and den. That's when a figure comes from the mudroom. It isn't the Coachella clown, but I make out the frizz of the clown wig.

"What do you want?" I ask, trying to sound tough.

Lightning illuminates the other clown. This one has on a black-and-white-checkered jumpsuit. The face is coated a grayish tone. Black diamonds are painted around the eye sockets, and clear-white irises peer through the slits. It wears the frizzed black and white wig.

This creature doesn't respond or even react to my question. I shout it again. Still no answer.

Then the clown from the front of the house appears behind the dark clown in the mudroom.

It has Rea.

The dark clown lifts its black-gloved hands and dangles Amy's keys. I look around, expecting Amy to pop up.

"Diet, help me," Rea sobs through chattering teeth.

The Coachella clown shakes Rea, giving a shrilling laughter at Rea's squealing. The dark clown only keeps the keys swinging from its fingers, unfazed by the commotion behind it.

I don't lower my guard. "Why are you doing this? Where's Amy?"

The dark clown lets the keys drop onto the kitchen's wood floor. He then pulls a long-bladed knife from behind his back. He spins its tip into another fingertip. In the lightning, I notice red smears along the blade. The dark clown glares at me. And I stare back.

I pace in place, still in ready mode but struggling between staying alert in the moment and watching images of what has happened to this point flash before my vision like a slideshow: the assault, the worthless campus security, what Dr. Ambaum said during the last therapy session, and the self-defense classes. All the scenes run through my mind in succession.

I remain in a defensive stance, ready for the dark clown's next move.

"You're no longer in a helpless situation ... You are no longer the victim. You're thriving ..."

A blinding flash erupts from outside, then a blast of thunder with more lightning. The storm viciously rattles the house's foundation. The two clowns flinch. Rea stomps the Coachella clown's floppy red boot just below the ankle.

A muffled shout yelps behind the mask as the Coachella clown loosens its grip on Rea's arms. "You crazy bitch!"

Rea cups a fist into an opened palm to provide force behind her elbow jamming the Coachella clown's throat. The clown releases her to grab its neck . Rea turns and delivers a knee to the groin.

The dark clown turns to its accomplice.

That's when I lunge.

I feel my blade slice through the jumpsuit and into flesh, and he wails. The dark clown calls me a whore and punches me in the face. I stumble backward but am quick to gather myself, replaying how sensei taught us to recompose yourself. The dark clown rushes at me, and I crouch. He topples over me. His knife scrapes my back, and I flinch from the sharp pain. I swing around and kick him in the face several times before he sweeps my legs and pulls me to the floor. The wind is knocked out of me, but my training kicks in and I keep thrashing my feet in the fucker's face.

Rea drops a knee into the Coachella clown's ribs. He's now in the fetal position, clutching his side. Rea wraps her legs around his neck and puts the squeeze on his windpipe.

My head is spinning. The Coachella clown reaches for his knife on the carpet, but I kick it across the room. I roll onto my side and get into position to punish him with several sidekicks. I get in a few more strong kicks to the chest and chin before he goes limp.

I rise to my feet, toughing out the burning sensation on my back. Rea rushes at me to inspect my cut. I look behind to see the Coachella clown curled up in a ball. I tell her I'm good and go to the kitchen island only to be reminded my cell phone is missing. I spin, scrambling to find it.

The creepy clown rises behind Rea. I scream when I see lightning reflecting in the knife's blade over his head. Rea turns just as the blade penetrates her shoulder. She cries out but uses the heel of her palm to strike the clown's face. He raises the knife for another stab, but she blocks it with her forearm. He catches her with a backhand across the face that knocks Rea backward.

I reach out to catch my friend, and the clown goes for me. But he suddenly stops, and starts spinning in place, trying to reach behind his legs. Lightning illuminates the room and I can see that Charlie has dug his claws into the clown's calves. I seize the opportunity. He finally flings Charlie off him, and I head to ram the creep. There's an *umph* from the clown, and he stumbles backward, slamming into the wall and then sliding to the floor. I gather Rea from the ground and practically drag her toward the front door.

I open the door to the foyer. However, the clown who had glared through the door still lingers in the exact position as before. Rea is ready to flee to the back of the house. I wrap my hands around her arm and instruct her to wait. I jog to the door and open it. The being is only a prop hooked onto the window.

I step into the storm and motion for Rea to follow me. I reach for her and impatiently encourage her to come toward me. Something runs between her legs, and she high steps, making me hop in terror, too.

Charlie had darted between her legs and is now running through the rain, across the street, and into the woods. More screaming pulls my attention back to the house. I'm thinking it's from the television again, only to remember the house's electricity is out.

Fluffy yellow sleeves encircle Rea's body and pull her back into the house. I follow her cries to the living room. Rea squirms and shrieks in the monster's arms. The Coachella clown grows aggravated and slams Rea onto the floor. It then pulls a knife somewhere from its side while leering down at Rea.

I yell for the clown's attention. It looks up just before I ram my shoulder into its stomach. The thing stumbles all the way into the dining room. His blade catches the side of my face before he drops it.

I snag the knife, help Rea to her feet, and assist her to the front door.

The dark clown blocks our pathway to outside.

I glance behind me to see the Coachella clown marching toward us. The dark clown steps into the entranceway between the den and foyer as we run past him and down the hallway.

II

Rea limps into my bathroom as I lock my bedroom door. I rummage through the dark to the nightstand. I grab the flashlight and battery-operated lantern before joining Rea.

After locking the bathroom door behind me, I place the lantern on the floor. I search the cabinets below my vanity and find my miniature first-aid kit.

I place it on the counter and help Rea ease on to the closed toilet lid. I gather all the towels I can find, then rip the sleeve of her bloodied Ice Queen dress and apply an alcohol-drenched hand towel over the cut.

Rea cries out through gritted teeth, and asks, "Who the hell are they?"

I hunch my shoulders to my ears while still nursing her flesh wound by recalling the steps from the survival guide. My vision is blurred by the steady stream of tears, but I'm able to stop the bleeding and get her bandaged up.

"Okay," I say. "We need a plan."

I scan the bathroom for weapons. I smash a hand-held mirror against the corner of the counter and wrap a washcloth around the base of the biggest shard I see. I hand Rea the kitchen knife, molding her hands firmly around the handle, and I keep my makeshift shank.

"Okay, Rea," I whisper. "They're going to be right outside this door any second now. We need to fight our way out of the bedroom, okay?"

Rea nods with tears in her eyes.

I count to three with my free hand, and we fly out the bathroom. I scramble toward the bedroom door, but then realize Rea has been snatched up. I turn to see a tall figure. She turns and stabs the clown. His scream is muffled by his mask. The other clown charges from the closet and grabs Rea, slamming her against the wall. She crumbles to the floor. The Cochlea clown jumps at me, and I slash his arm.

"You fucking bitch!" The muffled voice sounds familiar.

I jab again, but the clown is quicker. He grabs my arm and slams it against the wall. I keep hold of the shard long enough for it to dig into my palm before I drop it. Blood seeps through my clenched fist. The clown backhands me across my face.

Stunned by the blow, my vision is compromised. I resist the clown while he's trying to pin me to the wall. Everything's a whirlwind, and the lightning bolts only amplify the intensity. We are in a fight for our lives. I regain my focus and spot the dark clown on top of Rea.

I knee the Coachella clown in the crotch, and he drops to his knees. Then I charge at the dark clown and knee him square in the chin. It's a flush shot that twists his head and he tumbles off Rea.

Two thick arms envelop my torso from behind and my training tells me to stomp down on his foot; the Coachella clown wails but keeps hold. The dark clown regains his footing and runs at me; I spring off the carpet and kick him squarely in the chest. The dark clown tumbles backward and trips over Rea, hitting the back of his head against the dresser.

The Coachella clown snatches me up like a ragdoll and body slams me to the floor. The pain vibrates through my body, and the clown now has its weight on my chest, making it hard to breathe. I swing my arms wildly trying to land a blow to the face, but the clown takes hold of my frail wrists with one grip. It uses the other hand to slide a gloved finger down my chest.

All I see is red and lift my legs before thrusting my waist. The clown falls off me. I jump to my feet, and before the clown can collect itself, I kick it in the head … four times.

The fucker doesn't move. I give one more vicious kick to the head just in case.

I look at the other clown, who seems lifeless.

I lean in and remove the Coachella clown's mask and recognize Aaron—the Groceries-on-the-Go shopper.

"Oh, shit!"

I run to Rea and slap her a few times to wake her up. "Come on, sweetie. We need to get out of here and call the cops."

I sling Rea's arm around my neck and help her out of my bedroom, giving the dark clown's now smeared make-up face one more glance while exiting my bedroom.

We're both groggy but feeling our way down the hallway in the dark. I hear some kind of laughter. I again mistaken it for the television, but a high-pitched crackle bellows past Amy's room.

We reach the foyer and see a short clown standing near the shattered candy dish. The clown's wearing a pink-and-black diamond jumpsuit with a matching jester's cap. A pink and black bandana is hiding the lower half of its face, which is caked with white powder, and its clear eyes are intensified through painted black diamonds around the sockets. The pink clown cradles my carved jack-o-lantern—now lit—in one arm and has a sledgehammer in the other.

"Just fucking go!" I scream, and we both dart toward the mudroom.

I push the carport button while Rea unlocks the back door. We both scram out of the house.

We nearly run into the rising garage door, moving quicker than the mechanics. The door gets stuck about two feet from the cement.

"Oh, shit!" Rea cries.

I quickly push her to the floor. "Crawl under!"

I glance behind me and see the pink clown at the back door, watching us struggle. Through the tinted windows, I see the black clown's silhouette behind the pink one. As Rea slides underneath, both clowns start down the stairs with knives in the air.

I drop to the cement, ignoring the pain from scraping my knees and chin. I roll under the stuck door, barely evading the black clown's swinging knife.

Rea helps me to my feet, and we sprint up the driveway.

The rain has reduced to a sprinkle. The lightning's flashes are dim, and the thunder rumbles in the distance. We reach the road and stand by Amy's Bug. I turn and face the house.

The dark clown had made its way around the house and stood in the driveway. The rainbow clown—Aaron with the mask back on— stood on the front stoop. The pink clown stands in Amy's bedroom window, with a soft light illuminating behind it.

All three stand, glowering at us. I'll be damned if I let these sons-of-bitches terrorize me. I take a step toward the house.

Rea snatches my arm. "Diet, don't be stupid. Let the police handle this!"

Dr. Ambaum steps from the woods behind us: *"Trust your gut instincts. If you're not certain about the situation, then don't put yourself in it."*

A petite figure runs through her image, and she evaporated in the humid night sky. It's Charlie, trotting at us with haste.

Shattering glass grabs Rea's and my attention. The pink clown had broken Amy's window and began climbing out the damn thing. The other two clowns trudge toward us, and we run like hell down Anderson Street with Charlie in tow.

Subdued Gales

I

Rea and I scare several trick-or-treaters as we run up the walkway of the closest house around the corner, screaming bloody murder. The lady holding the candy bowl at the front door quickly steps into her house. Rea and I are begging for her help in the mist; a once-slouching scarecrow in a porch rocker has now come to life and stands next to her.

Their faces turn to pure fear as they yell for us to hurry into the house. Rea and I quicken our pace. We hear the scurrying footsteps and the shrills of trick-or-treaters behind us. Rea and I enter the couple's house and the scarecrow slams the door; he activates the house's automatic door locks.

The scarecrow commands all of us to go into the living room. I walk backward, with Rea pulling me down the narrow hallway entrance. I watch him go to the hallway closet and retrieve a handgun.

The ranch-style living room is dim with soft-lit table lamps. A horror movie plays on a flat screen nearly as large as the wall it hangs on. French windows cover the back wall.

"Oh, sweetheart," the little lady says while she holds my bleeding hand with a motherly touch. "Let's clean that up."

She leads me into the kitchen, still holding my hand. She requests for kitchen lights, and they flood the gigantic room. She pulls out a first-aid kit from beneath the island and gets to work.

I look at Rea. She's studying their entranceway. I hear a husky man's voice inform the banging on the door he's calling the police.

"We're the McKenzies. I'm Marsha, and that's my husband, Marty." She pours peroxide on my open wound, and it sizzles.

I wince. "I'm Diet. I live down the street. This is my friend, Rea."

Rea weakly waves.

I continue. "Thank you so much for—"

Rea's scream stops me in mid-sentence. She points past us. We look.

Through the kitchen glass door and the back porch, I see my jack-o-lantern's propped on a yard table. The candle flickers through the eyes and mouth. Something's moving behind the table. I look from the pumpkin to find the pink clown waving at us.

She's dangling Charlie by the neck with her other hand. He struggles to wail and wiggle out of the clown's gloved fingers.

We all scream. Tears blur my vision.

Mr. McKenzie runs into the living room, cell phone at his ear and gun in the other hand. "Oh, shit! One of the them is on the back porch too, Officer."

Some residual lightning blinds me for a moment. When I regain my vision I witness the sledgehammer impact the glass. The window splinters, like a spider building a web. The clown struggles but pulls the sledgehammer from the window. The pink clown slams the glass again. Her dancing feet steps on Charlie's corpse.

Mr. McKenzie tells us to get upstairs and lock ourselves in the bathroom. We head that way, but the two clowns kick in the front door just as the sound of glass shattering explodes behind us.

Gunshots ring out.

Then a girl screams. I know that voice …

Rea grabs the dark clown's arm that held the knife coming at her. The Coachella clown violently shakes Mrs. McKenzie, banging her head against the wall. I run toward the Coachella clown and spin a high kick to the back of the head. The clown staggers backward, and the now unconscious Mrs. McKenzie wilts.

I rip off the mask, showing Aaron's face. I slam his face into the mirror above the coat hangers. Blood pours from his forehead and over his eyes and nose. I force one more good smash before releasing his head. The Groceries-on-the-Go driver joins Mrs. McKenzie on the floor.

Rea is wrestling with the dark clown, and I grab the clown's shoulders and knee him in the groin. He wails and drops to the ground. I remove his mask just as I hear police sirens in the distance.

It's Rea who recognizes his face. "Oh, fuck me! That's the Landon dude Amy likes. From the picture she sent me."

I grab the back of his head and knee his face. Blood spews from his nose. I slam his head into the wall, and he's out cold.

I hear crying in the kitchen. I motion for Rea to comfort the now coming-to Mrs. McKenzie in the corner of the hallway and head to the kitchen.

Mr. McKenzie is standing over the pink clown. Tears are streaming down his face. "She left me no choice. I had to shoot. She was coming at me with that hammer."

I look over Mr. McKenzie to find a pink clown taking her final breaths. Blood stains the rosy silk outfit. The ribbon on the sledgehammer isn't black after all but blue, like the silk band for the bonnet to Amy's Bo Peep costume.

I hear the deep, authoritative introductions from the police at the McKenzie's front door. I plop next to the dying pink clown, crying. One of the officers eases toward the three of us. He looks at the clown taking her last breath. He kneels to remove the bandana.

I don't need to see the unveiling to know who it is. Instead I look at Charlie, who's circling between my legs.

A Night for Jack-o-lanterns and Scarecrows

PARTY SMASHERS In The PARK

Faye beelines for the middle swing. She's claimed that one ever since we began our late night hanging at Oak Park years ago. I step out of her car and take the swing on her right this time.

"Jessica," Faye moans as she lifts her feet into the night sky. "This is totally depressing. How could we let Halloween sneak up on us this year?"

I groan. "We've just been busy, you know. This semester at Midlands Tech is no joke. And you've been doing that cosmetology apprenticeship."

Faye huffs, and her breath rises into the atmosphere. "Adulting sucks. I want to go back to high school. No. Kindergarten, where our only stresses were coloring in the lines and making it to naptime."

I roll my eyes.

"I mean," she continues, "we've been grooving all summer. Since August."

I draw lines in the dirt with the tops of my sneaker. "I guess we're partied out."

"Oh, hell no, Jessica. We're always ready to party."

I laugh, still ogling at my shoe altering the dirt. "Apparently not since we ended up here."

Faye swings with the wind's current, gazing into the distance.

I glance at my watch. "It's nearly eleven, anyhow. Halloween is almost over."

"You hush that nonsense, Jessica!" Faye taps the jack-o-lantern face on my long-sleeved shirt. "Halloween is a lifestyle, not a holiday."

I laugh again, heartier this time. "I hear you."

Faye points in front of us. "Who's that?"

A Beretta putters and turns onto the side street in between the park and Oak Middle School. Dim orange flood lights shine. The vehicle turns into the carpool lane and halts in front of the school's entranceway. The motorized silhouette remains sputtering in place. The school's scarecrow display in the middle of a bundle of haystacks blocks my line of sight, so I can't see who's in the car.

I return to my shoe drawing. "Okay. It's a car, Faye."

"But why are they at the school so late, Jessica? And on Halloween?"

I shrug and kick the dirt. "I think you just answered your own question. It's Halloween. Maybe some teenagers doing a prank."

"Jessica, really? Teenagers? We're only eighteen."

I suck my teeth. "You know what I mean."

"Next year, we need to seriously plan a road trip to Atlanta."

"I'm cool with that. We can go check out that Netherworld haunted attraction."

A pickup truck rumbles down the side road, with no lights on. It parks behind the car. There's faint movement in the cabin, and the limited activity puts my mind in a hypnotic hum. I stare at the two automobiles until their bodies blend into the night.

"How's college?" Faye asks.

I share my experience and how it's completely different than high school—much more challenging.

Faye says she's enjoying cosmetology classes. I state that she'll do way better than I was with college because she loved her studies, whereas I was taking basic courses that seemed like child's play.

"How long do you think we'll continue to do this?" Faye asks.

"Well, if you don't quit your classes—"

"No." Faye stops swinging and gestures toward the shadowy park. "I mean, come hang out here at midnight and talk like this. I mean, tonight I had to pull you from those textbooks and convince you to come out with me."

I go back to my dirt-doodling, my eyes watching the progress at work. "Don't talk like that, girl."

We had met occasionally throughout the summer, but because of my studies and her apprentice, seeing each other every other day faded into once a week in August. And before tonight, we haven't hung out since early September.

"Well," I say, "how about we try to do what we talked about, before high school graduation? Let's look for a place together. We would still be busy with our lives, but at least we'd get to annoy each other every day."

Faye's beautiful smile returns—a smile I haven't seen since we walked that stage to get our diplomas. "Sounds good, Jessica."

A mechanical roaring shakes us from our connection. The truck rolls in reverse, and the other car pulls forward. Instead of turning toward the main road and leaving, the two drive past the middle school and travel down the hill to Old Oak Elementary School.

"Okay," I mutter. "I think we need to find somewhere else to chill for tonight."

"No way! We've been hanging here since sophomore year. We're good."

Before I can argue, Chief Addle's patrol car, slash, personal-vehicle creeps onto the side street.

It passes the middle school and rolls down the hill, toward the elementary school. Once it disappears, the atmosphere hushes and I can hear my heartbeat in my eardrums.

"Okay," I whisper. "That's totally our cue to leave, Faye."

"Oh, chill, Jessica. That's Addle. He's most likely doing his usual patrolling around the area, it being Halloween and all."

I shake my head, still looking down the street. "No, I'm sure he would've had that rookie work tonight."

"Oh, yeah. That new guy from the military. I'd be naughty just for him to handcuff and frisk me."

I snicker. "You're bad, Faye."

"You can't disagree, Jessica."

I shrug. "Anyway, this is getting odd."

"Let's go watch Addle bust their little drug deal."

"The hell, Faye?"

She hops off her swing. "Why not? At least we can say we did something this Halloween. Plus, might be something worth talking about when we invite others over to our apartment for the Halloweens-to-come."

I look at my watch. "It's past midnight now, so technically it isn't—"

Faye hooks onto my hand and snatches me off the swing. "Come on, Jessica!"

I nearly lose my footing, and stumble into balance. Faye releases my fingers and trots across the park. Before I register our new plans, she steps out of the park's lighted area and vanishes into the night. I look around, and my core trembles when I can't find her.

I call for her, but only crickets chirping answer.

The wind swirls around the shack by the baseball field.

"Come on, Jessica!" Faye's voice echoes from the surrounding darkness.

I stare in the direction of her voice and see leaves tumbling in the noisy wind. My whole body shivers.

Before I can recognize it, a shadowy figure beyond the park charges at me. I'm ready to dart back to the car, when Faye's petit figure reappears in the light. She stares back at me. I huff and follow her through the bushes and down the hill. We find a spot where the shrubbery separates just enough for us to have a clear view of the school campus.

The three vehicles are exposed in the well-lit, vacant Old Oak Elementary parking lot. Chief Addle is standing in the center of the cars. Soon, we watch a much younger beefy guy exit the pickup truck. The compact car remains occupied.

"Hold up," Faye whispers. "Isn't that the rookie?"

They're a good forty feet from where we're standing, so the details are still sketchy. The jeans and tucked flannel shirt seem too tight on the guy's firm build. I notice a clean-shaven face and a buzz cut.

When my vision confirms Faye's question, all I can say is, "Oh, shit."

Soon, a couple of guys exit the third car to join Chief Addle and the rookie's huddle. The steam of their breath puffs from their mouths as they talk. We can't understand any of the words, only hear their deep tones traveling through the crisp air.

The more I look, the more my eyes adjust to the distance and the weirder the strangers appear. The burly one has the upper section of his face cover by a bear mask, and baggy overalls stretch over his large stomach. The scrawny figure has on a wolf mask and is dressed in denim and black leather that glistens in the orange streetlights.

There's an exchange of small items between Chief Addle and the bear. He pockets whatever Chief Addle handed to him, while the chief seems to be counting some papers. Money, maybe. He hands some of them to the rookie after a second tally. Then one of the strangers lean into the rookie, hug him, and then they peck kiss on the lips.

"What the hell?" I blurt, and quickly cover my mouth.

Faye glances at me with clenched teeth. Then we look back at the activity.

Chief Addle tongue kisses one of the strangers, his arms around the burly man's chest.

The other stranger has the rookie pinned on Chief Addle's hood.

The cold wind adds to the chills traveling my body, but I can't shiver because I'm paralyzed by what I'm witnessing.

"This is some weird, crazy shit," Faye mummers.

I grab her sleeve and begin to step backwards. "We seriously need to go, Fa—"

Something catches my heel, and I tumble to the ground. Pain radiates through my shin and calf. I do my best to control my growls.

"Oh, shit," Faye says, leaning over me. "You okay, Jessica?"

I wince, pressing both hands around my ankle and squinting as if it'd hurt to peel my eyelids apart. I'm able to see the huddle in the parking lot, but the guys aren't embracing anymore. They're now looking in our direction.

"We seriously need to go, Faye," I repeat, but my tone quivers this time.

Faye hurries me onto my feet as I watch the men jump into their vehicles. I attempt to walk, but the agony is intolerable. So Faye slings my arm around her shoulders and guides me behind the bushes. The vehicles are raucous behind us and not too far away. When we reach the park, we hear roaring and squealing up the paved side of the road.

Faye is about to lead us toward the park's streetlights, but I squeeze her shoulder before she takes another step toward the light.

"Faye, they're driving too fast. We need to stay in the shadows."

Faye nods and searches the scene, jerking her head and darting her eyes left to right.

"Okay, but where?"

I glance behind us to see if there's anything to huddle behind, but I only see headlights, illuminating brighter by the second.

Faye pulls me with her. "Behind that shed by the fields."

It's at last fifteen feet from us. With Faye dragging me, we won't have enough time to hide before the cars get to the open section.

I spot the random small cement block erect from the ground we used at base when we played tag as kids. "Faye, put me behind that and you run behind the shed."

"No!" Faye hisses.

I slack my weight and become too heavy for Faye. I drop to the ground and behind the cube. The pain at the base of my spine travels down my legs to join my pulsating calves.

Faye cusses me but starts running. She darts behind the shed just as a bright light floods the scene and passes me. The light remains seconds longer, before fading out. I pant a count to ten and then peek around the cement. I see Chief Addle's car rolling past the par, his handheld flood light surveying the area.

I hobble from my spot once the rumbling truck creeps up the road and passes the park. When I hear crumbling leaves behind me, I turn to see that Faye has hopped up from behind the shed. She only takes a step before blurting profanity. Then her silhouette drops to the ground and crawls to me.

I look around the block. The bear has exited the driver's side of the small car. I hear a click and dart my head back before the flashlight illuminates the spot I was just in. Behind the flashlight is the brawny figure.

Faye and I hold our breaths while hefty footsteps near our hiding spot. Soon, the edge of the light passes the block and grows brighter as the steps crumbling the dead leaves become closer. The light reaches the shed, and the stomping ceases. The beam roams over the baseball fields. Faye moves her foot closer to her body, and I know the searcher heard the rustling shrubberies.

Every ounce of blood drains to my feet, which my mind thinking this makes the pain from the twisted ankle feel worse. I suck in cold air through gritted teeth, and droplets of spittle spray over my lips when I try to stop wheezing. My left arm aches from Faye's hand squeezing my bicep.

The light goes over our head, and I close my eyes. I don't want to see the man's face, envisioning one of those nasty-looking brawny men with beads of sweat pouring over his chunky face, and his wooly chest heaving from using all his oxygen to get this far.

Darkness grows behind my eyelids. I ease an eye open and find myself staring at a unoccupied, murky park.

Footsteps fade from us. In seconds, I hear a car door slam and build the courage to look out from behind the hiding spot.

The car drives up the street.

Faye helps me back to my feet. When I put the weight on my ankle, the pain isn't as unbearable, but the injury still pulsates. I let her know I'm good to support myself.

We watch the last car take a right at the stop sign and peel away from the campus area. It vanishes into our dark Town of Oak. But we don't leave the cement block, just in case one of the vehicles turns back to find whatever they'd heard in the bushes.

We stand and stare into the night. No car travels down the main road for about five minutes, but feels like 25. When we're certain that we're alone, I limp behind Faye, into the light and toward her parked car.

IT'S JUST A GAME

Late Afternoon
"Joni!"

I hear Beth's loud mouth from the other side of the enormous double French doors. I'm already regretting this, but she saw me, so it'd be rude to leave for home now .... and Mom would be mad.

Beth swings both doors wide as if presenting a queen to the spirits of All Hallows' Eve. She glides the mask off her face, over the long floppy cotton ears attached to a headband,

and along her voluminous blond hair. A pink dot has been dapped on the tip of her pale nose, along with three thin black horizontal lines stretched across each cheek.

Royalty? More like an offering.

Beth bends to hug me, but her frail arms barely connect with my shoulders. "So, so glad you decided to come."

She escorts me into her home, and I can't miss how tight the white jumpsuit hugs her petit body, nor the fist-sized cotton ball perched just above her tail end. The mixed aroma of honey, moss and vanilla welcomes me into the main hallway. The foyer is wide enough to fit the house where Mom and I had lived near Cat Island, with space to spare. The gaudy pearl ceiling clashes with the off-white walls, and the minimal sunlight from the sunroof makes the chandelier sparkle.

Laughter amplifies from the spiral staircase, and Kannitha stops midway to twirl her arms in the air. "Yes, bitch! You came." She trots down the steps.

The black spandex and leggings accent her slim waist, yet doesn't support her jiggly plump backend or top-heavy front. The tiny pointy ears on her scalp are a great accessory, but her mask reminds me of Mardi Gras rather than Halloween. A short black plush tube bops behind her.

Kannitha takes hold of my shoulders, her gaze skimming me up and down, with thick mascara eyes. "Love the getup. A ... cocktail waitress?"

I hope my feeling of defeat doesn't show through my makeup.

"I'm a succubus."

Kannitha furrows her eyebrows and shakes her tilted head.

I struggle but manage to hold my grin. "They're seductive demons that target guys."

Kannitha pulls me into her bosom, and her hug is stiff. "Yes! Work it, demon bitch. And I'm your black cat. Tonight is going to be a blast!"

I force my smile to expand across my face.

"Hey, friend!" Stevie calls from the stairs.

Her earth-toned outfit perfectly accents her curvy figure. No drawn-on whiskers, no accented features. Simple, yet I get what she's dressed as; a creature more respected across most spiritual practices. Rather have Stevie be my spirit animal, than some damn pussy.

I've always admired Stevie's confidence since we met in drama class, and I'm glad she kept her hair down, with the hairband replicating half-moon brown ears..

Stevie removes the furry masquerade before bear-hugging me. Then she pulls away and cuffs my hands. "I love the siren look."

My heart is elated, and my smile is now genuine.

Beth grabs everyone's attention. "So I got some games lined up, and I have so many classic horror movies. The one with the creep that has sharp knives as fingernails. The masked one that died in the lake is in the mix, too. And Mom and Dad bought a pumpkin for us to carve before they left for the party at Dad's lodge."

"So, we're going to play some games, watch movies—"

"I already said that, Kannitha!" Beth glares at her.

Kannitha's cheeks blush through her thick makeup. "Oh, yeah. My bad. Anyway, we're also going to try to scare each other—"

"With ghost stories!" Beth claps.

Stevie must've read my confused expression. "We have an annual ghost story contest."

My face loosens. "Oh, I love ghost stories."

"Oh, yeah!" Beth links an arm with mine and snatches me from away from Stevie. "We're just going to be silly and have a fun night."

If I hear one more time about how tonight's going to be fun ... "Nice!"

Beth's frolic has me tumbling over my own feet as she chaperons me into the kitchen. I glance back to find Kannitha and Stevie trailing us. As Stevie and I make eye contact, she displays an expression of sympathy and humor. I smirk while trying not to burst into laughter.

Beth releases me mid-trot to hop toward the island stove. "You ever done candied apples?"

I shake my head and take a place at the dining table next to Stevie, who grabs the knife near the pumpkin. Kannitha and Beth hover around the dipping pots and fill large bowls with junk food, replicating witches hunched over steamy cauldrons.

I still can't believe I let Mother talk me into this ridiculous Halloween sleepover. Sleepovers are such child's play. And of all nights! I'd rather go back to Cat Island to hang with Amber than be here. She and I would do our traditional All Hollows' Eve events, like gathering at Samantha's and communing in the cemetery.

I've only known these three girls since registering for school in August. Beth and I had Mr. Ambrose's Biology II class together, and we were paired for an assignment. She nearly gagged at the thought of touching a dead animal, so I sliced the frog. After getting our high marks for the dissecting project, she invited me to join her, Kannitha and Stevie at lunch that day. And every day after. They always gossip about trivial topics—celebrities, boys on our school's sports teams, and where to visit for spring break. When they attempt to bring me into their conversations, awkwardness overwhelms me when I talk about what book I'm reading or the most recent episode from my favorite paranormal docuseries. They're sweet to show interest, but I don't feel much connection with the girls. Well, not with Beth and Kannitha, anyway. Stevie and I share the same tastes in literature and television. And we seem to have a similar concept for the pumpkin tonight.

Kannitha snips a peep while retrieving apples from the pots. "Oh, that's a creepy face."

Stevie and I exchange smirks.

• • •

Twilight

We all climb the spiral stairs, Kannitha, Beth and I with the snacks. Stevie totes the jack-o-lantern. After strolling down the hallway and entering Beth's suite, Beth turns on a movie as the rest of us plop onto the bed spacious enough for two families. Beth joins us on her bed and pulls the sweets toward her while scooting away the bowl of popcorn and gluten-free candy corn mix from Stevie. We don't pay much attention to the masked guy slashing at the babysitters on the screen, but the film's eerie music emphasizes the ominous vibe by what is happening before us.

"Here, Stevie," Beth says nearly shoving some fruits toward my friend. "To help with your diet."

The urge to cuss her out flares in my chest, and reading the hurt in Stevie's eyes only adds to the rage.

Kannitha jumps into a game. "Okay, Beth. Truth or dare?"

There's a teasing hesitation before Beth answers. "Truth."

The two giggle. Stevie and I exchange spiritless glances before flashing thin smiles. Kannitha bops onto the bed and some of the popcorn/candy corn mix spills onto the comforter.

"Is it true, Beth, that you and Mitchel Anderson made out in the closet during Seven Minutes in Heaven at Rebecca Chamber's Labor Day party?"

Beth stares at Kannitha with a stoic expression, and Kannitha leans toward her with anticipation. Stevie fidgets with the plush pillow she's cradling.

Beth giggles. "True."

Kannitha squeals in her hands, and Stevie buries her face into a cushion, groaning.

"Who's that?" I asked.

"He's in our AP English class." Kannitha was still looking at Beth. "He sits behind me, in the back row."

"Oh, wow." I grimace at the image of the baby-faced Adonis in my head.

"You were all over him that night when we played partners with sexy charades," Kannitha says. "And that kiss did linger between you two during spin-the-bottle."

Stevie scrunches her face. "But Mitchel Anderson is so secretive. And moody looking."

With the winks he flashes at me and *everyone* else in class, that jock doesn't come across as secretive. And his behavior isn't appealing. Nor is any of this conversation.

"You can't deny the demands of the spinning bottle." Beth grins as if she should be praised for reciting the rules to a children's game.

Stevie and Kannitha giggle. I'm still lost about what's happening, but I still force myself to join the schoolgirl coyness while boredom floods my being. I feel like going home, and I'm not even worried about how rude it'll be. They can talk their gossip all they want at school. I'm only concerned about having to persuade Mom that these girls aren't the ones that'll—

My cell vibrates in my pocket. I remove it to see a text from Amber.

What u doing 2nite?

I glance at the other three girls and see that they're involved with gossiping about classmates.

I actually went to that sleepover.

For real Joni! That's Gr8.

Don't start Miss Cheerleader.

Shut up. I could eat you! You've been moping around being lonely and no one will be open about us. Now you have 3 wanting to get to know you. So show them.

I suck my teeth and glance at the girls to see if they heard me, but they're still engaged with the childish commanding game.

I guess but they aren't you Amber. We've been celebrating All Hallows' Eve together forever. They won't get it. I need your hug. Lol.

Well no one will ever be as awesome as your bestie. Lol. But at least you won't be solo tonight. Plus when I visit you and Mother soon we'll have more fun with them.

Ugh, I can't believe she even said that. I don't want any others invited into our group.

Need to get ready for Brandon's party. HAVE FUN 2NITE. I'll text l8r 2 check on u. Luv u.

"Joni!" Beth bounces on the bed to grab my attention. "You've been quiet. Truth or dare?"

I give a narrow grin. "Truth."

Beth stares as if she's trying to read my mind. "It is true that your dad's in jail for murder?"

Warmth heats my nerves, and every ounce of superficial joy I've invoked for tonight perspires out of my pores. The unsettling quietness makes my skin itch.

"Are you serious, Beth?" Stevie says.

Kannitha says, "OMG," but she doesn't sound shocked.

"What?" Beth's blunt tone contradicts her innocent expression.

"Jeez, Beth," Stevie says. "Be somewhat of a human."

Beth sighs. "*Jeez, Stevie.* Joni chose truth."

More silence before Beth turns to me. "Well, Joni? Is it true?"

"Shut up, Elizabeth!" Stevie jumps off the bed, hands thrashing.

I can't decide what to do—hide from the embarrassment or smack Beth.

"You can be completely unreal sometimes." Stevie gathers my hands into hers. "I'm so sorry for my airhead friend here. Just ignore that."

Kannitha giggles. "Don't be witchy, Stevie. It's just a game."

My stomach and chest contract as Beth's question repeats in my mind, and the room is spinning. Except during therapy, I haven't talked about my dad since relocating from the Charleston coast, not even with Mom. But I know that with my new high school being so small, people have seen me regularly visit the guidance office. I couldn't play the new-transfer-needing-to-complete-registration act for too long before some people became suspicious.

"No, no." I raise my hands to ease the tension in the room. "It's okay. It's fine. But that's not true, Beth."

Beth drops her grin. "What isn't?"

I want to ask the stupid, rude bitch if she had forgotten what she'd just asked. Instead I say, "My father isn't a murderer."

Stevie squeezes my hand. "Joni, seriously. You don't have to share anything."

I laugh, nervously. "Where did you hear that anyway, Beth?"

Beth grunts and moans but doesn't say words.

"That's just what the rumor at school is," Kannitha says, too willingly.

I chuckle. "Seriously?"

They nod as if listening to a keynote speaker, and I suspect this was why they'd invited me to the sleepover.

I adjust myself on the bed. "Well, let people know they're wrong. All right now. Stevie, truth or dare?"

Stevie's smirks and then shakes her head. "I'm tired of this game now, girls. Let's move on to something else."

Beth rolls her eyes. Then they grow wide, pupils dilatated. "I know!" She hops off the bed and disappears into her personal bathroom.

I glance at Kannitha by the private balcony's glass door, watching Beth with glee. I look at Stevie and she exhales as if to say, *What is this crazy girl trying to get us into now?*

• • •

Night Time

Beth reappears with half-filled glass bottles and plastic cups.

"What, we're going to play spin-the-bottle now?" I tease.

Stevie bursts into laughter, and Kannitha even snickers in amusement.

"No," Beth taunts. "We're going to lighten up the mood."

"Yes, bitch!" Kannitha starts dancing in Beth's direction.

Stevie gets up from the bed. "That's the way to my heart."

I get off the bed and join Stevie. "Sounds good to me."

"Really?" Beth said, shocked.

I take a cup from Beth. "Of course."

Beth pours my drink first. "My girl."

She distributes the other plastic cups and commands a device on her desk to play music.

Once the first song starts, we sway and sing the words in unison. When the chorus hits, we raise our drinks and toast, bellowing the lyrics. I wish Amber could join us now.

I retrieve my cell phone to see that Amber hasn't messaged me. I want to take a selfie. Still need to show her my costume, after all. I walk over to Stevie and hold the phone above us, and Stevie puts her arm around me. We give goofy looks before I snap the picture.

"We're sexy," Stevie says as we review the photo.

"I'm going to send this to my bestie, Amber, if that's cool with you."

Stevie holds her cup into the air. "Yes! To besties."

I toast with her before hitting Send.

Beth orders the music to change to something ominous. "Storytime!"

She stops the movie marathon and displays a video of a crackling fire dancing before a dried-up cornfield. The shape of a scarecrow lingers deep in the corn shucks and stands before a starry night image. Kannitha turns off the bedroom lights. Beth collects pillows and places them in a circle on the carpet. Then she puts the jack-o-lantern in the center. The scene is starting to resemble a conjuring sphere.

"We do this every year," Stevie says to me.

"Yeah," Kannitha says. "We conclude every Halloween with who can tell the creepiest ghost story."

Beth giggles. "The winner gets to choose the spring break trip."

Vacation trip? Seriously? That explains why they obsess over spring break at lunch.

I don't want to be a part of this nauseating discussion, but if I were to tell Mom and Amber that I couldn't connect with the girls after being here this long, I know they'd be disappointed. I send Amber a quick text while the three are still organizing themselves on the cushions around the jack-o-lantern.

Now we're competing for the best ghost story and whoever has it chooses the spring break vacation destination.

I expect Amber to respond with something sarcastic or a retching emoticon.

Well u r sure to win. U have the best ones.

Beth lights the candle in the jack-o-lantern and pats the pillow next to her for me to join. "Kannitha won last year, so she goes first."

We're all settled, and Kannitha tells her story about two friends hanging out at a playground one Halloween night, when some random cars pull into a nearby elementary school parking lot. When the friends investigate who's driving, they discover a mini-orgy of costumed bears and wolves desiccating the school grounds, all being ordered by some guy in a sheriff's uniform. They're caught spying and run for their lives. The story isn't scary as much as disturbing, but the other two praise Kannitha's story.

I can't stop thinking about wanting to text Amber, but I join in on the compliments. Then Beth says it's Stevie's turn.

Stevie's tale is titled *Whose Child.* It takes place at an autumn festival in a community park which is packed. A mother has taken her child to the carnival, and as the park grows more crowded, the mother has a tough time keeping track of her son. Each time the mother finds him, he would say that he thought he was just with her, pointing in random directions. This happened about three times, and each time the mother reunites with her child, he complains about his mother becoming more and more irritated with him getting out of line for the bumper cars. The mother is always relieved to find her son, but she's also confused when he references that she was just fussing at him for disappearing. The last time the boy's mother finds him, within a swarm of people waiting for the bumper cars, he's talking to a woman with uncanny features similar to hers. The story ends with a casualty—a derailed go-cart runs over a child. The mother fears that it was her son who got hit, but she finds him in the chaotic swarm of witnesses around the tracks. As she swoops her child into her arms, the mother spots her doppelganger kneeling over a lifeless boy with the same features as her own son. The mother is so petrified of the surreal moment that she flees, speechless, dragging her inquisitive son by the arm, out of the park.

I commend Stevie's creepy twist.

"Not bad, Stevie," Kannitha genuinely says.

"That wasn't even about Halloween," Beth scoffs. "Anyway, what about you, Joni?" Beth dons her hollow smile. "Would you like to tell a story?"

Kannitha's face lights up.

Stevie reaches for me. "Joni, you don't have to participate if—"

"No, I'm good." I reposition myself on the cushion, stretching my neck. "I have a few stories in the vault." I laugh to help with my uneasiness, but no one laughs with me. I tap my chin, looking at the ceiling. "I have a good one for this occasion."

Barely noticeably leans toward me within the jack-o-lantern candlelight, with squinted eyes and pursed lips.

I begin the tale.

***

"The daughter wanted nothing more than to be accepted by the group of girls, simply to please her mother. But she was fathered by the highest patriarch of the coven. This alone provoked animosity from the other girls, because the majority went through dehumanizing initiations. Her mother received her share of bitterness from the coven as well because her heart strode for a silver path and she struggled with the coven's sinister habits.

"One day the mother fell in love with a man from outside the community. She wanted to elope with him rather than having the priest marry her to the patriarch. The coven forbid her to be with the stranger, so the mother had to sneak to see him. The hostility grew unbearable, and the mother secretly left the community, with her daughter. By the time the others knew, she had purchased a Victorian house, and the man could spend time with them without any barriers. The mother and daughter still fulfilled their obligation to attend the coven's engagements, so the committee couldn't charge them for disobeying regulations. But most of the vicars made unexpected visits to the house, quizzing the mother and daughter on their daily events outside the community. The mother kept her responses vague. She even answered for her daughter when they directed questions to the child, and the process became easier throughout the years.

"The stranger—no longer one—proposed to the mother, and the daughter chose to befriend a common girl in the secular community. The two girls quickly grew close and remained so during their teenage years. The man and the mother remained close as well, but the mother feared eloping with him because she was afraid for his life. Still, he patiently remained a part of their lives, and the two didn't share their secret with anyone.

"The daughter invited her friend for a sleepover one night. The mother allowed it, and they all settled before the television in the den, with pizza and movies. There was a knock on the front door around midnight, and that's when the mother remembered that it was her turn to host the coven's gathering. It was a struggle, but the two of them had the friend practice a mantra to fall into a deep sleep. But the sleeping spell didn't last for the entire night, and the friend walked into the coven assembly in the den, but the TV had been replaced by an altar.

"The coven members became irate with the mother and daughter, saying that they've betrayed the circle for the last time and will cast them from the coven to their demise. The mother pleaded for the coven not to end her only child and the pure mortal friend. The clan's headmaster allows the friend to join the group, and all three had to create a sacrificial triangle on the next full moon for the friend's ritual—which was only three nights away—to convince the rest of the coven of their undying dedication. The friend wouldn't stop crying, and the daughter and mother attempted to console the child. When the meeting's facilitator added that the mother's fiancé had to be the offering, the mother began wailing.

"When the husband-to-be visited during the next few days, the mother remained distant. When he heard the school's voice messages about the daughter missing school, coupled with the friend's family calling them about their child not attending classes, he demanded the truth from the mother. The mother sobbed and handed him an official invitation to a full moon dinner she claimed to be hosting. The fiancé grew more furious with his demands, but the mother just pointed to the invite. He opened it, and after reading, he gave the mother a wild stare. The mother nodded and pleaded for him to come to the dining room.

"On the night of the ritual, the coven arrived at the mother and daughter's Victorian home. Everything was set, with candles as the only source of light. The fiancé lay unconscious and nude. The daughter, friend, and mother raised sacrificial knives over the man. The coven began the chant for blood shedding, and the three penetrated the man's torso. The chanting grew louder, and the man rose. He pulled out a gun he'd hidden—no one knew how, but some say it was mother's magic. He shot the headmistress while the other three turned and stabbed the witches. The mother quickly placed a protection spell on the man afterwards, so his wounded flesh quickly healed as his pores absorbed the blood that had seeped from his body.

"The murders were grizzly, and the mother, daughter and the man had to flee their hometown. They wanted to bring the friend with them, but it would only cause more havoc, especially with the friend's mortal parents. The three thought they were free, but the friend would tell the daughter that she keeps seeing the images of the witches they'd murdered about the hometown. The daughter shared this with the man and her mother, but the adults reassured her that all was good and they were be protected.

"But they weren't. The man went back to their hometown to wrap up some business, and he was robbed and killed. The mother and daughter knew it was someone from the coven, the robbery was a red herring. The three ladies had developed a charm to keep the forces in hell as long as they sacrificed every autumn, the night before All Hollows'."

***

Beth, Kannitha, and Stevie remain silent for a moment.

"That's it?" Kannitha asks, as if wanting more.

"That wasn't even a ghost story," Beth says. "Besides, it was too long."

"Well," Kannitha says, "the guy came back from the dead—"

"That's a zombie, idiot!" Beth yells. "Not a ghost."

Kannitha flinches as if Beth's words had slapped her.

"But the witches coming back are apparitions, demon spirits," Stevie says. "I think that counts as ghostly. And the guy had a spell that kept him safe, so he wasn't even a zombie. Who say there were rules to our stories, all the sudden, Beth?"

"Oh, look at the bestie," Beth taunts. "Defending her girlfriend."

Girlfriend? I give Stevie a glance. She looks out the balcony glass door, cheeks flushed.

"Don't matter." Beth throws her hands in the air." My story is bound to win anyway because it's a true ghost story. The story is called *Trench Coat Phil.*"

I shudder at the name, not sure because of chills or disappointment.

"You good?" Stevie's now able to look into my eyes.

I nod. "Yeah, just still thinking about your creepy story."

Stevie smiles. "Yours was good, too."

"Um, excuse me, lovebirds," Beth demands.

Damn, I'm ready to slap this white witch.

"So my story begins while a few girls who are waiting at the bus stop. The overcast makes it seem like it was still night time, and the wind made the air feel like the abdominal snowman was breathing on their flesh."

resist rolling my eyes at the weak analogy.

"Their bus was running late," Beth continues. "Before they knew it, a man runs up from behind them and opens his trench coat, and blood gushes from tattered clothing. He screams, 'I'm Trench Coat Phil. And I'm ready to kill.' Before the girls could pull themselves out of their shock, the rotting corpse grabs one of the girls and pulls her into him. With his free hand, he pulls a knife out of his coat pocket and stabs the girl repeatedly in the back. The other two run off while he keeps gashing the girl. When they get back to the bus stop with the authorities, they only see puddles of blood. And the officers were never able to track the murderer or their friend. The case grew cold, and the story became a vague memory to the town. The legend is that if you stand in the spot at the same time as the girl was killed that morning, a figure emerges from nowhere and screams, *I'm Trench Coat Phil. And I'm ready to kill!* Then he'll charge you.

"A recent high-school graduate, Mandy Sheridan, told us cheerleaders last year at State that when she was a sophomore, the team dared a freshman to stand in that spot the morning before she began practicing with the team. Nothing happened that morning, but the freshmen wasn't at school the next day. Or the day after that. So the captain called the her house. Her father said that the freshman was hospitalized because of some trauma that happened two nights ago. Some of the cheer team visited the house, and the father told them that a guy in a too-large trench coat stood outside her window all night, chanting that his name was Trench Coat Phil and he was ready to kill. When her dad checked it out, he never saw anyone. So she slept in the living room that night, only to see a tall, dark figure standing at the end of the hallway. She said she heard, 'I'm Trench Coat Phil. And I'm really to K-I-L-' Beth jumps at Kannitha and yells, "L!"

Kannitha hollers and then giggles with Beth. Stevie and I fake our laughter.

When we vote, I write Stevie's name on my paper and place the slip in the ceramic scarecrow bowl with everyone else's. The tally adds up to one for me, one for Stevie, and two for Beth. I apologize to Stevie that she didn't win.

She shrugs. "It's just a game."

• • •

Late Night
I plant myself on the loveseat in Beth's room and scan my phone.

Amber had texted just before midnight, *Being a party pooper?*

This girl knows me too well.

B4 the booze. Lol. This Beth girl asked about Dad.

Are you serious Joni? That bitch.

The reference to Beth triggers me to look up from the screen. Beth has disappeared again.

Stevie reads my face. "She's in her gaga walk-in closet." Stevie plants herself next to me. "Swear that thing is as big as my bedroom." She looks at my phone. "Who's Amber?"

"I'm realizing she's your doubleganger back home."

Stevie smirks. "She sounds cool, already."

We laugh.

Kannitha's flailing arms grab our attention. She's trying to find the beat to the music while spilling some of her drink. She stops to look at the spill. Looks at us and then laughs.

We join her in laughter.

"Alcohol abuse!" Beth says, with a boardgame box in her hands.

That better not be Candyland or Shoots & Ladders. I'll so walk home even though it's late.

"Oh, God," Stevie groans. "Not this again.

"You know I don't mess with that shit." Kannitha's tone becomes grave and stern.

"Come on," Beth pleads, and places the box on the floor.

I look at the large tan letters across the box top. OUIJA. I blow out a breath, relax my muscles, and purse my lips.

"Look!" Beth lights some candles and places them in a circle on the rug. "Joni looks interested in this."

"Really?" Stevie asks me. "You'd play that?"

I shrug. "I think it's something different. And I mean, 'tis the season, right?"

Stevie and Kannitha laugh.

Beth turns off the bedroom lights. "Come on, girls."

We join her on the floor again.

"She bought this thing back in fifth grade," Kannitha slurs to me. "Been trying every year to get us to play. I guess with you here and interested in it, it shouldn't be too bad."

"Okay," Beth says. "We all need to put our hands on this thing together."

"The planchette," I say.

They look at me, stunned.

"What? I'm a reader."

"Nerd." Stevie giggles.

"Now," Beth continues, "we cannot remove our hands from the ... planchette once the spirit begins to communicate. And we need to make sure we have the spirit say goodbye to us with the board before we conclude the summoning."

At least Beth had done her research.

She clears her throat. "Let's welcome someone to talk with us."

"Huh?" Kannitha asks. "Like who?"

"Whoever, I guess," Beth blandly replies.

We all place our hands on the planchette—well, our index fingers. There was still hardly enough room for all of us to touch it.

"Good evening, spirits," Beth says in an animated voice that's so cheesy my face flinches.

Her odd tone reminds me of that rip-off fortune teller Amber and I once visited on the Myrtle Beach boardwalk. I see that Stevie is also squinting, and we exchange grins.

"We're trying to summon any spirits around us," Beth says.

We sit in silence. The dim light of the flames dance behind my closed eyelids. The central unit clicks on, and a rush of hot air brushes the back of my neck.

"Beth," Stevie says, "this is dumb."

Beth shushes her. "Don't break the concentration." She attempts to beckon ... whatever once more, to no avail.

"Let Joni try," Kannitha says.

"Come again?" I say.

"That'd be cool," Beth says. "Give it a try, Joni. You even have the gypsy outfit on."

I shift, pretending to get comfortable for the bull. "Okay, um ... please, essences among us, join us in our gathering this evening."

"Damn," Stevie's murmurs impressed.

"We commend you for your strength to rejoin the living among the Earth on this Hallows' Eve," I continue. "We would be appreciative your blessing us of your presence."

Silence except for the heat running through the vents.

Then there's a vibration below my fingers and a faint scratch on the wooden board.

"Oh, shit," Kannitha moans.

We open our eyes to watch the planchette come alive under our fingers. The wooden communicator shifts over the letters H ... E ... L-L ... O.

"Oh, wow," Beth mutters. Then she yells, "Okay, Joni did you do that?"

"Huh?"

"I'm sure this is you, Beth," Stevie says, unamused. "You're always the one doing mean tricks."

Beth denies it. We all look at Kannitha.

Kannitha throws her hands off the game piece. "You've lost your mind thinking it's me!"

"So go on, Joni," Beth says.

I willingly continue. "Who's with us?"

Nothing moves for about five seconds. Then the planchette staggers across the wooden board, to the letter "P".

In unison, Beth and Kannitha say each letter that the planchette hovers over, like they're kindergarteners learning the alphabet. " ... *H* ... *I* ... *L*."

"Phil," Beth mutters. Then squeals, "As in, Trench Coat Phil?"

Before anyone could respond to her, the small instrument slides across the board to the word Yes.

Kannitha whispers, "This is getting too creepy. You did that, Stevie."

Beth says, "Yeah, you're the jokester, Stevie."

"Nuh-uh. If anything, it's you, Beth. That was *your* story."

"It had to have been Joni." Kannitha glares at me. "The thing started moving when you started talking all wicca."

I snicker. "You're kidding, right?"

The planchette moves again.

Kannitha and Beth spell aloud again. "*K* ... *I* ... *L-L*."

"Oh, hell no!" Kannitha jumps to her feet.

Beth's eyes go wide, but her hands remain on the planchette. "You can't take your hands off, Kannitha!"

"Forget that shit!" Kannitha heads for the bedroom door.

Stevie fidgets in her spot, and her eyes grow wide, too. "We do need to close the session."

Kannitha refuses to rejoin us on the floor, and when she's a few feet from the door, it slams shut.

The force is strong enough to extinguish the candle flames and rattle picture frames. We all scream, staring at the white door, waiting for something else to happen.

After staring for a while, Kannitha reaches for the door handle. She looks back at us as if she needs support or permission. She turns the knob, but she can't pull the door toward her. She tugs the handle with all her strength, and the door shakes in the frame. One of the pictures jangles off the wall.

"This isn't funny, Beth." Kannitha says. "You've gone too far this time. You're always doing this."

"What the hell, bitch!" Beth hurries to her feet. "It's just a game."

"Um, Beth," Stevie murmurs while looking at me. "Didn't you say not to take your hands off the thing?"

Kannitha approaches Beth. "You're always going too far with everything!"

Beth snatches Kannitha by the arms and shakes her. Stevie and I have no choice but to abandon the board as well.

"Okay, okay," I say, pulling Kannitha toward me.

Stevie collects Beth. "Let's just go back to the board."

Beth yanks away from Stevie. "Game's over, Stevie."

Kannitha pulls from my grasp. "Let's just go to bed."

Stevie and I are baffled, and the other two get into bed. Stevie and I unroll our sleeping bags and ready our pillows by the balcony glass door. Then Stevie blows out the candle in the jack-o-lantern.

• • •

All Hallows Day

The clock reads 2:31 a.m., and moonlight is coming through the glass doors. I need to text Amber but need more privacy than Beth's personal bathroom, so I go down the hallway and into the guest bathroom. Push my cell's side button. Amber had responded to my text from a few hours ago.

How would they even know about your dad?

I respond, *Good question. And they tried to do some Ouija game junk and spelled out his name and shit.*

I didn't think Amber would respond this late, but my phone vibrates and the screen illuminates.

Summoning board? Armatures. What did they say about your dad?

I text, *They guessed the name right. Well not really. They told ghost stories first, and Beth told one about Trench Coat Phil. Still, really eerie.*

I'll be there soon ok. You think the Stevie girl will be cool?

Rumbling in the hallway pulls my attention from my phone. Then I hear footsteps. I ease into the pitch-black hallway. At the end, a dark silhouette is lurking.

"My name is Trench Coat Phil," someone growls. "And I'm ready to *K-I-L-*"

I take a step backward.

"*L!*"

The figure stampedes down the hallway. It charges too fast for me to decipher anything but long, twirling fabric. It raises an arm, and something shines, reflecting the moonlight. I scream just as the figure lunges for me. I jump to the left, and the figure stumbles into the bathroom. The figure gathers its balance and turns to come back at me. I raise my hands and mutter the chant. I gently and stealthy ease both open palm forward, and the figure is shoved into the wall, through mid-air. The figure crumbles to the floor, and I jump over the body. I try to get back to the bathroom, but fingers grab my left ankle. I jab my heel into something boney. The grasp is loose now, and I break free and slam the bathroom door behind me.

"Joni, it's a joke!"

The hallway light flickers alive from underneath the bathroom door. I open the door to find Beth recording with her cellphone.

The hooded person removes the covering to reveal Kannitha. She rubs her side. "That hurt, bitch!"

Stevie comes from the bedroom. "What's going on?"

"Joni tried to kill me, that's what." Kannitha rises from the floor and removes the trench coat. "How'd you even push me, being at least four feet from me?"

"No way!" I step away from Kannitha. "You came at me with that thing." I point to the plastic gray knife on the floor.

"You two ..." Stevie shakes her head. "I'm glad Joni knocked the shit out of you, Kannitha."

"Oooh," Beth taunts. "Stevie protecting her girlfriend again."

"Shut the hell up!" Stevie snaps. "Your black girlfriend always worships your scrawny white ass like you're some overseer."

Kannitha lunges toward Stevie. "The hell did you say, you spic of a sow?"

Banging makes me throw my hands into the air and demand everyone to stop yelling—the energy escape my fingertips, and I feel them all obey a command. Then there's silence before more knocking booms from Beth's room. I creep into the bedroom while the other three tiptoe behind me. Amber's on the balcony, waving at us. I wave back, smiling with elation, and skip to the door. The other's mouths have dropped.

"Who the hell is that?" Beth asks.

Stevie says, "That's Amber, isn't it, Joni?"

I nod and open the glass door. "I thought you'd never get here. It was getting to the wire of witching hour."

Amber enters and embraces me, her purple cloak floating behind her. "I know, right? The community's hunting us hard this year since you and your mother dismissed yourselves from the coastal region. I'm lucky to still be standing."

In a high-pitched voice, Kannitha says, "How the fuck did she even get up here from outside?"

I pull back from Amber's hug. "Oh, we have our ways, Kannitha."

Amber hands me my crimson cloak. "Here. Your outfit didn't look right in that pic without this."

Stevie approaches me and Amber.

I wring my arm around Stevie. "This is the one I've been telling you two about, Amber. I think she'd be a great addition to the coven."

Amber sizes her up. "Oh, yes, I see it now. So gorgeous." She kisses Stevie's cheek. "Good to finally meet you, sister."

Beth and Kannitha try to run out of the room, but they bump into my mother standing in the doorway, beautiful as ever in her white cloak. Amber closes the glass door as Mom steps forward, forcing the girls to retreat into the center of Beth's room. My mother passes them and approaches Stevie, who stands confident before our master enchantress. The other two try to run out of the room again, but Amber and I telekinetically slam the door in their faces. Mom pulls the wood-handle knife from her cloak and holds it over Stevie's head. Stevie doesn't flinch while taking the knife, but she does seem confused.

My mother grips Stevie's shoulders. "Child, my daughter has spoken highly of you since the beginning. And I sense the divinity within you, sister. Would you like to join the circle?"

"Sure." Stevie accepts as if being invited to the party of the year.

Mother continues. "If you're true to your word, child, then you must make a sacrifice to demonstrate your devotion to Philip, our patriarch."

"Sacrifice?" Stevie mutters.

Amber and Mom surround Beth and Kannitha to convey Mom's meaning. I'm amazed by how composed Stevie is as she brings the knife near her heart.

I step next to the new member. "Stevie, you choose which one you'd like to use to show your loyalty to the sisterhood. The other will be our offering for this coven's immortal protection from the community's hexes placed upon us until the next All Hallows' Day."

Amber looks at her iWatch. "It's 3 AM, too. Just in time, Mother."

Amber help Stevie into a thin brown cloak.

Beth and Kannitha shiver and bawl, cradling one another. Moonlight shine upon them, like the spotlight that was always meant for just them two.

I secure my hood over my head and walk before Beth and Kannitha. "Now, now. Don't be worried. It's just a game."

PUMPKIN SPICE TEA

The grocery store having everything related to pumpkin spice *except* tea annoyed Kacey Smith. They carried pumpkin spice oatmeal, cereal, cakes … even coffee—but no boxed pumpkin spice tea bags on display.

"OMG, Kacey." Jessica Hightower sighed, putting the weight of all of her 115 pounds on the buggy's handle. "Just get some of those cups to make coffee from the Keurig and let's check out. I'm super bored."

"But I don't do coffee anymore, remember, Jess?"

"Ugh, come on *Kacey* ..."

"Fine!" Kacey grabbed a box of twenty-four-count mini pumpkin spice coffee capsules from the shelf and followed her suitemate to the cash register.

"Do you know why they don't have pumpkin spice tea this year?" Kacey asked the cashier as she and Jessica placed their purchases on the conveyer belt.

The teen-aged cashier apathetically shrugged without looking up from the scanner. "I know we did last year, but I think they were marked down for close out before Thanksgiving last year because it wasn't selling or something like a default or whatever ..."

Kacey and Jessica exchanged disappointing expressions before thanking the cashier for the help.

•   •   •

Jessica and Kacey carried plastic grocery bags in both hands while they strolled the sidewalk on Gervais Street on the way to their apartment.

"It's Halloween and you want to study," Kacey moaned. "We should go out tonight. Let's get it girl!"

"I have a major bio exam tomorrow, Kacey," Jessica explained for what seemed to be the hundredth time.

"Fine, fine," Kacey said, exasperated in defeat. "Can we at least binge on some horror movies tonight?"

Jessica opened the door leading into their apartment complex's lobby. "Well, *duh!*"

Both giggled as they entered the building.

Jessica spotted Berry from Apartment 6-D exiting the elevators, looking hot in tight, gray sweatpants and a snug tank top; a towel rested across his broad shoulders and, as always, he carried a water bottle. The two girls quickly approached the hunk, and Jessica smiled at him, but Berry remained fixated on his cell and kept his earbuds in. Jessica dropped the flirty grin from her face, and secretly hoped Kacey hadn't seen that awkward moment of humiliation.

The two entered their sixth-floor apartment and placed the sacks of groceries on the island in the kitchen. Kacey stored the perishables in the fridge and Jessica opened the cabinets so she could stack the shelves. In the process, Jessica stumbled upon an unfamiliar box.

"Hey Kacey, look what I found." Jessica held four individually wrapped packets of single-serving tea bags in the air.

"Shut up!" Kacey snatched them from Jessica's grasp. "Get out." Kacey sniffed the pouches. "*Yes.*"

Jessica returned to stocking with arched eyebrows. "You're welcome?"

After completing the chore, they split into their own personal agendas. Jessiac settled at her bedroom desk with her textbooks and notes, prepping for a lengthy study session while Kacey boiled hot water and poured it into a black, customized mug with THIS IS MY PUMPKIN SPICE MUG printed in orange-cryptic lettering and a toothy jack-o-lantern smiling beneath the message. Kacey consistently dipped her coveted pumpkin spice bag into the mug.

Jessica entered the kitchenette to brew some coffee while watching Kacey carry her mug to the sofa.

"Kacey, you're seriously going to drink *that*? I was joking … "

"What?" Kacey asked before sipping on the pumpkin spice tea and turning on the flat screen.

"Those bags have been up there since *last* Halloween. You don't think that stuff went bad? Did you even check their expiration?"

Kacey rolled her eyes and disapprovingly blew air through pursed lips. "Girl, please. You sound like my Mom."

Jessica shrugged and went back to her bedroom with her own mug of pumpkin spice coffee. Kacey had one of those annoying reality TV shows blaring from the television, so Jessica closed her bedroom door to muffle the noise.

● ● ●

Jessica opened her eyes and lifted her head from the desktop, glancing out the window to discover night had fallen over downtown Columbia skyline. The desk lamp was the only source of light in her bedroom. She must have dozed off while studying about how micro-bacterial fungi and viruses invade their hosts; it could easily be a cure for insomnia. When she reoriented herself, the apartment felt too still for Jessica.

"Kacey! You hungry?"

Jessica rose from her desk, stretching and rubbing her stiff neck, and approached her bedroom door to find it slightly ajar. Jessica figured Kacey had propped it open after finding a sleeping roommate and returned to her own business.

Jessica entered the open living area. "Hey, Kacey. I thought maybe we'd go the Halloween haps at the student union. Even be fast and scope what costumes the frat boys and athletes are strutting! I mean they'll most like leave little to the imagine—"

The only light in the living room came from the flat screen displaying the selection menu from one of the many streaming programs Kacey had her father add to their smart TV. Jessica walked behind the sofa thinking her suitemate had drifted into a late afternoon nap. Before she attempted to call for Kacey again, Jessica found only her mug lying on its side, with the letterings THIS IS and PUMP facing upward from the couch. The cushion had a fresh tea stain. Jessica went to the whiteboard on the fridge but didn't find a message. Kacey wasn't in front of the TV, standing on the balcony, or in the kitchenette. Nor did she write a note about leaving the apartment.

Jessica knocked on Kacey's bedroom door. "Hey, Kacey! You in there?"

She knocked once more before opening the door to a vacant bedroom and empty en suite. Jessica could feel her heart starting to pound; she was now worried about her roommate.

Rustling came from the kitchenette, then a loud *thud* followed by shuffling feet. Jessica scampered to the living area to find a bar stool lying on its side and a shadow lurking in the desk lamp's casting glow on her bedroom wall.

Jessica inched toward her room. "Kacey, did you need something from my room?"

A muffled groan came from the room.

Jessica stopped in her doorway to find Kacey staring in the far corner of her bedroom, swaying back and forth. She clawed at Jessica's bedroom wall.

"Kacey, hey. Are you feeling—"

Kacey's thin figure spun. The movement startled Jessica, and she stumbled into the doorframe.

Kacey's eyes were bloodshot. Saliva drooled from her lips. The veins in her neck protruded, pulsating beneath her pale, damp flesh and up her thin cheeks into her forehead. Blood oozed from her nostrils.

"What the fuck, Kacey!" Jessica took a step forward. "What happened?! Okay, we need to get you to the emergency room."

Unresponsive, Kacey charged at Jessica, growling through clenched teeth.

Jessica called Kacey's name once more but quickly surmised Kacey wasn't in her right mind; Jessica's suitemate seemed like she was possessed by a demon. Jessica ran out of the bedroom and attempted to close her door, but Kacey's gnarly hands clasped the wood before the door could reach the frame. Jessica furiously attempted to slam the door a few more times, smashing her roommate's hands in the process.

Unfazed, Kacey used her power to pry open the door. Her hand bent backward, and her twisted left arm dangled. Kacey shrieked and charged at Jessica again.

Jessica used the sofa to maintain a safe distance. "Kacey, girl, please. You need some medical attention or a priest with holy water or something—"

Kacey lunged over the couch.

Jessica screamed and darted to her left. She ran behind the kitchenette's bar while Kacey laid lifeless after tumbling over the cushions and slamming head-first on the wood floor.

The room got quiet. Jessica stared into the living area, looking for any signs of movement. The only noises Jessica could discern was her panting and the television. She leaned across the counter, hoping to peer over the sofa.

Kacey sprung up from the floor during Jessica's mid-lean. Teeth were missing, and blood sprayed from Kacey's snarl. She raised both arms over her head.

Jessica yelled again and sprinted to the front door. Jessica yanked the door closed and held onto the knob once in the exterior hallway. A thump came from the other side, and the frame shook.

Jessica stepped backward from the door, in traced of the beating from the closed door. The pounding rattled the doorjamb. Jessica shrieked when the wood cracked in the center of the door, and something grabbed her shoulders.

"Hey, hey," a guy's voice said behind Jessica, dodging flying fists. "It's me, Berry."

Jessica locked eyes with her neighbor before wrapping her arms around him and burying her head into him.

"What's going on? Are you okay?"

"It's my roommate, Kacey," Jessica sobbed. "I really don't know what's wrong, but she's possessed or something—"

Jessica heard the splintering and turned to see that Kacey had rammed her head through the door. Crimson liquid oozed down her nose bridge, her lips and chin. It didn't take long for her to spot Jessica with Berry, and Kacey let out a blood-curdling shriek before ramming her shoulders into the door.

"Isn't that your roomate?!" Berry blurted.

Jessica desperately clung to Berry's body. "I don't know and we need to get out of here, find help."

Berry grabbed Jessica by her upper arm and guided her briskly toward his apartment. He removed his cell from his pocket and called 9-1-1. Once they reached Berry's apartment, Jessica began to contemplate how close she came to death at the hands of her blood-thirsty roommate.

Berry hung up the phone and offered comfort to Jessica. "You're okay. You're safe in here now."

"No," Jessica said, rubbing her triceps as if she was cold. "I mean, my friend—"

A scream erupted from the hallway. Jessica didn't recognize the voice, but shortly after, she heard a snarl and knew that was Kacey's work. A shrieking female voice desperately cried out for help and begged Kacey to stop biting her.

Berry wanted to assess the situation to see if he could help. Before Jessica could convince him otherwise, he stepped into the hallway. Jessica remained a few feet away but on the inside his apartment, watching Berry through the peep hole while he looked both ways.

Then he spotted Ms. Someone slumped on the floor.

Berry cursed before gaining his composure. "Ms. Apple, how can I make you more comfortable? Help is on the way."

He knelt next to the elder lady, holding her chewed-on hand. Blood was running down her neck and cheeks from the bite-marks. Her eyes were wide and locked on the ceiling while she trembled.

Movement down the hallway caught Jessica's eye. She looked past Berry to find the contorted Kacey, who started banging her head against the side wall while she made her way down the corridor. Berry continued to comfort the lady laying on the hallway floor. Jessica flapped her hand on the closed door to get Berry's attention but he remained focused on the wounded woman.

Ms. Apple began to convulse and let out a guttural moan. Berry was frozen in the moment, not sure what to do to help this dying woman. He wondered his eyes about the hall, looking lost.

Kacey cocked her head back and let out a battle cry before charging them. Her broken arm dangled while she snapped her jaws.

"Oh, shit!" Berry shouted.

Jessica opened the door for Berry to get back into the apartment. She looked down to see that the elderly lady had opened her eyes again; a yellow film fogged over them. Before he could pull away from her, Ms. Apple grabbed Berry's arm and bit him. Berry wailed in pain. He punched the old lady in the head with his free fist, but it didn't faze her. She maintained her bite on his arm. Berry stood up, and Ms. Apple rose with him, but then collapsed onto the hallway's runner.

The elderly lady's dentures remained planted in Berry's arm until he slung them to the floor.

Berry darted for the door to his apartment, yelling for Jessica to get inside. But Ms. Apple grabbed Berry's leg and gnawed on his calf. Jessica backpedaled into his apartment as Kacey jumped on Berry's back. She bit into his neck and then his shoulder.

"Jessica," Berry said in strained voice through gritted teeth, "Get out of here!"

The living horror sent Jessica into shock. Kacey looked up from Berry's cheek, chewing on his flesh. She hissed and then growled at Jessica, who slammed the door and locked it before Kacey could react.

She took a few steps back before pounding came from the other side of the front door. The banging got louder as the pace picked up. Jessica yelped every time the hinges shook, wondering if this would be the time the door frame would give way. While backing away from the door, she wasn't paying attention to where she was going and bumped into the balcony's sliding glass door.

There were more bnaging from the hallway. Too many of them.

Jessica opened the glass door, shut it behind her, and laid the mop formerly resting on the balcony railing along the glass door runner to keep the door from sliding. She kept her eyes inside the apartment that she nearly tripped over a jack-o-lantern beneath her, and would've tumbled over the railing.

She saw people in costumes traversing the sidewalks below. She yelled for help, but the passersby merely hollered back, assuming she was pulling a Halloween prank.

She saw a scarecrow and a genie on the sidewalk approaching the complex. She surveyed her situation, looking for a way to get their attention, and picked up the pumpkin before throwing it over .

The costumed couple hopped in place when the melon shattered just a few yards in front of them. The scarecrow used a flurry of curse words while looking around for the source. The genie screamed and they both looked above them at the same time in Jessica's direction.

Jessica flailed her arms. "Oh, please help me! Help me please! I'm trapped up here!"

The scarecrow asked her if this was a prank.

"No!" Jessica wailed. "My neighbor has been attacked by my roommate. And Ms. Apple … an older lady needs some help, too—"

The scarecrow and genie looked at each other and then burst into laughter. They returned to their walk down Gervais Street, trying to decide if the girl on the balcony was drunk, high or both. "I'll take two of whatever she's having," the genie muttered to the scarecrow.

The genie shouted "*Happy Halloween*" while the scarecrow flipped a middle finger.

The door frame could no longer withstand the steady pounding, and the hinges finally relented. Jessica turned to see Berry standing on the flattened the front door. But he wasn't Berry. His mangled face snarled at Jessica. He flung his arms and legs into the front door. She saw Kacey not far behind him.

Finally, the sirens arrived. Jessica glanced toward the street to see two Columbia Police cruisers screeching to a halt in front of the entrance to the apartment complex.

Jessica waved her arms over her head. "Up here. Up here. Please help."

The officer spotted her and shouted "We're on the way!"

"I'm on the sixth floor. Apartment 6-D."

The officers sprinted toward the complex.

She turned back to find Berry approaching the sliding glass doors, Jessica leaned back against the balcony railing. She looked over the railing once more, measuring the distance between her and the where the shattered jack-o-lantern remained on the sidewalk. If need be …

Gunshots rang out from inside the building, setting off a panic on Gervais Street. Jessica watched a crowd huddle across the street as more cop cars arrived at the scene, along with paramedics. Many public safety officers had taped off the section along the sidewalks. There were more gunshots and now screaming with it. Just too much for her to handle, and Jessica screamed and cried.

Berry stood only two feet from her, separated by the thin sheet of glass. He held eye contact with Jessica, his chest heaving while his hot breath fogged the glass. He punched the glass twice, and Jessica recoiled each time. She heard someone yelling at Berry behind, but his groaning and the squealing form him scratching the glass became unbearable. Jessica covered her ears and screamed.

Blood spewed against the glass and a milli-second later it cracked like a spider web. A hole emerged from Berry's forehead, blood trickling from it. A bullet lay embedded in the center of the already splintered glass. Berry's body crumbled to the ground. Behind him, police officer stood stiff with narrow brow and squinting eyes, pointing his gun at the lifeless form.

• • •

The officer holstered his gun before escorting Jessica through the sixth-floor hallway. She only saw portions of the chaos in the hallway through the cop's firm, arms cradling her, but the rancid, iron odor provided what her eyes missed. Mostly uniformed officers flooded the hall, while medical examiners in white jumpsuits and hoods knelt over the two covered bodies. The mixture of fear, reassurance, and grief forced her to burry her face into the officer's broad chest after seeing the smaller of the two blanketed figures. She didn't loudly sob but couldn't fight back the tears of recognizing the body form. She heard the examiners rambling about another outbreak, but was too flabbergasted to really hear much of anything, even the officer ushering her.

The cop helped Jessica into the back of an ambulance and two paramedics took her vitals, asking about her current condition. They asking if she was certain Amber, Barry or the Ms. Apple lady didn't touch or attack her anywhere on her body. As soon as the officer step to the side, one of the two medics cradled the cop's wounded arm.

She latched onto the blanket as soon as the medic wrapped one around her shoulders. Jessica took notice of the other paramedic dabbing ointment-smothered gauzes over a the officer's bloody arm before finding his dark eyes

Jessica glanced at the cop's nameplate on his blood-stained uniform. "Officer Jackson ... thank you."

The tall officer nodded with a smile full of white teeth, slightly wincing at the medic's gauze matting. "Just glad we got to you in time, Miss Hightower."

Jessica flashed a soft, yet warm grin at him.

The medic finished cleaning Officer Jackson's wound and disposed the soiled cloths before gathering fresh bandage wraps. Droplets of blood continued to ooze from what appeared to be a set of teeth marks in the cop's forearm. Jessica couldn't resist caressing her fingertips on Officer Jackson's flesh around the indentions.

"It just burns," Officer Jackson said, as if responding the questions in Jessica's mind. "It's annoying more so than unbearable, you know?"

The medic nursed the arm before excusing herself. The costumed bystanders became rowdy, making both Jessica and Officer Jackson search for the cause. Bodies were being rolled out the apartment's front doors on gurneys—the same doors Jessica and Kacey had just entered only three hours before, picking on one another, having the best time of their college lives ...

"I should go help," Office Jackson said. He then handed his business card to Jessica. "Call me sometime, to get coffee ... so I can follow up with your well-being of course, ma'am." He cleared his throat to reset his stoic tone before saying those last few words.

Jessica exposed a wider smile. "Sure. Thanks again …" she read the card, "David."

Office Jackson excused himself. Jessica continued to smile and watched him walking from her … first examining his firm, plump butt, but then how thick and dark the blood from his bandaged arm seeped from the wrap …

ONE LUCKY SOUL

Ten Minutes Until …

The scarlet and indigo haze dissolved from my vision, and a dim, musky area settled before me. Unclear imageries bathed in dirty orange hues invaded my mind, and a nearby deep voice constantly repeated my name. I took a few breaths to gain composure.

The first thing I noticed was Gen's closed bedroom door. I cocked my gaze to the right to confirm the second-floor main bathroom was there. I reassured myself this was the Dunns' upstairs hallway. My head throbbed.

I went to raise my hands to my temples, but that's went I registered something oblong occupied them. They held a bloodstained wooden baseball bat. Crimson droplets splattered below me ... and into the pool of blood around Bubba's motionless body.

I slowly stepped backward and gasped for air, but I inhaled the metallic odor through my nostrils and mouth. The smell mixed with the familiar yet encrypted visions in my mind rumbled the acid in my stomach and I gagged.

Something snatched my arms from behind, reaching around me and clasping the bat. The force yanked me much farther from the lifeless Bubba.

"Sammie! It's me. It's Bruce. You're okay, man. Give me the bat. It's okay."

I spun to find Bruce pulling on the bat. He had lesions on his forehead and a busted lip. He kept saying it was okay and begged to let him have the bat. He said I did what I had to do to Bubba or he would've taken me outside.

Bruce saying Bubba's name seemed to invoke memories of how Bubba ended up on the floor. I recalled my hands removing Bruce's high school bat from the wall. I observed myself bashing the bat into Bubba's head as he charged at me in the hallway. But it seemed I had no real control over myself. I only watched the events unfold, like looking through a camcorder with a skewed violet lens.

Bruce tugged the bat from my grip—I must have loosened my grasp while grouping the actions.

He took my hand. "Sammie, listen to me. We need to keep to the plan, alright, man? I want you to stay behind me and keep your eyes on the back of my head—"

A bloodcurdling shriek came from downstairs. Some cackling, chanting, and humdrum music followed. The rest of the noises were just unnerving.

Bruce squeezed my fingers before putting one of his own to his lips. I nodded, glaring at the cerise smear on the side of his finger. I rested my hands on his shoulders, and Bruce lifted the bat. He lead me down the stairs.

Thirty-Five Hours Until ...

The name Geneva Dunn flashed across my cell's screen. This couldn't be good. Gen hasn't called me in years. I mean *literally* call. The last time she *actually called* me was about six years ago to inform me that her father had passed. Since then, our chatting had reduced to occasionally replying to one other's social media postings.

"Hey, Mahogany!" Gen resurrected the old high school penname for me.

"Sup, Gen?"

"Can you believe it's been *fifty years* since that old geezer Frank opened that dump, the DIrty Dark Dog?" I knew my coworkers heard Gen's hollering through the receiver—Gen's voice echoed like how I'd imagined black cherry would sound like. "He's throwing this *huge* party to commemorate!"

This was an odd way to start the conversation, even for Gen. "You mean when he converted the lodge into a pub? That place's been running before our parents' time."

"Whatever. People want you to come down tomorrow to party with us."

"Hold up. Tomorrow? Gen, that's a bit … sudden."

"But you know he opened on Halloween, so it has to be on Halloween. And Frank insisted I get your chubby ass down here. If Rocco think he's going out do us this year, he got another thing coming …"

I leaned forward in the desk chair fumbling with my clip-on tie. "Chubby? *Ahem!* Apparently you haven't seen my gym pics on Instagram, Miss Thing," I said, resorting to my old alias for her, hoping to ease the weirdness of her sudden call. "Besides—and I'm flattered now—why would Frank even think of me—"

"Are you coming tomorrow or not, Samuel?" Gen's tone converted from inviting to demanding.

And Samuel? Gen saying Samuel sounded like she spoke in some foreign language. Sammie's always been my childhood name, and Gen knows I always referred to her, Bruce, Erma, and Mr. Dunn as my real family.

"Um, I'm not sure, Gen. I think Darius made plans for Halloween and—"

"Bring him."

"But I think he works during the day—"

"Then come without him."

Gen's abrasiveness annoyed me. And simply not her character—she might had changed, though. It has been a while since we've chatted.

"Or can he not just call out, Sammie? If not, I'm sure he'll be fine with you coming down here without him. Bring him, don't … *You* just need get down here."

I didn't know how to reply. We haven't spoken in years, and now she'd arbitrarily called and practically ordering me to come home.

"Just let me check with Darius, okay, Gen? I'm sure he won't mind postponing if he planned anything."

I wasn't sure I even wanted to go now with how this conversation was headed.

"This's going to be a once-in-a-lifetime celebration, Samuel. You really need to come home and enjoy this event with us, the neighbors, your parents—"

"Geneva, what the hell?"

My thumb slid toward the End button on my cell, but Gen's burst of laughter startled me from proceeding.

"Jeez, Sammie. Chill. I'm just offering. If you can come, awesome. Hit me up. If not, that's cool, too. No hard feelings either way."

Thirty Hours Until …

"The entire conversation was just odd, Darius. I mean, I know we hadn't chatted in some time, but Gen acted … different. Granted, I'm sure her father passing changed all their dynamics: her mother losing the one she's been with since high school; Bruce moving back home to help them out; Gen's newfound persistence. But things like calling me *Samuel* and being all demanding was just weird."

Darius monitored himself stirring the sauce in the steaming pot. "Weirder than her usual self?" He takes a sip of his merlot.

I smirked. *"Anyway.* I think going back home would just be bizarre *all together*, you know?"

Darius licked his fingertips and grabbed a towel. "I don't know. You really didn't make much contact even with your parents since you moved here—"

"And that's another thing! She said I could party with her, the neighbors, and then said *with my parents*."

Darius leaned over the kitchen island with a wooden spoon, unphased by what I just shared.

I sampled the sauce and wiped the dribble from my lip. "That's good, babe! But what she said made no sense."

Darius returned to his cooking, and the light perspiring forehead sweat dripped and glistened his salt-and-pepper mane and tiny chest curls in the overhead lights. "Maybe she's finally snapped, like you said. You probably need to visit and check in with her. I'm sure being cooped up with her mother and brother under the same roof can be crazy. Plus, this shindig sounds like it'd be the best time to do so. I mean, isn't that Dusty Doggie—"

"Dirty Dog." The name's Dirty Dark Dog, but didn't want to get into that.

"—*Dirty Dog* you and Gen's childhood spot or something? Wouldn't that make you more obligated to return home?"

I went to say something but didn't had nothing. I hate when he's right … which is, like, always. Instead, I rose from the seat and approached our balcony glass door to admire the Queen City's skyline.

I've always enjoyed watching the city. Charlotte's colorful lights had always symbolized my freedom from Maple's Edge. I hoped surveying uptown now would bring serenity.

A firm grip tightened on my arms, and I nearly jumped out of my skin.

"Don't get worked up, baby," Darius cooed with his baritone voice—that and him massaging my shoulders instantly consoled my tension. "I mean, you didn't even go back after she called you about your parents."

I withdrew from Darius's embrace in utter shock.

"I'm thinking that's what Gen meant about your parents," he continued but minded his words now. "You didn't go down there, even then."

I spun on my heels to storm from him. "I told you many times how they were to me—"

He clasped my wrist and twirled me into his torso and planted a kiss.

"Don't be like that, Sam. I know, I know how they were. But still, I think you need to go back for that closure if nothing else. Even with all the therapy and everything, you haven't let yourself be fully cured from the pain—and don't deny it."

I attempted to pull from him again, but he made sure his hold was secure this time.

I retorted with a huff. "You mean the screaming and crying in my sleep?"

"Yeah, Sam. I mean that. Maybe going back would resolve some of those demons."

I faced the city, guiding his arms around my waist. He kissed my neck and rested his chin on my shoulder.

"Baby, I just think it'd be really healthy for you to go back, just this once." He swayed us both to the music in his head—the music between us. "And partying would make the closing smoother, you know? More importantly, I'll still be here waiting for you when you get back."

I told him I concurred.

He lay his plush lips upon my thin ones once more, and this kiss lingered. He locked his brown-colored eyes into my hazel ones. "Samuel. Go."

He interlocked with my fingers and led me to the kitchen island. He leaned me over it and sucked the base of my neck. He whispered in my ear, "Is my baby boy going to go for Daddy?"

I dug my fingertips into the back of his head to withstand the heat from his bated breath tickling my nerve endings. My fingertips trailed down to caress his beefy upper body. His abs shivered beneath my hands.

"I'll go." I panted, gently clawing my fingers down his bare, broad back and then inside the waistband of his gray sweatpants.

"Just please don't call me Samuel; total turnoff."

Eighteen Hours Until ...

The Southern autumn weather wafting through the open windows made the ride down Highway 77 perfect. The music's buoyant tempo wanted to control my speed, but I kept myself conscious of how fast I drove—I'm sure South Carolina State Troopers haven't changed during my seven-year absence. When I turned onto the crumbling freeway leading into Maple's Edge, my buzz was killed.

I hardly recognized any of my old haunts along Highway 321. Most of the buildings had their windows either boarded or shattered. A few of their walls had toppled to the ground as well. Battered *For Lease* signs struggled in their worn stands before the vacant shops. No greenery embellished their foregrounds, only dehydrated earth.

The only two familiar places I spotted still in service were Ms. Ann's Country Kitchen and Uncle Earl's Stop-and-Shop. However, they were lodged among the sole massive, glitzy strip mall I've seen since traveling along the throughway. Even with the flimsy paper Open signs dangling from their windows, the more modern stores' neon lights stole all the attention from any passerby. If it weren't for the jack-o-lanterns and scarecrows hanging outside their entrances, I'd had assumed Ms. Ann and Mr. Earl had joined the other out-of-service mom-and-pop stores. Regardless, there wasn't any traffic along the freeway for any of the businesses to make any profit. The deadness hypnotized me so numb that I nearly missed Maple's Edge's welcome sign emerging from the intersection of Highway 321 and Fishery Road (*est. 1852. Population: 1,021*).

Towering distribution warehouses had replaced the luscious woods Gen and I had explored many times before. In fact, public works had altered the entire street to circle the gigantic business park. Nothing from my childhood seemed to have survived the construction: the sprinkler park we visited in the summers; the little white store Mr. Sampson ran; even the many junkyards where I had tagged along with Bruce when he searched for car parts. All the historical landmarks had been uprooted with the trees.

I rode Fishery Road for another fifteen minutes before some pine trees finally emerged. They quickly created a canopy that blocked the sunshine. It wasn't long afterward that the dirt road that trailed into the old neighborhood appeared.

The remains of rusted fences fought to remain erect and segregate the exact same corroded trailers from my childhood, even though it was obvious the mobile homes were going to crumble off their tires at any moment There had always been four separate mobile-home parks in the area, but I could barely read the first three weathered and neglected signposts before their proper developments to recall their official titles. I didn't spot any vegetation throughout the lots.

The final section still had its name sign standing at full attention, despite most of the letters had peeled from the browned metal: THE HEN'S NEST MOBILE HOME PARK. I rode around the main dirt street outside the trailers, and the deteriorated panel titled 7-A dangled from the side of the last trailer in line. The seared trailer still lingered even after the fire, five years ago.

I halted and studied the burnt markings on the outside of the shattered windows. I saw no indications where the fire had started at first glance—not that I was some expert. The sporadic patches of dead grass dawdling about the nearby open meadow only made the site resemble more of an isolated tomb than a demolished trailer park home.

Something stirred from one of the side gaps. Or maybe? I couldn't distinctly see anything from the main road. It could've just been my eyes playing tricks from staring at the old place for too long. Either way, I didn't want to find out, and I shifted the vehicle into Drive to continue down the dirt road.

Nearing the end of the subdivision, a dozen or so kids infested the corner where many of us had waited for the school bus over the years. Some had chased and hurled pine cones and stones at one another. Others had stooped in a semicircle and poked sticks into the ground.

My car bobbled over stormed-based potholes in the dirt road, and the disorderly ruckus distracted them from their play. The kneeling children rose to their feet while the rest stopped running. They all stood like statues and observed me struggling up the road. My core trembled from their prolonging stoic glares. I covered a good ten feet before they began to tread in my direction.

The SUV continued bouncing, making it tough for me to maintain a stern watch on the kids. From my shaky sight, it appeared the children kept a steady yet determined pace. The ones who chased each other still carried rocks and cones as they filed behind the ones with the sticks. Their arms swung, and their legs took wide strides. The rocking became intolerable, and I could only guess as to when they'd reach me. I readied my foot to slam the brakes. Just as I got a good look at them, the children stopped at the bank of the road as I passed them.

The littlest girl from the kneeling group stood ahead of the entire clan. She wore the dirtiest sundress that matched her muddied face—why would her parents let her wear something so short and thin in October?

She rose her hand, and she wasn't displaying a stick. Instead, she held a matted kitten by its neck with only her petit thumb and index finger. The runt didn't squirm in agony, it only stared catatonically in the distance. A sudden rush of lightheadedness stunned my vision—at another look, I saw dark oozy liquid coated the tips of the held sticks.

I didn't want to lose sight of the children for fear of their volatility, so when I couldn't turn my neck any more, I promptly looked through the rearview.

The children had merged into the middle of the street without me observing when or how they'd moved—some rested their twigs on their shoulders, others cradled the stones and pine cones. The filthy, little girl dangled the motionless feline by her thigh like a ragdoll. I took the turn, unable to see any of them anymore. I pulled myself from the reflection to see the Dunns' driveway before me.

Seventeen Hours Until …

The colorful leaves from the vast and luscious trees shaded the Dunns' place, like partitions separating their land from the rest of Maple's Edge. They looked so brilliant, one would've mistaken the season blossoming into spring rather than fading into autumn by the sight alone. I heard the SUV's wheels rolling over the pebble driveway.

My mind became swamped with so many memories of my youthful, pudgy self struggling up the stone pathway just to escape my parents' lavish carousing or dangerous brawls. I mean, there were good times too, when Gen invited me over. However, most of the time, I came unannounced, and they welcomed me without any repugnance.

The driveway encircled the apple trees before the two-story farmhouse. Gen's mustang came into view, and I parked behind it. I stood between the two the vehicles, hardly recognizing the place.

Overgrown limbs and vines from dying shrubs climbed the side of the house. The off-white paint had been peeling for some time. It stung knowing Mr. Dunn wouldn't even allow a weekend of no mowing, much less this. This didn't look like their home at all.

I dialed Gen's number. The only sounds were some chirping through the wind, dried leaves rustling in the breeze, and the porch swing's rusted chains groaning from the frigid gusts. I pulled the phone from my ear to discover no service. Baffled, I pocketed it and approached the porch steps.

The boards dipped beneath every step I took along the entryway, as if they were made of rubber instead of wood. I steadied myself before knocking on the door. No one answered, and I banged again only to get no response. I sidestepped, but the discolored and tethered window curtains made it tough to pry into the desolate living room. I returned to the door and dove into my pocket for the phone. A faint cackling sound around the house stopped me from removing the cell.

I stood, waiting for another noise. When I only heard an airstream, I yelled for Gen, then Bruce and Erma. The breeze tumbled under the porch's covering, and a more wintery-than-autumn atmosphere embedded the front of the house. Again, I only heard the birds, leaves and chains in response to me. I rechecked the front door before circling the deck.

The bundled shrubbery infestation extended to the backyard. Some of the thick, untamed vines scaled up the columns that elevated the relic of a clubhouse. Despite a well-kept firepit mounted where the sandbox once occupied below, some bliss fluttered my heart in discovering something from my childhood had survived this unfamiliar town. Before the putrid hangout, freshly carved tiki torches had been pitched into the dirt—Gen and Bruce maybe wanted to have an after party once we're done at the DIrty Dark Dog.

Beyond the treehouse, Mr. Dunn's blue 1971 Ford pickup was parked in the stilted carport at some good thirty-something feet from me.

Unkempt shrubbery draped from the shed's overhang only verified the vehicle had been there since Mr. Dunn's passing. The overran wildlife practically blocked any source of natural light from the truck.

Yet, clear as day, light reflected off the dangling silver crucifix from the rearview, like the last star before dawn.

The firm grip on my shoulder made me hop and spin in place.

Gen giggled from my reaction. "Hey, Sammie!"

Pure happiness flushed any nervous feelings from my pores as we embraced one another.

• • •

Geneva gathered the steaming mugs from the kitchen counter. "How was the ride down?"

Apparently, she was done convincing me she had been in the house the entire time and had no idea what the cackling sound could've been besides woodland critters.

I thanked her for the hot tea—the resonating heat knocked the house's cold from my body. "Well, you know me when I get my jams going."

Gen hummed in agreement and planted herself on the other side of the table with her coffee— these chairs have always been our unofficial assigned spots since … well, forever. We both blew away the steam and took our first sips in unison. Gen slouched when she drank, and her posture had me inspect her appearance since seeing her.

Now, I'd always respected her effortless emo-pop style since grade school. Her father's

Cherokee bloodline blessed her with defined cheekbone structure, and her long auburn hair only complimented her heavy yet flawless makeup among her pastel skin. What's more awesome about this chick was she Frankenstein-ed her own outfits from the rags she bought when we went thrift shopping. It was entertaining to observe how our envious classmates would gawk at her attire, demanding the name of the designer or the store where she bought them. It was apparent she had an eye for fashion design, and I always encouraged her to peruse it, knowing she'd get far from Maple's Edge with her talent.

Her appearance before me wasn't the gothic supermodel I'd always envisioned. The bags under her green eyes were darker than the faint eyeliner. Edges of her cropped blue-and-purple tinted hair frazzled beneath the hoodie. A black tank top and platted pants drooped from her thin, pale figure, like how clothes hung on hangers.

I asked if she was seeing anyone, which she answered with her being "between boyfriends." I wanted to know if she had ever enrolled into the community college. She blandly stated she didn't then was quick to ask about my work and Darius. I told her both were all right and how I swore everyone in the office had heard her loud mouth when she called yesterday. This caused the hearty laughter between longtime friends.

We continued the idle chitchat, but I couldn't shake the kitchen's lingering chill. It didn't necessarily stem from Gen and me not having spoken in a while; we'd always resumed like we had hung out only yesterday. Our banter bundled warmth between us.

The room's unsettling cold felt like something unearthly—not from the weather outside. And heavy. I mean, it was visibly just Gen and me, but it was as if another presence hovered in the kitchen with us.

I scanned the area. "You said it's just us at home, right?"

Gen confirmed and peered pass the tatty curtains. "Bruce and Mother should be here soon. Then we can get going." When she said the last few words, she shimmied in her chair with delight.

"Do you know who's all going to be there?" I asked, trying to shake off the creepy vibe.

"Oh, Samuel, everyone!" Gen's voice climbed an octave as she flapped her hands. "We've been prepping for this ceremony since last year."

"Oh, jeez." I winced while setting the cup on the tabletop. "Does that mean Bubba Price's going to be there?"

Gen flashed a sly grin. "And Eddie."

I shook my head. "Oh, we were so bad …"

"Yeah. We'd *constantly* skipped Sunday worship, so I could make out with Eddie, the priest's son, in his daddy's office … and you with the curious older brother behind the lodge next door."

Our bursts of laugher traveled through the hollowed house. When the echoes died, I still heard some residual giggling trailing behind ours.

I jumped out of the chair. "Okay, you cannot say you didn't hear that."

"What?" Gen's tone was controlled as her eyes peered over her mug.

"You didn't hear that laughing?"

Gen just shook her head with a mundane expression. "I mean, we just laughed—"

"You said we were alone here, right?" I asked again.

Gen once more confirmed but with a concerning expression.

"But I just heard someone giggling. Like what I heard behind the house."

Gen lowered her mug. "Oh, yeah? Well, I don' t know. It's just us here."

I stood by the table, waiting for someone to enter the kitchen. Or even Gen to say something else. Anything.

Gen just attended to her coffee.

No one appeared.

Perplexed, I excused myself to the bathroom. Gen gawked at the curtains—not lifting to peer out the window but as if she could see through the thick fabric. She didn't even verbally acknowledge my departure.

Roving through the murky house didn't ease my worries. Shadows moved, and I kept convincing myself I was just scaring myself. The creaking of the house didn't help; it always sounded like someone was following me. I shouted to Gen for them to open some of the curtains so people could see through the house. Her lack of response only made the scene spookier.

I splashed water on my face and stared deep into my eyes through the vanity's mirror. "Sam, chill. You need to relax. You're just nervous being back here. You need to chill, Sammie ... Sam."

I washed my hands and stepped from the half bath built below the wooden staircase. I closed the door behind me, and something scurried across the mudroom by the front door, causing me to flinch and cuss. I looked down the extended hallway, waiting for something else to move. There was only stillness, and I noticed my labored breathing. I knew something had darted from the kitchen's direction and into the living room.

I called for Gen. There wasn't an answer. I hollered again, not moving until I heard her answer me. Only silence. I threatened to leave the house, saying this wasn't funny.

Finally, Gen answered me. "Samuel, what are you griping about now?" Her voice sounded weak from the kitchen.

But what I had seen now dashed into the living room. I practically flew down the hallway to follow.

The gloomy room was vacant. I looked past the sofa and through the windows to the bonfire setup near the clubhouse. There still wasn't anyone outside. I only heard the wind blustering and crickets joining the birds' singing. No laughing. The sun seemed to have found a break through the trees.

I baulked at the mechanical noise rumbling up the driveway. I crept toward the mudroom, listening to the sound grow louder and closer. When I reached the entranceway between the two rooms, Gen exited the kitchen and opened the front door. The sunset blinded me at first. Then I saw Bruce's pickup truck sputtering up the driveway.

"Yes!" Gen cheered. "Mom and Bruce are here with the burgers. We figured we could eat before going to the DIrty Dark Dog."

Fifteen Hours Until ...

Gen and Erma remained in the kitchen, preparing the condiments for the burgers. Bruce and I were manning the burgers on the patio grill he and Mr. Dunn had built years ago. Bruce approached me after flipping the meat.

Before sitting, Bruce got two longnecks from the Styrofoam cooler and handed one to me. "Mr. Veggie still drinks?"

I scoffed while accepting the alcoholic beverage. "Well, *it is* yeast. Seriously though, appreciate the black bean burgers. And thank you for the beer, man."

Bruce snickered. "Just make sure you shit in the first-floor bathroom."

My laughter was genuine this time.

He tipped his glass bottle toward me. "Good to see you back home, man. To being back home"

I nodded with a sincere grin and clanked my beer against his. "To home and being with you all."

We took swigs and savored the frosty liquid while enjoying the dusk. Bruce sipped again and held the beer in his mouth before swallowing.

He sucked air through clenched teeth. "Seriously, it's good to see you, man. I got worried."

I ceased mid sip and arched a brow. "Worried?"

"Just …" Bruce dawdled from the one word and drifted his gazed hazel eyes from mine. "Sammie, it's just … Maple's Edge hasn't been the same since I moved back home." He met my gaze again with a hallow grin. "Hell! Things really started changing when you moved." He slugged my shoulder and chuckled. "Dude, don't get all squishy on me."

I was lost but laughed anyway. "Whatever. You're the one saying the sappy shit."

"It's just you're like family—a brother. And you know this. We haven't seen you in so long—"

"Yeah, too long, Bruce." I meant saying that.

Bruce focused on the steaming meat on the grill and took another sip. "I returned home before your parents' place burned."

"Yeah," I responded. "You called me, remember?"

Bruce lifted his chin. "I did. Just thought you deserved more than Gen messaging you online."

I told him I appreciated that.

"I saw the smoke rising that night," Bruce continued. "I mean, after all, they only lived down the street. But it happened at night, so that smoke stood out with some grayish glow or some shit. Everyone was there too. It was a shitstorm, man. There were so many assumptions about how it started, but it was never officially determined how, you know."

I squinted and shook my head. "Gen told me the news said something like one of my dad's joints caught something on fire or some mess—"

"Yeah, that's what Chief Mills officially reported. But you know it wasn't—"

"How're the burgers?" Erma's words made both Bruce and me jump.

I caught her stoic expression a moment before she flashed her bright smile.

She set the items in her hands on the nearby patio stand. "Bruce, maybe you should go check on the burgers. You know I don't like my meat well-done. Besides"—Erma patted my leg before squeezing it too tight—"it's my turn to catch up with Samuel."

Bruce excused himself, and Erma took his seat. "Sammie, it's been so long since you came to Maple's Edge."

"I know, I know. I'm sorry, ma'am. Just, work has been demanding—"

"Remember he's a social worker, Mom?" Gen blurted while sitting next to me. "From what I hear, it's *very* demanding." How she emphasized "very" seemed a bit mocking.

Erma asked, "So, how's that? Do people even like you?"

I didn't know how to respond or even take the questions. "I mean, they *respect me* at work, if that's what you mean. We're really too wrapped up in our caseloads. And I really do enjoy my work, helping youth seek purpose. They seem to appreciate me"

Erma and Gen rolled their eyes at each other.

"You always had a way to communicate with tomorrow's generations," Erma said with an odd tone.

I didn't know what to say, so I just laughed in agreement.

"Well, are you dating?" Erma asked.

This question didn't make me feel any better. "Well, not really."

"Mama," Gen interjected, "I told you he shacked up with Darius."

"Shacked up?" I repeated in a wary tone.

"Darius?" Erma clutched her necklace. "Isn't that a boy's name? What part of Europe does that name come from?"

I choked on the beer and attempted to swallow. I looked at Gen, but she just blankly stared back. I glanced at Erma, and she had that look a grandma gives when she's being subtle about judging while donning a bright expression.

What the actual hell was going on here?

Bruce called for me. "Sammie. I'm going to need a hand, man."

I quickly went to his aid just as he flipped the patties.

"I figured you could've used some rescuing," Bruce muttered below the sizzle. "When do you plan to head back?"

These questions were getting more and more uncomfortable. I tried to not sound offended because it was Bruce asking now. "Not sure. Maybe I'll stay the night and leave tomorrow."

Bruce shot an unsettling glance at me.

"It's just …" Bruce searched for the right words. "I think Gen said you might have plans with Darius for Halloween, when she wasn't sure you were coming. I mean, if you want to dip out a little early to head on home tonight, we'd get it—"

"Need help?"

This time it was Gen who startled us. When did this family become stealthy and creepy?

"Um, sure," Bruce said.

Gen snuggled herself between us, serving the patties onto her plate without confirming if they were ready or not, and discussed what they should expect at Dirty Dark Dog's tonight. "Bubba's band, the many faces you haven't seen in so long. Shots, shots, and more shots. We're all just glad you're here, Samuel."

I wanted to address this *Samuel* shit, but she was swift to mention she was starving and ready to eat. She led the way and beckoned for us to join her and Erma. Bruce gave me another scornful glower. Gen requested us once more with a commanding tone. Then Erma became adamant with us coming to eat. I watched Bruce's stoned-muscle figure droop in defeat while heading to the patio table.

Eleven Hours Until ...

I followed Gen and Bruce into the Dirty Dark Dog. The aroma of lumber and booze and sweat hit my face. The streamers among the entrance reminded me of how grade school teachers decorated their classrooms.

Gen and Bruce led me to the bar section. Some paper décor was pried along the bar top. A handful of patrons sitting at the bar came to life when Bruce took a stool next to them. A nearby jukebox twanged some old-school county.

It was apparent Bruce had tried to hint at something back at the house. Maybe here we could be more discreet when the place gets hopping and no one could really hear us. I ambled to the empty seat by Bruce to whisper my idea to him.

Just as I approached, a much older man had just appeared from the end of the bar and behind the countertop, cleaning a mug as if he'd always been there. He wore a burnt orange tunic with frills around his collar. A dark emblem glistened around his neck. He and I made eye contact, and the way his dark brooded eyes naturally scowled unsettled me.

"Is that Sammie?"

Gen interlocked my arm. "You know it!" She practically dragged me the three more steps I needed to take to be right on top of the bar.

Her long black cloak nearly blanketed me as she twisted and bounced like a schoolgirl with her BFF. "Told you I'd get him here."

"Well, damn if you didn't, Geneva." The man grinned and extended his hand. "Little Samuel Haskell. How the hell are you, son?"

I hesitated but accepted the handshake.

"It's Frank."

I had to contemplate what he said, but then my mouth dropped, and my eyes stretched. "Oh, wow. Sorry."

"I know, I know. I look different. I lost weight from the colon cancer. But I fought the bastard. The power of worship does wonders."

Frank gave me a quick check. "So, you're going to be *that* guy, huh?"

His words made my chest wince.

"You didn't want to dress up with Gen? Neither did Bruce, huh? Party poopers."

I scanned the bar patrons. Two donned cloaks pretty similar to Gen's attire. The third customer wore overalls and a flannel shirt, which I was about to point out until I saw the werewolf mask next to this mug of beer.

Frank patted the countertop like Congo drums. "So, what's your poison, Sammie? On the house."

Still thrown, I ordered a drink. He pointed at Gen and asked if she wanted her usual, which she confirmed she did.

With my eyes adjusting to the dim orange glow, I realized the vast and spacious place didn't look anything like a classroom ready for a Halloween party. Eccentric crimson symbols had been embroidered on black cloths sorted along the timber walls. Also, an overabundance of animal heads were mounted on the walls. And they weren't just animals people hunt—like deer, fish, or rabbits. Heads of bears, oxen, and wolves vacuously stared from the lumber with protruding mouths—I waited for *them all* to start chattering at any moment. Fully stocked candelabras flickered with the tabletop jack-o-lanterns. Disturbing-looking scarecrows crucified on posts outlined the stage and dancefloor.

Families occupied some of the booths and were eating dinner. Flies swarmed around nasty-looking meat and burnt sides on their plates—I see why Gen wanted to eat before coming here. I caught some patrons leering over their shoulders while others just stared directly at me. Even with me eyeballing them, they ogled seconds longer before returning to their food.

I smelt the strong alcoholic odor before the glass was forced into my hand. Gen hollered for everyone to surround us, lifting her own drink, and they did. Bruce even got from his stool to join the gathering, but his eyes remained solemn when he looked at me. Frank grabbed his beer bottle and shuffled down the bar to be near us.

"Everyone get in closer for this toast," Gen called out.

They all closed around me. Not Gen and me. Just me.

I attempted to stand for the toast, but they swarmed so tight I couldn't lift from the seat. I rose the glass but only got to shoulder's height due to their crowding.

"Here's a toast to the Dirty Dark Dog lasting for fifty years, helping Maple's Edge stay afloat even after the recession. We all know the neighboring cities are still struggling. But not us. Not today."

Many yelled and applauded, repeating. One individual was way too loud in my ear. I turned to find the preacher of Maple's Edge Secular Practice.

"Father Patrick?"

He wore a muddy yellow tunic and winked at me. A dark emblem hung from the cord around his neck.

This wasn't happening. This man isn't in this unholy place. Oh, hell!--if any of these residents could read my mind when I said that ....

"And to Samuel coming home." Gen added.

They cheered and clanked glasses over my head. I tried to thank them, but they continued clanging their drinks and chattering among themselves. Some bumped my glass, and beer froth sloshed over the rim and into my face. I pleaded for them to chill while still trying to express my appreciation, but the zeal of their chanting grew. I couldn't even make out what they were saying anymore. Most seemed to barely move their lips, but my core vibrated from their humming.

Someone outside the horde released the high-pitched cackling, reminding me of the odd noise I heard at the Dunns' place. I tried to rise again to find its source, but the bodies had constricted too close by this point—Father Patrick was the tightest of them all, with his hands on my shoulders and lips padding the back of my head. I kept attempting to stand from the stool, to lighten the mood by saying I wanted to get up and laugh too. My head bumped into so many crossed arms, perspiring mugs and even a few damp chins. I pleaded for them to back off, practically screaming, but I couldn't hear myself over their rising hubbub.

And the jukebox blared now, and the music wasn't country anymore. The tempo was steadier, and the melody was more repetitive and mellow.

The patrons' eyes glazed, and their hefty jumbling settled into a unison of murmurs. The clanking glasses became a beat for their chanting. I didn't know when it occurred, but a high-pitched ringing boomed over the invocations but remained smooth with the soft voices. The cackling broke through the ringing and the chanting.

I yelled for them to stop. Their chanting grew excited. The cackling became unbearable. The bell tone penetrated my eardrums.

"Shut the fuck up!"

All the noises ceased—the ringing, the cackling, the chanting, even the clanking. The jukebox switched back to acoustic guitars and whining singing.

Everyone remained around me though, no longer staring with dazed pupils. All their mouths were shut. Their expressions looked like they'd been smacked.

"Thank you," I stuttered, feeling the room grow hotter. "It feels good to be back home."

Some smirked, but the majority quietly wandered back to their claimed spots among the pub. Father Patrick said something like *bless you, child*, but I dwelled on the embarrassment.

When the brouhaha died down, I tugged Gen's sleeve. "What the hell was that about?"

Gen shook her head and squished her face while setting her beer on the counter. "What? People happy to see you home? Or you being ungrateful about your best friend's toast?"

"No, Gen—I mean … I am. Thank you. But why did they all just bundle up like that?"

Gen's expression remained stunned. "Because that's how toasts usually go, Sammie."

"No. I mean, those people were … just a bit too close for comfort."

"What, you mean Betty and Paul?" Gen motioned to one of the families in a booth. "We went to school with them two. You know them."

I glanced at them once more. I didn't recognize their faces. In fact, the husband looked a bit too old to have attended Maple's Edge High the same time Gen and I did.

They had a little boy and younger girl sitting with them. I continued to stare at the family, trying to place them, and only the children's faces were familiar to me.

I turned back to Gen.

"Okay. First off, it wasn't them alone. Best believe that. It was everyone in this damned place—"

"Oh, the place is damned now, Sammie?"

"And secondly," I rose my index finger, "those two are not *that young*, Gen."

Gen shrugged. "Well, they might have hung with our parents back in the day or something."

"They're not that old, either. Look, whatever, girl. Regardless, Gen, it wasn't them alone. The entire bar nearly suffocated me—"

"Samuel!" Gen tapped the bar hard enough for people among the general vicinity to look. "They've been here for a long time. They've been to Bruce's gatherings and shit. So many have been here for a long time, Samuel. Devoted to our home—"

"Okay," I said with raised hands. "What's with this *Samuel* shit, Gen? You've *never* called me that."

"Huh?"

"Yeah. I mean I've always been Sammie here. Not Sam. Not Samuel."

Gen glared at me with a vacant expression. "Sammie, Sam, Samuel—what does it matter? It's your name."

Before I could continue, Gen blurted out that she had to use the bathroom and stormed from the bar.

A few guys along the bar still watched the entire time. When Gen left, their gazes lingered on me for a few moments longer before returning to their drinks and chatting. I turned back to see Gen walk around the booths toward the restrooms. She passed the Paul and Betty people with their children.

The little girl sitting next to the mother kept her glower on me. Her face was filthy. How could her parents not even wash her up before coming— oh, shit.

This was the little girl from this morning. The one with the dead cat. She wore the same expression she did when they all watched me drive past them.

Eight Hours Until …

People continually stopped by the bar to express their eagerness that I'd returned home. They stated we attended school together, or they wanted to give condolences for my parents. The majority of which I recalled only their faces. Some I don't think I'd ever met before. Nevertheless, everyone who entered the Dirty Dark Dog bought me a shot. The rest wore either the black cloaks or some hick-themed getup with some creepy animal mask—a few sounded disappointed I didn't dress up for Halloween.

Even Chief Mills got me a beer. He wore some ruby red tunic with a dusky emblem.

"Little Sammie ain't so little anymore, huh?" He chuckled while squeezing my arms and chest.

By the time the digital clock behind the bar read *7:00*, the Dirty Dark Dog had nearly quadrupled with patrons. Gen never returned, and the place spun around me.

●   ●   ●

The band prepping on the stage sounded off kilter over the blaring house music. I scanned the musician lineup while nursing a cocktail some lady who could've been someone's grandmother had bought me. Mark Faulkner strummed his guitar, and Todd Singer sat behind the drums— they were two grades ahead of me, I think. Jeff, the front man, diddled with his acoustic. He had married Bridget Peppergrass, his high school sweetheart—she had told me she's now Bridget Meadows and they had four kids when she bought me a drink on behalf of Jeff.

And to the far left stood Bubba Pear tuning his bass. His biceps and triceps flexed as he maneuvered about the bass. It'd been a while, but it seemed he had massively toned his husky figure since the last time I saw him. Not that he was a disgusting blob then, just the true definition of big boned. Now, he rippled through the tee-shirt and jeans like he was made of pure rock. His physique came across like some road worker with that bushy beard. After a few moments longer, he rested the bass on a stand and helped with the rest with soundcheck.

He peered over a microphone he was fiddling with and did a doubletake when he caught my gaze. He flashed a half grin—the same half grin he'd always given me since the night of Bruce's eighteenth birthday party in the clubhouse. I went to reciprocate the smile, but a glimmer from his left hand stopped me; a wedding band circled around his ring finger. My grin fell flat, and I turned back to the bar.

Gen had yet to return, but I figured she joined some of the patrons on the dancefloor, so I'd catch her later. I scoped the mirror behind the bar to observe the boogying, but caught Bubba hopping off the stage. The crowd parted just enough for him to cross effortlessly through the pub.

Bubba propped onto the bar next to me. I kept goggling the mirror. The tingling sensation traveled through my body, and the alcohol rushed to my head. He nodded at Frank, and I watched Frank nod back before diving into the coolers. He nonchalantly turned in my direction and gave me a thorough up-and-down check. "You gonna be like that, Sammie?"

I couldn't not grin. Nor stop my cheeks from blushing. I could only mutter a *hey*.

Bubba got his beer from Frank, thanked him, and then ordered me a drink. He seemed to remember my favorite without needing to ask. Bubba took his first swig. "So, finally decided to come home, huh? That's good." He didn't make eye contact but instead studied his frothy bottle.

I accepted my drink from Frank. "Is it now?"

Bubba took the neighboring stool and toasted with me.

He sipped and gritted his teeth, exhaling his enjoyment of the alcohol. "What you been up to, Sammie?"

I told him about working in Charlotte, not minding having to repeat myself for the umpteenth time since entering the pub ... just for him. He showed genuine interest in my life outside Maple's Edge.

"Well, I'm an auto mechanic," Bubba shared.

"I figured a lumberjack." My stupid statement an indication that all the booze had finally taken over my thought process.

Bubba chuckled again. "Okay, then. Well, I even run own my own place off Busbee Road—Bubba's Garage."

He tapped his fingers around the glass bottle, and the ring clinked. He saw I noticed it and told me he had eloped with April McIntosh—she was in Gen's class. I asked where she was, and he explained she wasn't feeling well. He added she was on disability due to some medical issues, so the fucking hadn't been great for the past few years. Too many emotions and thoughts flooded me from him sharing very personal information. His brought the longneck to his lips, did a sideward scan of me, and then flashed a wink and a smirk. This only screwed with my inebriated head more.

He quickly changed the topic to about his two kids finishing at Maple's Edge Elementary and how funny it is to go in there for assemblies and teacher's meetings all grown now, with the urinals and chairs so tiny and low to the ground.

In fairness, I shared how I lived with Darius in one of the high towers in uptown Charlotte. He asked and I told him Darius was a banker. Bubba smiled at me when he said my partner's name. I asked what.

"So, he's a black guy, huh?"

I felt my sly grin stretch too wide, and I slurred, "And? Don't tell me you're jealous?"

Bubba's laugher was overbearing … and nice. Bubba looked forward, occupying his mouth with his beer bottle. I sensed he urge for me to compare. I quickly changed the topic and asked long he'd been playing in the band.

He pulled out a self-wrapped joint and lit it. He took a few puffs and offered it to me. I was too floored about his boldness but waved my hands in refusal. He looked down at me while taking another hit and winked again. Why was he fucking with me like this? His face turned stern when he pulled the cig from his lips, and he passed the pot to his left. He bent his index finger for me to gesture toward his puffy cheeks. I did so and, without asking or any hesitation, I parted my lips. He exhaled some smoke into my mouth. I had to wave to him to indicate I had enough. Only then did I realized how opened we were. I scanned the scene: no one could not care less if we made out right at this damn bar.

Bubba humoredly grinned and exhaled what remaining smoke he had. "Shocked you showed, Samuel. I mean, I heard you didn't come home when your parents' trailer burned with them in it. I'm sorry about that, by the way. They were okay people. But I didn't think we'd ever see you again, especially after not showing up for their services."

I took the rest of my cocktail to my lips. "Yeah, well ... So, everyone else bought me a shot to welcome me back. I think it's your turn."

Bubba bellowed another of his hearty chuckles. "Alright, man."

He ordered two Jägermeister shots. He handed me one and then lifted his. I cringed at the choice, but I toasted with him to my homecoming. Bubba took the shot with no hesitation. The liquor burned as soon as it touched my taste buds, and I nearly flinched off the stool. I had to sip it in strides. My reaction to the alcohol entertained Bubba so much that he ordered two more. I waited a moment before attending to the second shot. This one I gulped in its entirety.

Bubba slapped and rubbed my back. "There you go. Swallowed it all like a good boy."

His words embarrassed me, but I felt tightness in my jeans, nonetheless.

Bubba ordered himself another beer and me another Long Island—top shelf this time. He leaned into me, clinking his beer to my glass. And, even though the place was too loud for anyone to really hear him, he whispered in my ear, "To our good times."

My blood flustered through my entire body, my tongue tied, and I couldn't fight becoming semi-hard.

His beard and lips practically engulfed most of the longneck, his eyes watching my reaction in amusement. He turned and headed to the stage without even a goodbye.

• • •

I don't recollect when she had returned, but Gen took the stool Bubba had just vacated. "Who got you that?"

I was still sipping on the Long Island. "Bubba."

Gen grinned. "Seems like he wants a little reunion. He married April McIntosh, you know? Two kids." Gen took the drink from me as soon as I put down the glass.

Mark Faulkner blared into the microphone, "Happy Halloween, Maple's Edge! Are we ready to welcome this night or what?"

The crowd stridently responded. The house lights dimmed, and the band struck notes that sounded ominous together. More patrons gathered onto the dancefloor. The candelabras and jack-o-lanterns provided a faint glow over the pub. The animal heads seemed to jerk in the candlelight, but I knew the flickering was what made them appear to wiggle.

Gen grabbed my hand. "Let's go dance. Like old times."

I didn't answer either yes or no. She pulled me through the crowd faster than I could object. The speed made the head spinning hurt.

I told her a headache was coming and wanted to sit. She pulled a small pill from her pocket. She took some random person's drink to give to me. I took it. I dropped the glass when I realized that wasn't a pain reliever.

It was shoulder-to-shoulder mayhem. I noticed many familiar faces among the crowd—some from school, some from the neighborhoods. People flashed huge smiles at me as I passed them, giving high fives. Loose hands and arms flooded my vision.

Gen began to spin me to the beat. My stomach curled from the many drinks so many in this crowd had bought me. So many eyes were locked onto me, waiting for me to hurl or something. I yelled for Gen to slow down but knew the music was too loud for anyone to hear anything else. I still tried to tell her and yanked her hands.

The music grew somber. Bubba locked eyes with me while singing with the lead, but he just mumbled some syllables I couldn't necessarily decipher.

People closed in on me, forcing me closer to the center of the dancefloor. Hands rested on me. I tried to excuse myself from the mob, but Gen kept her grasp on my wrists while tossing back her head. More hands did their best to find some exposed part of me. Voices joined Bubba and the band's chant. The syllables were choppy. The chanting powered over the instruments, but the music became a tantric tempo for them. Gen kept spinning me, faster and faster.

I faced the stage, and three dark figures emerged from behind the band members. Their grotesque masks hid their faces. Their tunics were of different colors than the patrons: red, yellow, and orange. Onyx emblems hung around their necks.

I refocus on telling Gen to quit spinning me. Her eyes went dark. I couldn't make out any white from around her pupils. And her grin molded into something jagged. I demanded for her to release me, trying to yank my arms from her hands, but she continued to cackle and twirl.

"Damnit, Geneva! Let me go."

I stomped between her legs and broke her grip on me. I was unable to gather my own balance from the release, and my back end hit the wooden dancefloor. Everything still spun, but the velocity finally slowed to a halt. I cradled my stomach before the acid liquid burned my esophagus's lining. The liquor bubbled up my throat. I crawled onto my hands and knees before vomiting.

. . .

Gen clucked her tongue from across the booth. "Jeez, Sammie. If you didn't want to dance—"

"I'm sorry about that." I took another sip of water. "But that was an odd song the band played."

Gen's brow frowned.

My spinning head now throbbed. "That rambling they were doing … You seemed to be … chanting or whatever with them. You all did," I said with a wave to the dancefloor.

Gen shrugged and took a sip of her beer. "I'm sure we've all heard it too many times, since Bubba and them play here *every* weekend."

"But you all just … swarmed me—"

"Well, it is a small dancefloor, Samuel—"

"Seriously, Geneva. Chill with the *Samuel* shit."

Gen's tongue clucked again. "Well, you don't need to be missy prissy about it."

"It's just everything and everyone has been so weird towards me tonight. Even you. I mean, what gives?"

She chugged her beer, staring ahead of her at the crowd in the flashing strobe lights. Bubba's band still played, but it sounded more like a rock song than some tantric mantra. Even with the music and the hollering in the Dirty Dark Dog, the chaos did no justice for the unsettling silence between Gen and me.

Gen finished her drink's last drop. "Have you visited there?"

The question threw me, but I knew what she was asking. "I rode by it before going to your place."

She disapprovingly shook her head. "No, not good enough. Let's go there now."

I nearly choked on my drink. "Now?"

Gen shrugged. "Why not? I mean, we can come back here afterwards. And I don't think anyone will notice if we're not gone too long."

"No," I spat. When she huffed and asked why not, I responded with, "Out of all the weird shit I've gone through since pulling onto Fishery Road, that'd be the creepiest bullshit."

Gen demanded for me to look into her bloodshot eyes. "You need to know the truth. You have the right to know. And I don't think if we don't go now, there won't ever be another time."

These were the first set of genuine words I had heard from Gen since we reunited at the Dunns' house. She sounded like my best friend, the sister I grew up with all those years. But even with her wholeheartedness, I still felt uneasy with her suggestion.

"Gen, I'm not ready. I mean, Darius and I spoke about me coming back here just to do that. But it—"

"When will you ever be? When are you ever going to come back? I mean, it seemed like pulling teeth to just get you to come tonight. This is your moment to amend everything."

The words hit my heart, like how Darius's did. "But ... on Halloween? That would *really* add to all this creepiness."

Gen laughed. "What? You're scared?" She flipped her hood over her head. "This had *always* been our night, Sammie. You know that ghosts and goblin junk is just hocus-pocus bull." She gathered my hands. "You need to do this, Samuel. Then you can leave again."

Two and a Half Hours Until ...

I was wrapping up a phone conversation with Darius when Gen and I entered The Hen's Nest Mobile Home Park. "So, let me go, because we're here."

Darius said how proud he was of me. I thanked him and concluded by telling him I loved him and would see him in a few.

I followed Gen carrying the lantern—I had a flashlight. There were no streetlights throughout the development, and the moonlight alone wouldn't had been enough, so I made sure my still-intoxicated self didn't straggle from her pace.

I flinched at every moving shadow snatching for me—I knew that damn pill Gen slipped to me was still fucking with me. It was around 9:30, so most likely every single citizen—even the minors—of Maple's Edge were still prepping and getting fucked up at the Dirty Dark Dog. However, the time when the veiling between the living and the undead opened was only a couple of hours from now, and I couldn't be too certain we were completely alone in the otherwise vacant trailer park.

Gen stopped at the end of the dirt thoroughfare, but I took a few more steps before ceasing in front of the piled cement and wooden blocks that led to the entrance of Lot 7A—or where the front door once existed. I looked through the opening, and the charred interior resembled a scene I recalled from those horror-themed videogames. The atmosphere became so still I heard my heartbeat in my ears. Random gusts shifted things I couldn't see, making it sound like someone or something was rummaging among the place. The disturbing notion that my parents' ashes still lingered inside this vault exaggerated the creep factor.

I turned to find Gen's hood trapped enough of the lamp's light for me to see parts of her face. She didn't meet my glance but took the cue to begin.

"That night was so unreal. When I got here, most of the neighbors were already here and had provided their offerings into the fire. The flames had blocked the exits. Even with the mantras and commotion, we still heard their screams. Your dad didn't last long because I only heard his cries for a short while—"

"Goddamn!" The October chill had my tears stinging.

"But your mother fought to the end. She banged the hell out of that window"—Gen pointed at the hole where I remembered the kitchenette would have been— "pleading for forgiveness to the elders. She tried her damnedest to break the glass with chairs, anything she could grab."

My teeth chattered and steam escaped my mouth. "No one wanted to help them? *Her?*"

"Bruce did." Her tone sharpened. "But after leaving like he did, he knew doing anything would only stack against him with The Great One."

My neck muscles ached from the tension when I shook my head. "Bruce came back for you, Gen."

"He came back to appease the elders."

"No, Gen. Bruce and I met in Huntersville and Davidson so many times, planning how to get you from this nightmare—"

"You two sure were taking your sweet-ass time. Hell, you seemed to not have any problem leaving me behind yourself."

I couldn't believe what she just said. "That's bullshit, Gen, and you know it. It hurt me—after all those years of meeting downtown at Cool Beans, doing research with you on fashion programs instead of actually studying for my classes—you didn't attempt to follow through before I moved. We knew once I finished USC, it would've been only a matter of time for Maple's Edge to figure a way to lure me back. I should've gone to that school in Boston, but I got scared. Also, I feared if I got too far, I'd never hear from you or Bruce again."

"You know Bruce and I both couldn't leave Maple's Edge. Could you imagine Mom's turmoil if we *both* had left?"

"Don't go there, Gen. Your mother's grown. She needs to take care of herself as you do you, as grownups."

"You know Mom's too simple to defend for herself." Gen's tone rose. "After Dad offered himself, Mom was a sitting duck. I had to stay here to take care of her for Dad, and Bruce had to come back—"

"Stop with the excuses, Gen! You know your father wanted us to get out of here. He pushed us to study hard in school just to get into a good college, get that education, and get our asses from this madness. That's why he encouraged Bruce to enroll in that auto school in Mooresville—"

"Dad turning a blind eye rather than demanding Bruce to stay home was rough for Mom and me. But when everyone told the elders about Dad bringing home the Bible from that Cayce church, Dad knew he had to sacrifice himself for the sake of Mom and me ... even for Bruce. He had me promise to offer new life before the community during the ceremony—reproduction is the ultimate devotion. Dad said if I did that, then Mom and I would be immune to the recoiling. I just haven't been lucky with getting pregnant, Sammie. We went to the medicinal vicar in Maple's Edge and all. That's why Bruce had to come back—to procreate."

"There were plenty of people back at the Dirty Dark Dog." I gestured behind me as if the pub was nearby. "I waited for the damn fire marshal to burst into the place. Bubba and April had kids, and that Betty and Paul couple did too. And I saw a shitload of chaps this morning at our old bus stop. I think this place is doing just fine with maintaining a healthy population."

"You know that's our responsibility after our eighteenth year ceremony—contributing to the community's survival. Offering life is the ultimate gratitude and devotion to the Great One, the practice, and the community. If you had just stayed and assisted in the community's strength, Samuel—"

"Gen … *I'm gay*. How the hell was I going *ultimately offer* to this hellhole? I couldn't deny that part of me and fuck some girl just to get her pregnant." I recoiled at the mere thought of pussy despite the intensity of the moment.

"You know your parents suggested to utilize your unique intelligence to educate the younger generations on how freewill is the illusion of the damned. Your parents convinced the elders to let you study the divinities under Elder Patrick for you to teach—"

"You know that alone wouldn't fly, Gen."

"Damnit, Sammie! You were always so fucking stubborn. Dad always said you were too smart for your own good. Do you know how many *would kill* for the pass your parents' offered and sacrificed for you—"

"Yeah, but their devotions didn't seem enough for the goddamned place." I gestured toward the dilapidated trailer. "And they wholeheartedly *believed* in this shit. A gave their all—literally— for this fucked up lifestyle. I remember them eagerly allowing the community to come to our cramped home for the procreating gatherings and the offering rituals. Sure they did it in that meadow in the back, but still. I have night terrors to this day from witnessing all those sacrifices and the orgies. I flinch at the sight of skulls and rodents, and those black cloths still flood my mind." My gaze found the ruined window where my parents' bedroom once resided. I controlled my frustration. "They believed in this place, Gen. That's why I just don't get why no one helped them that night."

Gen stepped to my left. "Others never cared for them, Sammie. You knew your mother and father were just ... beyond control." Gen shifted her weight. "And how the elders agreed for your parents to sacrifice themselves for your autonomy from Maple's Edge pissed off so many. They felt your parents and you got off too easy. Our primary mission is to understand that freewill is delusional and dangerous for life. The community saw that blessing you with the freedom to choose contradicted what Maple's Edge had been built from."

"Did you?"

Gen continued rather than answering me. "We met before the ritual that night, pleading to the elder's how offering your parents and then commencing a benediction of your immunity wouldn't appease The Great One with terminating the lineage of the Haskell's. But they had spoken, and it was final. They knew this, but that enduring fury from all those years had finally blinded them. They tried it tonight, but their anger skewed their ability to consider that none of the coven's mantras and spells would work on you tonight."

"Hold up." Those words brought everything full circle. "Is that why you pleaded for me to come tonight, Gen? You think if you got me to come back to Maple's Edge, you'd be forgiven by the elders and the demi-gods? That's fucked up, Gen. You know you cannot get pregnant because of the—"

"The disease is the Great One's punishment of Bruce and my dad, to truly test my devotion to the community. The elders informed me if I got you to come, then maybe, maybe …" Gen planted her face into her hands—she let go of the lantern, but the flame had extinguished before hitting the ground. "Oh my stars, Sammie. What did I do? This was fucked up of me. I got blinded too. This place. You know how this place fucks with your head. What the hell happened to me—"

I grabbed her wrists. "Forget that. Here's your chance, Gen. Everyone's still back at the Dirty Dog. We can get into my car and get the hell out of Maple's Edge. *You* can finally leave."

"And what about Bruce?"

I shook her. "He'll be fine until we can come back. But you need to leave with me right now. Because, if we stay, I really don't see you and me surviving tonight. You know they offer people like me as sacrifices to the Great One. And, even if the Great One's forgiving, you know these elders aren't. Your illness will be the excuse for them to sacrifice you."

Gen's words were incomprehensible through the sobbing, but she nodded.

Just then, some uncontrolled noise blared from the direction of the Dunns' farmhouse.

Fifty-Two Minutes Until …

I had called Darius as we left the trailer park, but it got harder to carry on a conversation with him over the ruckus as we approached the Dunns' farmhouse.

"Wait, what now, Sam?" Darius's voice distorted. "You said Gen's coming home with you?"

"Yes, yes," I emphasized my words to make sure he got them. "I can't get into it now. But she's coming back to Charlotte with me."

"What happened at the trailer? What just—"

Static interrupted his words.

"Darius?" I covered my other ear with my free hand. "Are you there?"

I heard his voice but couldn't make out any other of his words.

Then I heard a digital click from the phone. I pulled the cell from my ear—I'd lost service.

I heard Gen trying to warn me about something, but my concentration to reach Darius again and the damn noise from the farmhouse distracted me. My knees rammed into something, and agony radiated through my legs. I rushed to rub the pain, not thinking about the phone in my hand until it was too late. I heard the screen shatter without needing to look.

A muddy jeep was parked before me. Gen had sidestepped it and seemed too amazed by what she saw beyond it. I shambled around the vehicle. Endless twisted clusters of cars, trucks and other vehicles were parked along the Dunns' driveway.

Their lawn resembled one of those auto junkyards Bruce and I used to search through many years ago. Even more bizarre, people danced on the car roofs and in the truck beds and about the yard.

Gen and I maneuvered around the collection of automobiles and noticed buses and shuttles too. In the distance, I saw an eighteen-wheeled oil tank. Gen and I got around a Lexington District Two public school bus graffitied with symbols similar to the ones on the cloths at the pub and discovered the volume of people in her yard had quadrupled.

Sporadic bunches of people swayed between the vehicles, lost in mumbling to the tantric melody coming from the farmhouse. Gen and I struggled through the sweaty bodies. Some wore dark cloaks with black hoods covering their heads. Other wore solely latex animal masks resembling the mounted heads on the Dirty Dark Dog's walls.

"How the hell are we going to leave in your car with this mess?" Gen muttered. "Should we just turn around and run down—"

The echo of a bloodcurdling shriek somehow fought through the music and chanting and yelling and laughing.

"Mom!" Gen charged up the driveway.

I screamed for her, but Gen was already deep into the locomotive clusterfuck. I used the lit headlights and bonfires to maneuver through the automotive labyrinth.

Herds of cloaked or nude citizens drank alcohol around the ample blazes in oil drums and ignited torches. The pot odor was strong too. Some even had the audacity to snort off the vehicles' hoods—to include mine and Gen's when I finally reached the front porch. No one seemed to notice me.

I cursed at the ones on my SUV to step from it. They only shifted to the side thinking I wanted some blow. Their adjusting exposed the slit tires.

"Fuck!"

This was only getting worse. I needed to go back down the driveway and run like hell from this place, like Gen had proposed. I scanned the faces and couldn't spot Gen. I didn't want to leave her, but I had no choice. I could come back with authorities. I turned to flee.

Two heavyset, burly nude men grinded on one another, making out through their bear masks. I tried to part them, but they had their arms and legs tangled. I tried to get around them, but there were just too many other people swarming and chanting. A cloaked female nuzzled her head between the parted legs of a nude lady wearing a horse's mask. Two other people spun one another. The masses pushed toward the house, trampling the two girls on the ground, but they continued with their play.

I retrieved my cell phone, but then remembered I had shattered the screen. I still attempted to power it on, and the screen lit. Hope flushed through me.

Then someone elbowed me, causing me to lose my grip on the cell.

I bent to pick it up, and pairs of feet danced it onto the grass. Some even stomped on my fingers. I cursed at the idiots but managed to get my phone. I pushed the start button only to find a darkened screen this time.

I rose from the ground, and the bodies seemed to just keep multiplying. And there weren't just adults in the crowd anymore. So many teenagers were getting wasted by the burning barrels. Children frolicked while wearing plastic animal masks and twirling streamers. From behind the house, two bottle rockets zoomed into the night sky. People cheered for more fireworks. And more exploded.

I was scared for my life, ready to crawl into the fetal position and wait for them to take me.

In the commotion, I heard someone call my name. I scanned the chaos and found Bruce jumping and flailing his hands on the front porch. I shoved and elbowed many bodies—even two prancing kids—to fight through the chaos. Bruce reached with both hands for me. I linked his fingers with mine, and he used all his vigor to yank me past the bodies on the stairs.

"We need to get the fuck out of here, Sammie," Bruce said as he helped me balance on the delicate boards.

"I lost Gen. We got to the driveway, but—"

Bruce waved his hands before me. "It's too late for her. That's why I could never get her from this damn place."

Those words didn't settle right with me, but the community's chanting roared into howls and cheers, causing me to return to the current threat.

Bruce grabbed my hand and said to follow him. However, everyone stopped grooving and chanting. We both had to see what had ceased the ruckus. Every citizen faced down the driveway.

"Oh, shit," Bruce muttered.

Three heavily garmented figures with some of the most hellacious head coverings marched toward the farmhouse.

Bruce squeezed my hand and dragged me into the farmhouse. Surprisingly, no one had found their way into the Dunns' home. I followed Bruce into the living room. All the curtains throughout the house were wide open now, and I could see the people starting the celebration again, praising the elders for their presence.

The mass of bodies occupying the backyard mesmerized me toward the picture window behind the sofa. I couldn't even physically see the bonfire's barrel, only the orange glow radiating above the congregation. The clubhouse towered over all and was decorated with black embroidered cloths and animal skulls.

Bruce glanced at the grandfather clock. "It's not midnight yet. And everyone's too fucked up to really know what's going on around them. We need to escape through the kitchen backdoor and run like hell into the woods. Beyond are those warehouses. If we can cross the business parks, we're out of Maple's Edge and can get help. Okay?"

I frantically nodded. Bruce must have seen the fear in my eyes, because he grabbed my hand and led the way.

When we ran by the staircase, I spotted someone on the second floor. I didn't get a good look, but it seemed to be a figure wearing a dark red wrap or something. I really didn't want get more details.

I kept my pace with Bruce, but the area began to look fuzzy, and the pungent scents of dogwood and honey and decay went up my nostrils. My eyelids went heavy, and my vision merged into a hazy purplish-blue tint. I became woozy.

I heard Bruce telling me to keep up, but he sounded miles away.

The area became less and less familiar to me. I snatched my hands for whatever tugged, then surveyed the room. The only thing I recognized was the coffee maker on a counter.

Someone grabbed my shoulders. I saw Bruce's nose bulging into my face. He was yelling something at me, but his mouth moved slow, and his voice sounded like he was deep in a cave. His foul breath mixed with the other pungent scents. He pointed behind him. I looked passed his thick shoulders.

Bubba was in the doorway to the grill patio. He wore a black cloak and red shawl. He winked at me. Bubba's lips moved, but I only felt the tremors of his deep voice. The words I heard weren't matching with his lips' movement. These words were telling me to let go and allow whoever was speaking them to protect me. Bubba charged at Bruce with a raised machete.

A red-violet tent blanketed my vision.

The only thing I heard was, "Mama has you, baby …"

Midnight

My palms remained on Bruce's shoulder blades as we eased down each step to the first floor. My sight wasn't fully restored, but clear enough now. The iron odor from Bubba's blood had stayed in my nostrils. I constantly checked behind us, making sure Bubba wasn't charging at us again but instead remained dead on the second floor.

The small phosphorene light over the kitchen sink produced a dim halo around a lumpy silhouette in a bathrobe slouching at the nook. The figure swayed but wasn't in tempo with the chanting—when did the music ever stop? The head slumped, and I couldn't tell if the person was looking at their mismatched socks or the kitchen knife they had twisted into the tabletop.

Bruce pointed at the opened backdoor. I saw the patio grill and then the open field that led to the woods. He motioned for me to wait at the entranceway, and he inched along the stained tile floor, bat ready to swing at the figure any moment. He got about a foot from the body when he stopped and lowered the bat.

"Mom?" His voice sounded like an infant.

The figure stopped rocking and spinning the knife.

"Mom, are you okay?"

The stillness in the kitchen grew colder. Also, it could've been my sheer exhaustion messing with me, but the lightbulb seemed to dim. The metallic musk in the air thickened.

Bruce shifted on his feet, triggering Erma to spin on her heels to face Bruce. Her bathrobe was open, and Erma's sagging breast flopped back into place. Her head remained slanted. And she still held the knife. Slobber dribbled from her lips and down her chin.

Bruce crept toward Erma, softly calling for her. He reached his free hand to his mother's shoulder. Erma snapped her head toward him.

A dull yellow tent surrounded her dark pupils. She snarled, and sweat seeped over her upper-lip hairs. Her shoulders and chest heaved. Liquid suddenly trickled between her legs. An acidic ammonia odor filled the kitchen as the stream splattered and puddled onto the kitchen floor, soaking Erma's mismatched socks.

Bruce's face drained of color. Whatever ounce of bravery he had within him left with his firm stance. Bruce dropped the bat.

The flow stopped, and Erma collapsed onto the floor. Her chin smacked the tabletop before hitting the floor. The blood pouring from Erma's busted head mixed into the urine.

Bruce screamed for his mother as he finally ran to her body. His right knee skidded through the mixture of bodily fluids as his hands went under Erma's head. Her blood seeped through his fingers.

Something trembled beside Erma. It was the kitchen knife. I watched the rocking get heavier.

"Bruce, the knife!"

As if being exposed, the knife flew into the air. I shrieked as it darted at Bruce.

"God, Bruce!"

Bruce gradually turned my way, trying to speak. The knife had burrowed into his cheek. Crimson flesh and blood dropped from his cheekbone. The knife lost its hold and plummeted onto the dampened floor.

A breeze came from the opened backdoor and spun dust into the kitchen. It collected into a cyclone from the wood tiles. The dirt swirled toward the ceiling. It didn't take long for an entity to form. A crackling sound came from it. Some grime extended from the being to collect the knife.

I fell next to Bruce. "Bruce, you got to get up. Now!"

Bruce held his hands to the tear on his cheek. Saliva bubbled from the hole, mixing his own trickling blood with his mother's own on his stained fingers.

My throat burned from screaming. Bruce's frightened eyes pleaded for me to just run. The knife stabbed into Bruce's chest.

Bruce's eyelids began to relax as he looked from me to the ceiling. Blood seeped and bubbled from his torso as his final breaths were evident by the lack of his chest's expansion. Red spittle spat from his lips as his final breath was released. His eyelids dulled and didn't blink anymore.

The black smoke bundled within itself as the cackling came from the puff. The laughter distracted me, and I was caught off guard when the smog flew past me. Sulfur, iron and rot terrorized my nostrils, making my head spin and nearly lose consciousness … yet, again tonight. I fought to keep my vision from blurring yet again. I strained to find my hands were empty.

The sound of glass shattering came from the other side of the house. I ran and searched for the source. The living room window had been broken. The firepit was alive outside, and I could feel its heat. In its auburn radiance, so many figures surrounded the clubhouse. The smog floated above the people. I caught it holding Bruce before it released his body into the center of the coven. Embers and flames violently whipped from the bonfire barrel when the corpse dunked into the barrel. When it settled, Gen stood behind the barrel, arms raised toward the stars.

More beings emerged from the darkness surrounding the house to join Gen's incarnation. The dark fog hardened and formed into something more sinister. The figure grew nearly half the height of the immense clubhouse.

I needed to pull myself from this insanity. I needed to continue with Bruce's plan. I needed get to the warehouses outside Maple's Edge.

I ran to the base of the stairs and heard knocks on the front door. I continued into the kitchen, ignoring the banging. I ran around Erma but then halted.

Cloaked and nude-wearing-wilderness-beast-masks people lingered on the grill patio outside the backdoor. They didn't approach but gawked at me. I couldn't see their eyes—either because of the masks or the hoods hung too low—but I felt their stares. I backpedaled into the mudroom, toward the knocking sound on the front door. I stumbled into the living room again to find people standing on the porch watching me through the broken living room window.

I stood still, knowing I was surrounded. I didn't want to be cornered on the top floor, but if I wanted go out fighting, that was my only option other than to let them just take me now. I grabbed the railings, climbed the stairs and stopped on the third step.

At the top of the staircase stood someone I thought I'd never see again.

My mother.

She stood nude, but a thick crimson gooey substance coated her body like a nightgown. Her long, straight black hair rested around her shoulders. Her eyes were an icy blue.

I heard myself mutter, "Mom?"

She remained motionless, glaring at me. I stepped back onto the first floor. She continued to watch me, non-responsive, even to my movements.

I again mumbled, "Mom." This time more confident and aware.

The front door's handle jiggled, and the October gusts flooded the mudroom. Hands snatched whatever parts of me they could clasp. I didn't break my stare into my mother's eyes until I had been fully pulled outside.

An Hour and Twelve Minutes After

So many citizens of the community stood like statues just off the porch. They extended as far past as the vehicles and into the darkness beyond the yard. They turned only their heads to watch my escorting. Again, I couldn't actually see anyone's eyes. The swarm was so hypnotic I didn't look to see who had yanked me from the house until we neared the backyard.

My chaperons were the little boy and the little girl who had sat with the couple at the Dirty Dog. They held my hand as if I was the one taking them somewhere, like to a candy store or the amusement park. The little girl had a clean face and the brightest smile. She wore a pink tunic instead of the sundress. The boy wore one too, but blue

We got around the corner of the house. Beyond the swarm of hooded and masked figures, the three beings with the grotesque disguises hovered among the bonfire on the clubhouse's petit balcony. And a much shorter, dainty person stood before the fire.

We stepped off the porch and into the backyard.

Too many people surrounded the clubhouse. And more joined from around the house and from the woods behind the shed. The bodies—both clothed and nude—were crammed so tight I couldn't even see the ground below me. However, they parted for the two children to present me before the elders. I stumbled over a few feet. A few arms and hands smacked me—whether if it was accidental or on purpose. Everything spun and shifted and shook before me. The chanting nauseated me, and my stomach boiled. Tingles and jolts traveled through my head.

Just when I felt faint and ready to succumb to the weakness, a sudden bright rustic-toned light emerged before me as the final patch of people parted. It took me a moment to adjust, but I saw the bonfire before me. And before the barrel, Gen stood on a podium. Behind her and the flames stood the elders, still in costume. They held their hands above them, chanting.

The fog slowly lowered to the ground. It hardened and formed into a full being. It glared at me with those terrorizing eyes I thought the drawings were only emphasized to spook us into worshiping. His pupils were slit like a cat eyes, only miniature curling of gray and red flames lapped along the edges.

I cursed under my breath, realizing I was looking into the eyes of the Great One.

The children shoved me toward the barrel. The fire instantly heated my flesh. I knew it'd be stupid to try to escape, so I stood in silence.

The elders finally removed their helmets, revealing their identities—Frank, Chief Mills, and Father Patrick.

Gen only shifted her eyes down to look at me. The rest of her remained erect. The hood hid most of her face.

"Samuel, you betrayed your family and your community. You abandoned all that our ancestries had fought over the eons to keep the Great One among the living. Not only did you break your obligations, you've laid what's sacred to our lineages upon innocent ears, upon a being that's just as inhumane as yourself. For this, you must show your ultimate devotion to our Holiness before the community now."

The crowd whooped and cheered behind me. in a tantric unison.

"You must either bring the one you told about us before the community to offer to the Great One. Or sacrifice yourself for the one you love."

I was confused. My parents were dead. Who else could they—

"Darius?"

The entire scene became still.

"Are you talking about Darius, Gen?"

She only continued to glare at me.

"No!"

No one flinched. They most likely expected me to respond like that and were willing to let me ponder the options.

"I mean," I said with a more subtle tone, "how am I to even get a hold of him—"

The little girl approached me, carrying something with both hands—my cellphone. I took if from her petit hands. I looked before me—at Gen, at the hooded elders. I glanced at the Great One. His stare became too horrifying, and I shifted to the elders.

"But I don't think I even get sig—"

The cell beeped, and the screen illuminated, showing not only did I have a connection, but I was picking up Wi-Fi.

"I only told him about my parents."

No one gestured or said a word.

I stared at the screen, hesitating, before my trembling finger dialed Darius's number.

"Hey, baby," he said. "Are you and Gen outside the city?"

"No." I barely heard myself.

"What's wrong? Where are you?" I heard the worry and fear in Darius's voice.

"Nothing. Nothing at all," I answered, trying to boost my tone. "I'm still in Maple's Edge, actually."

"Oh, you partied that hard, huh? So, you're just slurring then, not crying." Darius laughed.

I paused. Gen and the elders didn't budge—an indication I was on the right track.

"Things got … fun here."

"Really, Sam? You weren't even interested in ever going back. Now you don't want to—"

"Yeah, yeah. Look. They want to know if you'd come down?"

"Huh? *They?*"

I looked at the elders. And the Great One.

"Gen and Bruce. They'd like to meet you."

There was silence. I only heard the crackling from the fire.

"*Okay* … Well, um. I mean, it's nearly three in the morning, so maybe I could come another time?"

I looked directly into Gen's eyes, stiffening my back. I knew my next line: I was to tell him he needed to come now. I needed to convince him to drive all the way to Maple's Edge now.

"Darius, I need you to … to forget coming. Don't come. Get help, Darius. I cannot—"

I lost connection.

An enlarged claw backslapped me, causing the phone to fling into the bonfire. I saw black spots and white sparks, and I felt my equilibrium go off-kilter. My already sore knees plummeted hard into the dirt.

Gen snickered. "You should've of done that, faggot."

Two Hours and Fifty-Eight Minutes After

The incantation resumed. The swarm closed around me. The Great One's physique seemed to swell the more the community chanted. Dark red jagged lines pulsated from its reptilian flesh as bright as trails of lava from a volcano

Gen grabbed my arm and twisted it to expose my wrist. With her other hand, she pulled a knife from her burlap string around her waist. She swung the blade above my skin. I felt the sting and thought it was my wrist. But I looked to see she had sliced a bit above.

She sneered in delight of my flinching and panic. She did it again, cutting another part of my arm. She raised the knife high, and I saw in her eyes she was aiming for the artery now.

I heard screams—so much screaming behind me.

The congregation around us started to flee. They ran in all directions. Some were pointing back at the house.

They were yelling in bliss; it was fear.

Gen didn't release me, but she lowered my hand and the knife and looked past me.

She whispered, "Holy fuck."

She loosened her grip enough for me to look behind me.

My mother came from around the porch, launching whatever torches or burning barrels she passed with I guess telekinesis—I was beyond done figuring shit out. Some fell back to the ground with an explosion. Patches of fires spread about the dry grass.

People ran and crawled from the porch. A few jumped over the railings. My mother somehow got a hold of four at once, and she snapped their bodies effortlessly at their waists and necks. They piled on the porch, and my mother continued to strut in my direction. She descended the steps with riveting elegance.

People fled for their lives. When she passed those attempting to escape, they went flying into the house or through nearby barrels. She didn't even raise her arms to jettison them.

The little girl charged my mother with a knife, and my mother descended her gaze to the child. The little girl's knees snapped, and she plopped onto the grass. The girl pleaded and sobbed for her own mommy, and my mother stepped on the child's head. The girl's eyeballs popped from her skull, follow by streams of blood.

Gen grabbed me and raised the knife with a tree knot as the handle. I pulled just as she slashed at me. She caught the side of my leg. I punched Gen in her face and headed to the wood line.

I got as far as the shed when the three elders came from the other side of it. They had replaced their horrid masks. I stepped backward, and they lunged at me. I turned and ran. There were too many people exiting the house that I couldn't resist the current. They were pushing me closer to the elders.

I caught something from the corner of my eye—Mr. Dunn's crucifix hanging from the truck's rearview. I squeezed through the swarm of bodies, using my arms as if I was swimming. I jumped the last few feet out of the crowd, limped under the shed, slung open the passenger door and hopped into the cabin.

The three elders stepped in front of the truck while their flock ran behind them. They stood still in their autumn-color tunics and in their demonic facades. One lifted the monstrous hood over his head.

Of course it'd be Frank.

"Little Sammie," Frank called. "You need to accept your fate. You were destined—oh, shit!"

Frank was lifted into the night. The other two elders turned to see what had happened, and they, too, vanished into the sky without a trace.

My mother stood before the truck and me, carrying herself with tranquility and poise.

And she smiled.

I smiled back and exited the truck. I approached her, ignoring the many more fleeing members. I got about eight feet from her when she convulsed. Gen stepped from behind my mother with a hand still hovering behind Mom's back. Gen twisted her arm, and my mother convulsed once more.

Gen was digging that damn knife into my mother's back. I screamed for the bitch to stop. My mom collapsed to the ground.

"You cunt!"

Gen's eyes turned black and her grin contorted into that jagged snarl. She charged at me with the knife high above her. She only got about three steps in before she was flung through the air. My mom sat on the ground with her legs out, using her hand now to do her telekinesis voodoo shit. Gen flew all the way into the side of the clubhouse and then ricochet into the bonfire.

I continued walking to my mother as she graciously rose from the dirt. We smiled at one another.

My eyes welted. "I love you, Mom. I miss you. I'm sorry."

She still smiled.

There was a rumble behind her. She turned just as I looked above her head.

The Great One had enveloped Mom. The creature stood nearly four times taller than her. And as thick as mountains.

"Oh, shit. Let's get out of here, Mom."

I don't know why I said that. But she turned and gave me a slight humored expression. I teared up but grinned back. Her face went stern then became the same look she'd give me when she was mad at me: *You better get the hell out of my face.* I wanted to retaliate her command. I wanted to stay and fight with her.

Instead, I turned and hauled toward the woods, weaving around the few stragglers who were still escaping. I got to the edge of shed and took a final look at my mother.

The monster flexed before my mother; his eyes looked like the snake that it was—orange, red, and yellow flames danced around its slit pupils. I saw my mom's reflection in its eyes as if they were made of mirrors. The untamed fire that had spread across the backyard from the exploded barrels flickered wildly behind the creature. My mom had her back to me, but I saw her curvaceous silhouette stand confident and graceful before the monster.

She was ready to fuck up that freak

I continued into the woods.

Seven Hours and Twenty-Two Minutes After

The doctor kept the penlight in my eyes a little longer. He said everything checked out, that my abrasions were shockingly superficial, and I just needed to rest. He told me he had to attend to others and excused himself. I remained sitting on the patient bed, acknowledging that this was the first time in over twenty-four hours I'd actually stopped. I sobbed so loud some medical professionals stopped to check on me.

Through the hustling and bustling in the ER, Darius's face peered through the bodies. He stopped far down the corridor. I stared at him and waited for him to lock eyes with me. When he finally did, Darius pushed everyone in his path out of his way. He embraced me in his arms, kissing me all over my face and forehead and squeezing me into his chest.

He kept asking if I was okay. I told him they found me bundled and unconscious between Ms. Anne and Mr. Earl's shops. He had no idea what I was talking about, so I just reassured him I was all right about four times. I knew he knew I wasn't, but he also knew to just take everything as that for now and kissed me again on the crown of my head.

Darius scanned the ER. "But I mean? Where's Gen? And Bruce?"

I looked at him, and more tears fell from my eyes as I shrugged—surprised I had any more tears. He did some more coddling.

I sniffled. "I mean, I asked. The authorities said there were so many burnt corpses throughout the woods and along the Dunns' property. Their house burnt to the ground. I think the paramedics are still collecting bodies, and they are still trying to control the flames. The news said the smoke can be seen all the way from Cayce to South Congaree. But no survivors have been found yet."

"Except you, baby boy. Except you." Darius kissed the top of my head again and firmly squeezed and rocked me. "You're one lucky soul."

A NIGHT
FOR
JACK-O-LANTERNS AND
SCARECROWS

1.

Tonight's PTO meeting was another total waste. With the organization's board scheduling the assembly at townhall rather than the school, I now have an additional twenty-six minutes to this evening's commute, traveling from one end of Bluff Hill to the other. Still, arranging the event there was a smart move. The parents were able to directly petition at the town committee rather than the school faculty this time.

It didn't even take our administrative assistant, Mrs. Emeries, ten minutes to shift the evening's agenda of planning this school year's fall festivities into an open forum on how to shut down the Township Lodge's Haunted Walkthrough this Halloween. The remaining hour-and-thirty-something-minute meeting focused on the parents mostly repeating one another's key points.

I wanted to leave when Tommy Shultz's mother blabbed into the mic about the values of family and America and the Baptist practice that founded this town, but the community spotting the school's assistant principal sneaking out of the place during the middle of a PTO meeting would've been *this* Sunday's church gossip. Instead, I settled in the back of the hall and absorbed myself into some emails on my tablet rather than listening to their complaints.

I don't mean to seem callous about their concerns. It's just their grumbling has been ongoing for the past six Octobers now. And I get it; the parents' legit worries generated from a dread hovering over our hometown of Bluff Hill even before my time. The Township Lodge should've known dangling their flyers throughout downtown would've stirred the adults' suspicions and the kids' curiosities … just like when Miles Wellington originated the stunt years before.

The students tell the history of the Wellingtons and the Haunting Décor and A Night for Jack-o-Lanterns and Scarecrows in the school hallways like ghost stories. The upper-grade levels take it further, teasing the younger classes about how they spot Miles Wellington among the recycled props from the former haunted attraction in the lodge's more modern walkthrough or when the tour guide escorts them through the Wellington estate halls, waiting to attack the offspring of those who never supported his family ... or some crap like that.

It's just Miles Willington can't roam the Township Lodge or the Wellington Mansion. He'd passed seven years to the date of the fire, and every Bluff Hill resident knows this. And sure, the Township Lodge does use some of the old props from the haunted attraction Miles Wellington established in 2005 in their own watered-down Halloween event, but it's more like a museum than a walkthrough maze from how they're arranged. It's all the jokes and pranks the kids use to hype one another for this time of the year.

No one can officially say anything bad has happened or that anyone has been harmed while going through the lodge's attraction for the past six years. People around the world still make autumn their vacation season to visit the Wellington Estate Ghost Tour with the Halloween walkthrough—the Township Lodge should be ashamed how they charge forty-five dollars per person as a bundle package, as if they're some Disneyworld ...

Hell, I can't say much. I was even a fool and took the wife and kids through the damn things last year. Can't say it was worth the two hundred bucks, but we had a blast! That spooky mansion seemed to never end, as if they tried to get us lost in the hallways as we followed the directions from the handheld tablets. And the Township Lodge Haunted Walkthrough was creepy and interactive, with the props programed to grab at us.

Yet, no one died.

No news stations has flooded our backyards for headlines since that tragic Halloween night in 2026. Well, some out-of-towners occasionally visit to commemorate the ones their own hometowns had lost that night. Also, our local news comes nearly every Halloween to run the same damn report about the Wellington's legend, like some ghost story—it's only a constant reminder of the family's blasphemy upon Bluff Hill.

It's ironic, even after the demise of their lineage and after the destruction of their warehouse, the Wellington's name still brings the tourists and revenue to our sleepy town.

Foundation
2.

When I was a high-school history teacher, prior to the school administration gig, I taught how the affluent and southern-elite Wellington family became the source of our hometown's origin during the Antebellum era, solely due to their plantation occupying what's now Bluff Hill's western region. Their land consisted of their immense manor, miles and miles of cottonfields, and the slave quarters. Also, their warehouse stood as long and wide as a football field not far from today's Savannah River estuary between South Carolina and Georgia. The family's patriarch during that time, William H. Wellington, III, ran his cotton gins and hosted his slave auctions in the warehouse.

Businessmen traveled from Charles Town— now Charleston, South Carolina—to attend his auctions. The regulars witnessed in amazement how William Wellington's pockets swelled between the two zones each month and wanted a part of the profit. William Wellington would settle to terms with them only if the forests that separated the family's territory from the rest of the town remained rooted. In agreement, the entrepreneurs submitted their contracts with Charles Town's slave market, mended a partnership with William Wellington, and founded Bluff Hill in 1789. Other than their accounting ledgers, there weren't any other official documentation about the Wellington Plantation during the pre-Civil War period.

When I attended the College of Charleston and then grad school at the University of South Carolina in the early 2010s, I found a few scholarly articles during my long nights in their libraries that revealed how historians had found some slave journals among the Wellington grounds. The researchers iterated the slaves wrote about their family members being selected as house servants due to their "bloodline shared with the Wellingtons." Their entries stated how intense their "light-skin kin" preached their loyalty to the "Wellington clan" and their practices were "the way to real freedom." The words scribed expressed genuine fear and concern for their families because they emerged their ancestral practices with the "white folk spirituals."

The documents noted how the slaves' relatives returned to the quarters less and less after being assigned to the mansion until they were only spotted in the fields just to join William Wellington's Sunday services for the fieldworkers. The writings described how their relations "stood tall, like warriors ready for battle" behind the owner himself while William

Wellington paced and praised on a wooden pulpit and would "no longer be in sight" once services concluded, as if they'd "died out into the skies above."

Other fieldworkers shared that the unsold slaves at the auctions returned to the grounds "not like themselves." Like the reassigned family members, they described this thick milky glaze "as white as the master's skin" had coated the returns' eyes, and they'd behaved as if "their souls done been drained from their bodies." The articles mentioned how many labors noted these unsold slaves worked in the fields "stiff and fast, like those shinny cotton gins in the master's hexed warehouse" during the day while "kept to themselves when night done fall."

3.

When the North's revolution heightened in the 1860s, the emancipation dented the Wellington's business. The family struggled to provide Bluff Hill with cotton sales due to the thinning of their labor crew. Yet, the mayor supported their cause regardless, saying how even if they had to terminate their industry, the Wellingtons still could test what other suggestions they'd brainstormed with the town council.

The September 1865 editions of the Charles Town newspapers ran quotes form the chief of law's investigation about "the wildfire" that had torched the Wellington's estate. Many witnesses reported they could see the flames' glow amongst the dividing trees and throughout the town's skies that night. The wildfire had burnt their buildings and crops to the ground, even incinerating the slave quarters. Only a handful of the surviving fieldworkers remained; most ran North. No one would ever learn the source of the arson, and, by October 1865, the newspapers reported the official ending of the Wellington Plantation era.

The only dwelling the flames didn't even flicker upon was the warehouse.

Historical documents in many regional libraries' Carolina Rooms archived the accounting books collected from the estate right after the death of the late Miles Wellington around 2027. The books showed the Wellington royalties covered the reconstructed of the Wellington Estate after the nineteenth-century fire. It reflected how they saved money by allowing the hands of the many prior slaves that "chose" to remain with the family to renovate the place.

Also, for whatever reason, the books reflected the town's establishers supported what financial auxiliary the family developed for Bluff Hill. The town committee welcomed William Wellington's youngest son, Benjamin, as the community's business officer, while his siblings and their heirs continued with the family corporation in the warehouse.

Construction
4.

The Wellingtons' bank books reported many failed commercial propaganda. No matter what merchandise they sold—candy, upscale machinery and technology, pre-season clothing—the Wellington's never seemed to uphold a decent profit. As a result, they constantly closed the doors to that horrid relic.

Each time the Wellingtons liquidated another business, Bluff Hill citizens petitioned to demolish the building at every townhall forum. However, rather than listening to the residents, the council grasped onto the plans the Wellingtons created to once again flourish the town's revenue like they did in the late eighteenth century.

And they never voted to demolish the warehouse.

Mom and Dad never wanted my brothers and me to attend church, because when *they* were kids, Bluff Hills Baptist Church was more so grounds for town gossip than a house of worship—a habit that transferred into today's PTO meetings. The congregation not only griped about how the council perpetually allowed the Wellingtons to fail all with each terrible scheme but how the family never had to file bankruptcy while the rest of the rural citizens barely survived from paycheck to paycheck.

Dad chuckled how the older and more superstitious Bluff Hill residents rumored how the entire Wellington estate was "the Devil's playground." Around Halloween, the Bluff Hill elders told haunted tales about how the Wellingtons sold their bloodline to the Devil, making the warehouse their sanctuary, and that platform where William Wellington preached the altar. Dad added some speculation that the Wellingtons' genealogy was rooted from New England, therefore coming from a long line of occultists who practiced witchcraft to invoke demonic entities for possessing their "more obedient slaves." The elders scared Dad's peers with how the ones who died in the massive fire haunt inside the warehouse's brick walls, cursing every

Wellington family business attem~~~yet, the deal with the Devil had aided the clan t~tay afloat all these years.

In the school hallways, Dad's classmates would always tease one another to snea into the remnant structure. Some embellished crazy experiences about hearing voices and footstep, in the different sections of the place. A few swore they saw shadows lurking around the building.

Whether the things people said were accurate or urban legends, their words' essence lingered among the streets, bedding the root of Bluff Hill's haunting existence.

Modernization
5.

One evening in the mid-90s, my family had settled in the living room to catch that night's episode of *Seinfeld* when a high-pitched whistle escaped from Dad as he lifted himself in his recliner. He looked from the newspaper to Mom, who nestled on the couch with her paperback, and said how the Bluff Hill Haunting Décor was growing nationally. Mom cursed in the book's pages. Dad teased her, asking how could she be shocked. Mom continued grumbling, with explicit language.

My brother and I exchanged shock expressions. We've never heard Mom sound so irritated before. Dad asked her to clam down and saw he needed to explain Mother's foul behavior.

• • •

He started w how all the men in his childhood home waited or Grandma to return from the monthly Bluff Hill ownhall forum before settling at the kitchen ta^{le} for supper one October night in 1977— we were affled to why he started so far back in time but wee too interested to interrupt with questions. Once seated, Grandma shared with Dad, my uncles and Gramps how the young bachelor Miles Wellington, an eleventh or twelfth descendent of that lineage, presented to the then mayor, chief, preacher and other Bluff Hill council members his bizarre marketing strategy: Bluff Hill Haunting Décor. Dad stated Grandma seemed disturbed when she continued with how vague Miles Wellington described the details but expressed how Halloween would be "the trend of the future."

Dad said Grandma sounded firm when sharing she was one of the many who grumbled absurdities behind "that ungodly man." Then Dad said Grandma's tone suddenly dropped to disgust when the council once more approved another "braindead Wellington plan"—I still envision Dad's annoying habit when he made those air quotation marks to emphasize Grandma's own words—without any thought or discussion with the citizens. Dad said Gramps quickly blurted how he wasn't shocked Miles Wellington pitched such a "disturbing product gimmick."

Dad explained how Gramps and my dad's uncles attended grade school with Miles Wellington. Gramps described the heir as one of "those peculiar only child" who remained a loner throughout school, and Miles didn't get involved with extracurricular activities or school functions. Yet, no specialists ever suggested Miles was low-functioning or anything. In fact, school records confirmed Miles stayed in the tenth percentile of their class rankings from elementary school all the way to graduation—I checked for myself after my administration promotion.

His grades were sub-impressive, because folders of disciplinary reports explaining he wouldn't participate in classroom lectures existed. However, none said he was disruptive or inattentive in class. Teachers described him as "disrespectful." They recorded he "read leisure books rather than school textbooks during class time." However, their marks on his progress reports testified with frustrated terms, explaining Miles answered with "eccentric yet appropriate responses during class discussions." Instructors seemed to grudgingly praise him but jotted remarks like "Miles will insolently flash a half smirk before returning to whatever book he's reading rather than continue to participate in classroom exercises."

In his files, Miles displayed some interests in his science and math classes. They seemed to reflect what his former schoolmates in those local new stations' Wellington documentaries shared about how he'd get "giddy" when they dissected in biology or experimented in the chemistry labs. Also, many shared how "Miles not only engaged but would monopolize the physics and calculus lectures." I recalled how this one classmate of his commented, "It was boring and weird at the same time how anyone, much less Miles Wellington, could be so … portentously nerdy, in carrying on the class topics. But he seemed to know what he was talking about, because the teachers couldn't say anything else, as if his remarks shut them up."

My dad and uncles responded to Gramps' story with jokes about how Miles was most likely that geeky study-buddy the jocks took advantage of; but Gramps reminded them how their peers keep their distances from Miles' aloof demeanor and odd behaviors, which seemed to not be challenging for them, since he remained withdrawn from school functions and clubs.

The only events Miles never missed registering for each year were the school district's autumn talent shows. He did these one-man shows, which most of the school faculty found sad. However, his elaborative sets impressed the judges and audiences. (I've seen those first-place ribbons dangling from the frames that hold those photos in our school lobby's trophy case; his lavish props and flamboyant costumes are beyond impressive— although, even today's students joke about how he used "dusty leftovers from his family's previous business failures" to create them.)

Miles' acts emerged into scenes from classic novels like *The Invisible Man* and *Dracula* during Gramps' middle-school years. His backdrops became gloomier, borderline macabre. Parents and some faculty expressed their reluctance, thinking they were "too scary" for the younger crowd. However, like with how they helped the town's economy, his family sponsored the county's school system, so the school board allowed these "horror sets." (And speaking as an educator, a sixth grader able to grasp the concepts from such books is mind blowing). It was noted his sophomore year was when Miles stepped from the books and reenacted scenes from movies.

One October night in 1962, Miles opened his skit by lurking in the shadows on the shared school district's auditorium stage. The audiences and judges expressed in those Wellington documentaries that it was obvious, even in the dim lighting, he was dressed as Frankenstein's monster that night. Still, no one knew where he was going with his performance and most quickly grew bored of his humdrum monologue in comparing Shelly's novel and Whales' cinematography.

When he referenced where the movie cut from the scene when the monster met the little girl by the lake, the stage lights illuminated upon a plush and vibrant meadow scene. A small mannequin in an elegant spring dress and blonde wig with stringy pigtails stood lifeless near what we'd consider today as a homemade kiddie pool. To me, the set appeared beautiful in the yearbook archives, but many in the autumn television specials teased the props were overstocked merch from the Wellington family's failed businesses—a common running joke.

Miles expressed how disappointed he was to not watch the rest of the pond scene. He explained the significance of the scene was critical to the foundation of the monster's character, its innocence clashing against the world's complex perceptions and expectations—those in the documentaries stressed how he motioned to the girl-like model at this part of his dialogue, like how the monster stiffly gestured in the motion picture. Dad said Gramps remembered teachers and parents later saying how young Miles Wellington expressing such worldly awareness was disturbing enough, but what happened next terrorized all in the auditorium.

Miles said something along the lines of how he'd simulate what might've happened if they had kept that section of the reel. Then, without warning, he "roared like a possessed lion," according to Dad's retelling of Gramps' experience. Miles' face appeared to alter before the crowd into something atrocious— Dad said Gramps remembered some in the audience covered their eyes from the teenager's disturbing snarl. Miles stomped on the stage, with each plod turning him toward the mannequin. His tautly arms flapped in rage. He froze in place when he faced the girly statue. He remained still for only seconds, but people who talk about that night described the wait as lasting minutes.

Then they saw Miles' stoic expression give "that half-smirk" many of his teachers eluded to in the progress reports. He twirled his stiff legs in the air as he unbendingly marched toward the life-size schoolgirl doll. The audience's anticipation quickly returned to boredom, but they'd soon be amped into terror within the next few minutes.

Miles snatched the mannequin by its arms and threw it into the makeshift pond, like one tossing a large log into a creek. All but an arm splashed into the water.

Miles' triumphant and joyful groans amplified in the auditorium as he rose the fake arm into the air like a trophy. Thick dark red ribbons dispersed from the shoulder-end of the arm. Miles seemed to channel his inner method actor that night, because people said he looked as enthused about the victory of throwing the mannequin into the pool as the monster did with the girl in now revised editions of the movie.

Nearly everyone in the auditorium either ran out the building, shrilling, or froze in their chairs in utter horror, only able to scream. It took a while for the talent show facilitator to remove Miles Wellington from the stage and regain composure from the guests. He announced how they had four more routines to get through that night and begged for no one else to leave.

Superintendent Spalding emailed me the documented parents' complaints when they attended the school and town meetings in an uproar after the night of Miles Wellington's alarming performance. However, no reports of any reprimanding happenings exist, and Miles performed in his junior and senior years. The church gossip gradually ceased—on that, anyway.

The only references Gramps and Dad's uncles said that people's chatter never seemed to die when talking about that night was how Miles' parents sat in the front row that night with overjoyed eyelids strained as wide as their toothy smiles stretched from ear to ear—primarily, the last time many Bluff Hill residences would ever see the couple alive.

• • •

David Letterman's voice lingered in the background when Dad continued how the town's eagerness to see what the young adult Miles Wellington had brewed in the warehouse during his childhood the mid-70s. The only advertisements were black-and-white flyers throughout downtown Bluff Hill with *GRAND OPENING: BLUFF HILL HAUNTING DÉCOR JULY 1ST AT 9AM* printed on them.

People peaked through the front door glasses after months of anticipation. However, they shared among one another in the streets that the only thing visible in the murky shadows were some massive front-store displays, reflecting much like his childhood skit sets, and how they blocked anyone from seeing further into the store. No one could form a clear concept of Miles Wellington's concoctions. When the *Bluff Hill Query* couldn't get anything juicy for an article months before the doors opened, townsfolks' anticipation shifted into concerns.

When the Bluff Hill Haunting Décor's grand opening finally arrived in July of 1978, the waiting crowd grew beyond control and had to be managed by town police. The citizens nearly busted down the entrances at nine a.m. sharp … and almost nearly shattered the bolted doors. It was as if the entrances were waiting for the people to stop pushing on them before prying apart. When the crowd calmed, a loud *click* echoed, and the glass doors rattled open.

No one stood behind the doors waiting to welcome the customers. It seemed the doors had opened themselves. Yet, the doors were wide and welcoming, but the unexpected and rather eerie lack of greeting spooked the patrons as they crept into the warehouse.

After the store's first operative hour, the majority stormed out the self-contained mechanical doors disappointed. They told *Bluff Hill Query* the walls and shelves exhibited typical Halloween paraphernalia that anyone could buy in other department stores "at cheaper prices," like era-appropriate costumes with matching plastic or latex masks, options for trick-or-treat candy pails, and cheesy outdated decorations. They even chuckled with the running jokes that Miles Wellington's products were most likely "leftovers from family's previous business." With the grownups uninterested in the place, Dad said the warehouse developed into the hangout spot for his classmates.

Dad wasn't really allowed to check out the Haunting Décor until October of 1979, when he griped to Grandma about how his friends' parents were *finally* allowing them to "shop" there. Grandma complained about what the ladies at church would say if one of the Tuner boys "hung out" there, but, on the Friday before Halloween that year, she reluctantly agreed, as long his older brothers accompanied him. Dad said he was cool with my uncles joining his crew—to this day, they still poke at one another after their first and only visit to the Haunting Décor in their youth.

Before then, he only saw the place from the outside, so Dad didn't realize how humongous the warehouse was until he entered. The floor appeared wider than a football field to him, and ceiling stretched so high Dad said he got vertigo during the initial upward glance. Dad expressed how overwhelming the never-ending shelves were stuffed with so much strange and wonderful things only relating to Halloween.

And, emerged within the welcome displays at the front entrance, were some nearly seven-feet-tall jack-o-lantern figures and scarecrow mockups oddly arranged as if to be greeters. The jack-o-lanterns wore drooping cloaks with wide hoods, whereas the scarecrows donned flannel shirts and too-large straw hats, but both had oblong stick arms protruding from ragged sleeves, as if trying to reach for Dad's squad. Their crater faces were barely noticeable under the headwear, but their glowering orange-red eyes illuminated as bright as fiery embers.

Dad said they all went bonkers over the scary models, even the friends who had already seen the junk before the Turner brothers were hyped with them. His buddies kept daring them to approach one of the props. All three hesitated, but the oldest, Uncle Ernie, built the courage to step up to one of the scarecrows.

Dad described how timid Uncle Ernie inched toward the display "like a scared bitch with her tail between her legs." When he got about two feet from the thing, the scarecrow's fire-orange eyes ignited a blood-red hue and bent toward Uncle Ray. Its pointy fingers and straggly flannel-covered arms thrashed at him while shrilling an unharmonious mixture of laughter and growling. Dad said Uncle Ernie "jumped so high that he fell hard on his fat ass."

Dad and Uncle Manny never stopped teasing him, but the picking never messed with Uncle Ernie, because he would always retort how Dad and Uncle Manny looked as if they would piss their pants when they heard, *Do you boys like that one?* whispered behind them.

Truth be told, Dad admitted only to me that he thought he "needed a new pair of jeans when the voice cooed hot steam" down his neck. Dad said his heart "thudded so hard that the organ could've burst through his chest bones." He spun on his heels, ready to run like a bat from Hell with the rest of the guys—and leave Uncle Ernie on the floor—but a scrawny, pale figure stood between them and the exit.

The thirtysomething frail-looking guy dressed like he was trying too hard in an oversized business suit that draped over his skeletal body. His ear-to-ear smile was so thin that jagged teeth protruded through his faint lips. His forehead was high due to a receding hairline. His bloodshot eyes with soul-piercing dilated pupils sunk farther into their sockets when he stretched his brow with glee. Dark circles hung below his eyes. Even the cliché fingertips Dad described tapping upon one another before the creepy guy's torso helped emphasize the freaky factor with the man's appearance.

Dad said they didn't even wait to hear more; they all ran around Miles Wellington and fled the warehouse.

· · ·

Dad snickered at the irony that he'd sworn with his friends how they'd never return to the store, and, yet, he ended up employed there during my childhood.

He referenced Mile's disturbing glare over Dad, my uncles, and their buds was the exact same glower Miles Wellington projected from his high-rise executive office when Dad and his coworkers maneuvered around the factory floor many years later when Bluff Hill Haunting Décor grew international. Not sure if he told anyone else, but Dad shared with me, after the layoffs, every nightmare he had were of Miles Wellington's scowls. Even in his deathbed at the assisted living facility, he would awake from his naps, screaming for Miles Wellington to stop staring at him like that. I wonder if Dad turns in his coffin due to still seeing that man's demonic grin.

6.

Whether positive or negative, the disturbing jack-o-lantern figures and scarecrow models were the talk of the town. Some dug them—the youngins—but most of the grown folks despised their threatening stature and upsetting designs. The naysayers went to *Bluff Hill Query* to share their options. The ones who couldn't get enough told their family and friends outside town about these awesome additions for their Halloween yard decorations. Either way, citizens of Bluff Hill developed enough attention for the animatronics to fly off the warehouse sales floors before every Halloween for the next few years. The sales seemed to earn Haunting Décor advertisements in South Carolina's *The State* newspaper.

The ones opposed of the props went berserk when residents outside Beaufort County came shopping at the Wellington warehouse. The residents expressed their fear that the "grotesque things would be bad representations of Bluff Hill." Every townhall meeting housed at least three citizens demanding to pull the ads.

To appease the residents, the townhall council suggested for Miles Wellington to make more family friendly animatronics for every season. They were more assertive than in the past with a Wellington with the request, but Miles Wellington stuck to his guns on maintaining Bluff Hill Haunting Décor's mission solely for Halloween. Bluff Hill citizens took matters in their own hands when the council folded in defeat and picketed before the warehouse with intentions to block customers entering the Haunting Décor.

The angry people must have got to him, because Miles slugged through town hall's pried doors during a 1987's August meeting. Mom and Dad said his silhouette cooled the otherwise hotbox of a structure when he stood in the open doorway before the setting summer sun. The place silenced—only hearing the swatting of hand fans—and those who stood before the microphone parted in the aisle for him to approach it. He said he'd like to establish a board for Bluff Hill Haunting Décor, since the town's name is part of the company name. People were content, until the board comprised of only the mayor, chief, and the one preacher of Bluff Hill—members from the council.

The townsmen waited for reports, but, instead, the "board" used tax money to attend regional conventions. The town was only more stressed about the waste of money for Miles Wellington and how much the board spent to take these "business trips." Miles Wellington didn't seem too concern about results though, which many residents added how his lackluster approach to this was just another major indication of how horrible his insane marketing scheme represented Bluff Hill.

They were worried about their image but guessed the expos trips would be horrible, thus finally ending Mile Wellington's crazy business. In July 1988, every Bluff Hill resident filled town hall, shoulder to shoulder, and wanted to hear how the committee once again chose wrong with supporting the Wellington company based from what they assumed would be lackluster auctions at the conventions.

The supposed board reported how most of the agencies at the conventions wanted to try the company's "high-techy jack-o-lantern figures and scarecrow models." Many were in disbelief with how "digitally advanced" Wellington advertised their props. Yet, when feedback told all how the merchandise peeked the expo guests' desires based on the rise of their numbers of guests visiting their own establishments, the organizations practically threw their money to Bluff Hill's Haunting Décor to stay ahead of the amusement park attraction game.

The big sales finally piqued the town's curiosity to know how these high-demand animatronics were manufactured. Miles Wellington was hesitant but agreed to let only the board to enter the factory. When they learned this'd be the first time the board entered the store, the citizens became more disinclined and demanded to join the board on the factory tour. However, the mayor reassured them that he, the preacher, and the chief would report all they noted during the factory tour at the next town meeting.

Again, the town hall was just as packed at the September meeting like in July. The committee touched on the usual upcoming events in Bluff Hill, but nothing about their visit to the Wellington warehouse. When the floor opened, the audience didn't wait in line to yell their demands. The mayor and chief simply raised their hands to ask for silence and shared that the warehouse's assembly lines were top notch, the sales were booming, and Miles Wellington was onto something big. Then they added how the Township Lodge agreed to assist with the logistics and development of business deals, becoming a part of the company's board.

The town became irate, and the police had to stand before the crowd while the committee snuck from the building through the cellar. But the board kept their smiles on their faces.

Those television documentaries shared how many residents went to the query dissatisfied with being told nothing about their visit. They said how the mayor really didn't even tell them anything about how the machines were made. But what stuck out to me personally was how the ones interviewed for the films described how the committee's behaviors were "odd, stiff, and frank." Some citizens who always sat in the front rows during the forums proceeded to describe how the committee's eyes looked "wide and dilated, as if they had been smoking something before the meeting."

Expansions
7.

Bluff Hill Haunting Décors' sales massively exploded the town's revenue by the hundreds-of-thousands in the late 1990s. The internet helped quadruple the national sales before the network became today's way of living, and other corporations were so wide-eyed by the "memorizing success" that they wanted to be partners. However, the more Bluff Hill's currency strengthened, the more Miles Wellington grew distant with sharing the achievements with the town meetings.

Citizens demanded to know what made their hometown globally noticeable. However, the council and township lodge met with Miles Willington behind closed doors and kept their conferences from the press. Some residents weren't accepting that.

The town's more meddling families were abrasive and brought their children to the warehouse on Halloween of 1999. They excused themselves as they got word the mayor, the chief, and even the preacher brought their own kids to the Wellington warehouse for Halloween, so "thought" it was opened for all citizens.

They were ready to fight, but Miles Wellington surprisingly welcomed the visits. My fourth-grade classmates came to school bragging about their peeks at next season's jack-o-lantern figures and scarecrow designs as well as how "radical" Mr. Miles Wellington decorated the warehouse hallways as they journeyed by lodge members through the showrooms. Some even referenced how the Wellington plantation home perched high on the hilltop behind the warehouse made the ambiance more unsettling, like how the Bate's home did over the hotel in that movie. And Miles Wellington's silhouette in the windows only added the creepy factor—the Township Lodge members ran the warehouse and store by this time, so he hardly left his actual home at this point.

Mom and some of the selected few who had yet visited the place questioned the holes in the business marketing and logistics on how Bluff Hill, both the Haunting Décor and the town, comfortably survived. How a company that sold Halloween props, of all things, would rake such massive net worth into the town's revenue flabbergasted them. When Mom's crew kept poking into the holes, the town committee posted on the townhall's bulletin board the community meetings were secluded to the ones who were employees for the company or those accepted as Township Lodge members. Meanwhile, Bluff Hill Haunting Décor hired Dad as chief electrician. Mom became furious. I was confused about how everything was going quick and chaotic.

8.

Dad attended the meetings now instead of Mom, and she'd probe Dad for information as soon as he got through the front door on those nights. Dad only shared how awesome the place is and how we needed to join the lodge. However, each month of his employment, Dad appeared more aloof from the family when coming home from the meetings. My brother and I wanted to ask Dad if he was okay, but he always had this dazed glare in his eyes, like even if we talked with him, he'd wouldn't give us any attention or remember what we'd said.

The handful who wholeheartedly protested the town supporting Bluff Hill Haunting Décor picketed before town hall the night of every monthly meeting. And on Halloween nights, Mom joined the crew to petition right before the warehouse where many waited in line to enter the Wellington warehouse.

Mom allowed some of the group's gatherings at our home—both she and Dad made sure he was scheduled to work those nights without directly confirming with one another. My brother and I weren't allowed to attend the in-house meetings, but we eavesdropped in the hallway anyhow. It didn't take long for us to realize the snooping proved boring and time consuming. Every gatherings' topic focused on more examples of how the town supporters' obsession advanced into something more "cultish and ungodly."

9.

In 2000, major entrainment corporations were mesmerized on how a small Southern town's makeshift attraction had such extravagant success. They traveled from other states to personally experience the excitement. The event enthralled them, and they became Town Lodge members as well—people from other states became associated with a small-town community organization; it was almost scandalous! Business representatives of other national attractions gave their own phenomenal testimonials, which sparked global attention for Bluff Hill Haunting Décor.

We heard on the news stations how top international vacation spots saw some drops in their proceeds during the Fall season—nothing critical, but enough for analysts to dig into the cause. The worldwide guests raved about riding through the ghoulish and precise decorative neighborhoods in Bluff Hill—sponsored by the families with memberships for the Township Lodge—on their way to the distribution center to wander more by foot through the many elaborate sets just see the latest jack-o-lantern figures and scarecrow models the company engineered for the next Halloween season.

This phenomenon transformed Bluff Hill Haunting Décor from a small-town business to an international franchise in 2005. Major international-city folk visited Bluff Hill too often that my older bother's then girlfriend who worked at the sole motel in town told us the out-of-country places sponsored the development for more hotels in town. And so many cities did: Guadalajara, Tokyo, Moscow, England, Dubai, and Montreal. They visited Bluff

Hill aboundingly and frequently. Before we knew it, Dad let it slip one night during dinner how they were assembling not only extensions to the warehouse but merchandise factories around the world.

The thing was, once someone or another organization were finally able to enter the place to see the secret to what made the animatronics function, they'd leave the warehouse amazed with wide grins and glazed eyes, muttering how excited they were about how next season's jack-o-lantern figures and scarecrows would be more limber and menacing. They didn't share anything else.

Enthusiasts loved the products but were confused with what exactly was Bluff Hill Haunting Décor. Retail or entertainment? Miles Wellington decided to spruce the company's name—Bluff Hill Haunting Décor, Incorporated—to represent the international collaborations. But, to separate the product from the glitz, he founded Bluff Hill's official haunted attraction: A Night for Jack-o-Lanterns and Scarecrows.

● ● ●

I know. That's probably the *shittiest* name anyone could create for an entertainment establishment. We picked the title as a tribute to the obsession over that weirdo's metallic creepy contraptions, but who would even consider such a pitiful name? It's too damn long and seemed like the first thing Miles blurted without anyone involved pondering it. I can only imagine what those sickening followers of his thought when he said the most random and total stream-of-conscious thing to call it: "Sure, anything you say, Mr. Wellington. Just keep bringing in the money!"

The guests just wanted the experience and souvenirs, so the name didn't phase them. Money talked louder than opinions, and how those animatronics couldn't even get from the warehouse onto the display floors without buyers snatching them before the store clerks' could stock them was what solidified the decision.

How this freaky fucker fooled those outside Bluff Hills was unbelievable and just ... scary.

Destruction
10.

The mayor and chief returned to the townhall meetings during my senior year in 2008. The worldwide Township Lodge members elected many international partners into the board chairs. No one living in Bluff Town were voted to join the board that year.

Many international partners brought so much help that the Township Lodge laid off the original employees. Few who the reporters interviewed in those local biopics said they were okay with this because "they were programming more innovative jack-o-lanterns and scarecrows animatronics to assist building next year's models, as if they were to replace the actual workers eventually." Some said how "humanlike" they traversed the warehouse disturbed them. That alone just sounded too bizarre for anyone, as if not ready for the future threat of household incomes to begin right in our own sleepy hometown.

Not having that, some citizens tried to force themselves into the place during off-seasons, but the place became only opened for the public during the months of September and October ... after paying admission to "journey through A Night for Jack-o-Lanterns and Scarecrows."

By this point, none of the original loyal patrons—Bluff Hills' citizens—were even muttering about the damn place. Nearly every one of my peers shared how they lost interests with A Night for Jack-o-Lanterns and Scarecrows. They griped how the queue wait time grew longer and longer. Mom and Dad even expressed how their friends phased out the annual autumn tradition to visit Bluff Hill Haunting Décor when they took their children trick-or-treating or to strike.

The few citizens who did bare the long lines shared bad reviews. They said the older animatronics showed their age, with their wobbly limbs flickering, as if the arms would pop off the robots at any moment, or the sparks were large enough to be hazardous. Some accused Miles Wellington of putting people into costumes and claiming them to be "the latest mockups" as a desperate and cheap attempt to freak out his patrons. The public shared the animatronics weren't convincing, because the new models that roamed the warehouse were too limber, like humans, when they walked off platforms or entered the walkways.

The few of my schoolmates who grudgingly admitted going, using the excuse their parents *made them* take their younger siblings, said the complaints adults grumbled weren't entirely true. They bragged how they grew bored in the damn place and approached the wandering animatronics to lift their cloaks or yank down their trousers. They were convinced those things were alive, because they only exposed robotic bolts and levers when doing the disrespectful acts.

11.

The town's lack of support didn't hurt Miles Wellington. So many visitors from across the oceans attended that he didn't even notice how the original fanbase had stopped supporting. Besides, it appeared it was how he wanted it; no one, not even the council, was aware of when he'd built the border wall between the forests and the rest of Bluff Hill. It was as if—most likely the warehouse laborers—had constructed it overnight.

The council hired attorneys to assist with legislations on their rights with Bluff Hill Haunting Décor; however, Miles Wellington seemed to have better representations from across the globe, and Bluff Hill lost all connections with the company. This would be the first time in Bluff Hill's history the town had no affiliation with the Wellington enterprise.

Township Lodge Members became irate and caused a public disturbance, acting like they were detoxing from some narcotic state. Meanwhile, the residents who never were a part of it seemed liberated to no longer be affiliated with the living nightmare.

When interviewers asked former lodge members and employees to talk about their time involved with the Bluff Hill Haunted Décor, Incorporated and A Night for Jack-o-Lanterns and Scarecrows, they couldn't really answer. I remember my dad telling me even, "It's all hazy, like some vague dream I cannot recall now."

Insolvency
12.

The news about Bluff Hill Haunting Décor, Incorporated became distressing in May 2014 when the mayor reported at the monthly town meeting he was being swarmed with many calls. He said former contracted customers of Bluff Hill Haunting Décor, Incorporated contacted him because Miles Wellington wouldn't respond to their emails and phone calls. He said they wanted refunds on some of the jack-o-lantern figures and scarecrows designs, willing to even buyout their agreements. The unanimous reasoning was a significant drop in their admission sales correlated with overwhelming number of guests' negative feedback.

Their patrons detailed how the parks' newest animatronics were beyond sinister and how their unsolidified behaviors were terrifying enough for their park guests to not return to the grounds, how their movements cut some patrons when grabbing for them. Some said they thought the props would assault their staff members during attempts to pull the things from the attractions. When the corporations did their research, every complaint led to the Haunting Décor's products.

I personally found the more-disturbing headlines were from the individual buyers. For the past decades, they'd been ordering the more unconventional, customized jack-o-lantern figures and scarecrow models just to wander and interact with their guests at personal Halloween parities, like AI. That Halloween, owners stated, while spooked by how bizarrely and aggressively their personalized robots engaged, their company laughed off the weirdness as some party trick. It wasn't until the props sparked and uncontrollably thrashed their arms when the buyers became concerned. The mayor went to quote some of the homeowners when they said they sworn the malfunctioning monstrosities behaved like they wanted to attack people.

But the most horrific headline didn't come from the mayor during a meeting.

13.

November 1, 2020, every news station reported an electrical fire demolished one of Asia's well-known Pacific Coast haunted attractions. It resulted in multiple causalities. By November 3 of the same year, federal and international authorities checked into some Bluff Hill's newer hotels.

The contractors and buyers took their allegations to the courts and to TV to avoid any collusion accusations. The press practically camped in our backyards and town parks. Bluff Hill became one of the world's greatest places to visit, to the origin of some of the leading and horrendous international headlines.

Reporters and cops with unanswerable questions constantly harassed the citizens. Some families went live to share their disturbing visits to A Night for Jack-o-Lantern and Scarecrows. However, most of us were done with the Wellingtons and Bluff Hill Haunting Décor, Incorporated. We just wanted to continue with our daily lives while the media acted like a wild circus and harassing authorities attempted to pressure us to tell them things we didn't have the faintest idea they wanted to know. Still, the town felt the stress from Miles Wellington abandoning his hometown as our small town went through a recession.

By end of 2020, what the town of Bluff Hill had feared back in the 1980s finally happened. The Wellington had another failing business. Just that the citizens didn't bet on this being the worst one yet.

14.

Miles Wellington no longer had a board and was solo with running the massive warehouse. Yet, it was apparent he thrived on the fame the company still had. He begged for the handful of remaining Township Lodge members to assist, like old times, with hyping 2024 as the comeback for The Night for Jack-o-Lanterns and Scarecrows. They agreed to help with the pre-sales and special holiday sales through Bluff Hill Haunting Décor prior to Halloween that year. However, that didn't seem to really help with anything.

During the November townhall meeting, the mayor reported how A Night for Jack-o-Lanterns and Scarecrow only made approximately seven thousand dollars, and the total sales from Bluff Hill Haunting Décor only made near sixty thousand in profit worldwide—the lowest since the warehouse doors opened in 1977. On March 21, 2025, Mr. Miles Wellington requested an international press conference in the front of the warehouse to officially share with the world, after nearly four decades, Bluff Hill's Haunting Décor would be closing their doors forever.

He announced a closeout sale would begin Summer 2025 and would have the ultimate haunted walkthrough for Halloween before terminating the company on the first of November. Until then, no one would be allowed to enter. He laid off all workers, and Miles bought out his contracts with partners.

This was odd to the world, because if no human beings were allowed, then who would help his big plan?

• • •

Miles Wellington spared no expense in the preparations for the "ultimate haunted walkthrough." Meanwhile, the entire town feared they'd need to file bankruptcy—not only because of the steep dip on revenue but also the lawsuits.

And the claims weren't just from outside buyers. Many former and current warehouse workers had been injured on the job from the malfunctioning machines and animatronics lingering about the floors. In addition, a lot of citizens went into Columbia and Charleston for therapy due to post-traumatic stress disorder, as if they were hostages or kidnapped victims terrified to run into their abductors in Bluff Town. I think one of my friend's mothers had to even be hospitalized due to the severity of her psychosis.

Gossip throughout the town mentioned how the police found a bloody and bruised woman outside the Wellington warehouse. She wore a shredded business suit and had three metal jugs of kerosene and a box of matches, about to torch the place. When they escorted her to the station, she told them she had to rid the source of the evil because one of Haunting

Décor's scarecrow props had "the spirit of a slave" and tried to kill her earlier that night.

Social media and those online dark-storytelling blogs had rudely shared later she had told her psychiatrist it was one of the deformed scarecrows that the company's engineers kept looming around the warehouse for spare parts—and it seemed she wasn't exaggerating about the looming animatronic. Other workers reported how she'd noted this particular scarecrow would appear in the same warehouse sections she was assigned to work during her final shifts before the layoffs, each time with another piece removed. She said, at the time, she didn't think much of it because she, as so many other employees—even my father—said those jack-o-lantern figures and scarecrow models were always blending in on the floors like another crew member. The morning of her last employed hours, the scarecrow was in the locker room. She said she couldn't miss it this time, because the thing's bottom jaw, right eye, an arm, and its crown had been removed, exposing the thing's hard wires.

A week after all had been being laid off, she went job seeking throughout downtown Bluff Hill. She strolled Main Street when something shiny in an ally caught the corner of her eye. She stepped back to find rows of garbage cans. However, she recalled they were too weathered for the sunlight to reflect how she had seen the sliver glimmer.

Later that day, she noticed a familiar metallic being stood before some coffee shop or other store fronts a few yards ahead of her. Her breathing grew heavy and short, her chest aching. She'd turn onto another road before she could get any closer to the thing.

There were times when she thought the image of a menacing and busted robot scarecrow reflected in the glass where some the store windows' Help Wanted signs hung, but nothing stood behind her when she quickly turned. The moment she claimed she knew the thing was after her was when she went into Bell's Boutique for an interview a few days later but only got as far entering the front doors.

She reported among a child-size welcoming mannequin in the midst of a beach scene was the animatronic scarecrow wearing a sweetgrass straw hat. Even without a bottom jaw and only one eye, she said the machine's expression looked so pleased to see her, waving with its one hand. She fled the place and called the owner, apologizing for not showing and needing to cancel at the last minute.

Then she asked why they have a scarecrow in the front store's summer display. The owner responded with, "What scarecrow?"

She ran back to the store so fast that the heels she had chosen for the interview broke. She burst open the doors barefooted, panting, to find no scarecrow in the display. She returned home in the setting sun, the asphalt burning the soles of her feet, convincing herself she was going insane due to the job loss and the chaos of everything happening in Bluff Hill.

She passed her backyard clothesline when one of her bedsheets wrapped around her. A force tossed her around like a rag doll. Punches and items rammed into her back and thighs. She heard over her cries what seemed to be rusted metal. She tripped onto the ground, and someone kicked her in the face and stomach. The sheet somehow uncovered only her right eye. The sunrays were in her left eye, but she saw the rays reflecting off something metallic. When the thing seemed to notice her exposed eye, whomever—or whatever—was attacking her darted from her sight. When she was able to remove the blanket, she was alone in her backyard.

She concluded that night she had to burn down the evil that resided in the Wellington warehouse.

15.

The final night of The Night for Jack-o-Lanterns and Scarecrows attracted so many Halloween and haunt enthusiasts from all over the world that the queue seemed to circle the entire downtown area. The press swarmed the town like gnats, and even some celebrities came to party, mostly from the music industry. The residents didn't understand why so many would visit that living hell. I took my family on a late vacation to Canada during that time, because I knew how crowded and chaotic the place would get. I just didn't realize how too true I was when I read the online articles afterward.

They reported the doors opened at the usual time of seven-thirty, and I heard it went great in the beginning. The first patrons remarked how the jack-o-lantern figures and scarecrows stoically standing in the middle of the walkthrough was a rather cheap scare. A few praised how the machines turned their heads and followed the guests with their glowing eyes as the guests had to wiggle and worm around the props.

However, the complaints grew creepy later in the night. One reported how a animatronic sparked, burning a few patrons. Then another nearly tumbled onto a group of passersby, malfunctioning from its repetitious gestures. I think it was eleven o'clock when the complaints became disturbing.

Some said they'd bet actors had dressed as the props and would step from the scenery. The scarecrows and jack-o-lantern figures grabbed people, tugging on the customer's clothes. When the time approached two-thirty in the morning, the visitors said a few costumed characters who resembled the original animatronic models chased them throughout the haunted attraction. The regular patrons stated they loved the surprise, saying making it seem like some animatronics were coming to life to chase them was thrilling and entertaining.

But a character brutally assaulted someone, and a patron called the paramedics from inside the warehouse. The police were soon to follow. They unexpectedly shut down A Night for Jack-o-Lanterns and Scarecrows for the last time.

Every on-duty Bluff Hill police officer rushed to the distribution center to search the premises, inside and out, on the hunt for the prankster who snuck into the warehouse. They only found the variety of Halloween props the company had manufactured throughout the years posing in the eerie yet beautiful horror scenes. They even located a scarecrow model that exactly fit the description the victim—a Japanese citizen—shared regarding her attacker posing in the haunted cathedral scene, like one of the undead props rising from the graves.

Days later, when the victim wanted charges placed on the assaulting actor, Mr. Miles Wellington told the authorities he didn't have any actors disguised as scarecrows in the warehouse. All his lodge volunteers wore black logo shirts and jeans, selling the remaining merchandise on the sales floor.

Bankruptcy
16.

Bluff Hill attempted to vend the warehouse as soon as Miles Wellington ended Bluff Hill Haunting Décor, and three manufactures did buy it for a distribution center. However, their businesses were short-lived. It was chaos, the town enduring many days in the state and federal courts when the first two wanted to break the lease, because they reported the leftover jack-o-lantern and scarecrow animatronics acted "hazardously wonky" when the companies attempted to clean out the abandoned decades of remaining products from the Wellington's previous businesses.

The reports continued with the witnesses saying it was as if the machines fought removal from the buildings. Bluff Hill agreed to breech the third company's contract when they lost two lives.

It remained abandoned afterward. Many neighborhood teens snuck into the vacant building on dares or to throw underground parties. But my daughter told me some weird things her peers shared that happened at these shindigs: echoing footsteps, rusted creaks, and mummers. I told her they were most likely the kids pranking one another.

My son said the scaredy cats told the wildest excuses to bail early on the parties. They were freaked about the unfinished scarecrows and jack-o-lanterns dangling from the high ceilings or lying on the conveyer belts. Some reported seeing the eyes glowing and a few limbs twitching. Electricity has not flowed through the place since 2026, so they're accusations about the humming and lights were their scared minds tricking them.

However, someone got hurt at a party in 2031. I remember the breaking-eleven-o'clock news that Halloween night. They reported live before the smoking Wellington warehouse. The flashing lights of police cruisers, firetrucks, and ambulances reflected behind the reporter. A few blanketed teenagers huddled before the premise, hugging and crying.

The reporter stated something nearly slashed off a young man's leg. The story went something like he stepped from the group, not saying particularly why—I figured to either set up a prank or take a piss—but few teens able compose themselves enough to be interviewed said they heard his cries echoing through the large rooms and hallways. Then their lips trembled when trying to describe how the abandoned animatronics flickered as they ran through the warehouse looking for their friend. They said water sprayed from the sprinklers without any warning, but it only caused more sparks from the robots. Their sparks ignited the cardboard boxes and leftover hardcopy reports.

The police attributed it to another drunk and clumsy teenager being somewhere they didn't need to be. That following Monday morning, the story hit digital news. And, somehow, one of the news stations acquired some "authentic footage." The reporter shared it might be disturbing to watch and viewer's discretion was advised.

The images revealed one of the teens who had searched for the kid. He had turned on the recorder rather than just the flashlight on their phone. I heard the screams as soon as the image appeared on my child's tablet. The shots were a bit disorienting due to the pixilation from the camera trying to focus while the phone's owner ran. A young male shrilled for help in the distance, and all the flashlights strobed about the walls and floors while rushing toward the cries.

The person responsible for the recorded footage approached a double door entryway. One door was opened and the other closed. The closed one had a worn, aged label reading TESTING AREA. The person's free hand pushed the other door open, and the flashlight shone on two young men.

One kneeled by another lying on his back and cradling his crimson-toned right leg. When other lights emerged behind the recorder, I noticed more red spots on the cement floor. The camera swooshed around, and yelling and howling echoed throughout the area about how someone needed to call the police. The last of the images were blurry and with lowlight, but I swore many jack-o-lantern figures and scarecrow models stood sporadically about the room. And all seemed to be glaring in the victim's direction.

The closest animatronic—practically three or four feet from the wounded teen—appeared to be a deformed scarecrow with exposed wires from a topless head. But then the falling sprinkler water made any machines around the kids spark, and the image became a bright blur before the screen returned to the news anchors.

Reconstruction

17.

Still, our horrifying past attracts people far and wide, and that's why the mayor, chief, and preacher overruled the parents' pleas tonight: out-of-towners and our children waste their money in Bluff Hill every October, long after our infamous haunted attraction had burned to the ground.

I applauded the lodge members on the phenomenal job with commemorating A Night for Jack-o-Lanterns and Scarecrows. I see us visiting again this Halloween. Maybe next time the PTO meeting gripes about shutting down the walkthrough, I'll give my two cents.

I recognized some of the older—now rather ancient—jack-o-lantern figures and scarecrows models when my family navigated the Township Lodge's Halloween walkthrough last year. I'm told they never returned the ones they had acquired when they broke tides with Miles Wellington and the board for Bluff Hill Haunting Décor, Incorporation. Seeing them in there was alarming and uncanny, but the family's enjoyment distracted my discomfort.

How the jack-o-lanterns and scarecrow models miraculously run like brand new, even the original replicas, amazed me. The older ones gestured really creepy too. I don't recall them moving as fluid as they did last year, but they did when they turned to watch my family pass them through the lodge's lobby and main areas. And how they moved like they planned to grab my children—chilling and entertaining.

Some speculated Miles Wellington is behind the scenes at the Township Lodge, helping with the sets. However, no one had really heard from the last of the Wellington clan when the warehouse burnt down. Most were content to believe he remained recluse or even withered until his death in that decrepit plantation house that still looms over the warehouse's ashes.

But occasional mummers come from the students in the school hallways, saying they noticed the silhouette in the windows while sneaking into the warehouse's crumbling remains. Even some of the visiting press have said they saw something standing in the windows when they stood before the place, but it vanished before they could go live. But no one from the Township Lodge have been up there. Nor the have police investigated when someone reports seeing something.

Who's to say if people's fear are playing tricks on their minds? After all, Miles Wellington would be over the age of one hundred now if he were still alive. People are just seeing things and letting their spooked mind get the best of them. The Wellington bloodline died with the burning of the warehouse.

Acknowledgements

I want to give a huge thank-you to Jennifer Givner, owner of Acapella Book Cover Design, for not only the awesome book cover but the general guidance for a wannabe writer. I want to thank Brian Paone, founder of Scout Media, for his supports and guidance. I want to thank Ashley Conner, from Ash the Editor, for her feedback. A huge thank you to Jerry Snow from the Enquire Journal in Monroe, NC—my words cannot express enough. A huge thank-you to the wonderful Serena Guest for the talented author picture. And many thanks to my beta readers.

My heart and soul goes to Antoine James for his everlasting devotion, unconditional love, and sacrificing valor from the beginning of this project. I appreciate my little kitty cat girl Carrie for pushing my drive. My prayers will forever go to my muse Coal—hope you broke from samara.

Lindsey Neal Stephens, Jr. was born and raised in Gaston, South Carolina, a rural town about twenty-five minutes from Columbia, South Carolina. He attended the University of South Carolina in Columbia and earned a degree in experimental psychology. He currently holds a Master's in Mental Health Counseling from Webster University and an educator's license by studying school counseling from University of North Carolina at Charlotte. He currently resides in Charlotte, North Carolina with his partner and their two cats. He's written poetry under the name Neal Stephens. This will be Lindsey's first collection of stories.

Made in the USA
Columbia, SC
07 March 2020

88621026R00231